Deathwalkers
Tales From Purgatory Book Two
Liz Roderick

TINKERBELL PUBLISHING

Dedication

For Juniper
Choose the right one.

Contents

Content Notification   VII

1. Cope   1

2. Death Will Not Stop the Party   13

3. Disney Princess and Fuckboy   31

4. Love is Literally the Worst   44

5. Plop, the Shoe Drops   60

6. Party at Heaven's Vista   77

7. The Midnight Limousine   93

8. Spoiled   102

9. The Boss   120

10. Answers Industries   147

11. Negotiations   171

12. Deathwalkers   181

13. The Web   200

14. Always Home, Never Home   218

15. Understanding   240

16. Love is Blinding 258

17. If Your World Falls Apart 266

18. And There's Gonna Be Trouble 286

Epilogue 303

Author's Notes 305

Other Books By Author 306

Content Notification
Read Me! No, really!

How do you do, fellow kids?

If you're on book two, you have *some* idea of what you're in for, but there's a couple other things to be aware of.

There's a relationship in this book that some might think is inappropriate. I'll let all of you decide for yourselves whether it is or not. Regardless of the intents and potential secret motivations of the parties involved, the relationship could remind some readers—or trigger memories—of the grooming of an underage person by a middle-aged person.

One of the main reasons I pulled this series out of contract and decided to self-publish it is because I didn't want to somehow sanitize this relationship. People who grew up or are growing up the way I did, this relationship is probably going to be all too familiar, at least in some respects.

I don't think teenagers are delicate flowers who need to be shielded from the realities of living in this fucking society. You all are living in it as much as adults are, and you're capable of navigating this shit within the safe confines of fiction, if you so choose. I mean, some of you won't be, and I get that. That's what content notifications are for. It's a chance to opt out.

There is also workplace sexual harassment. *Workplace?* you might be asking. Ah yes, Tales from Purgatory is suddenly going square and getting a job. We'll see how long that lasts.

This book continues to portray a girl's reaction to and internalization of abuse, and it doesn't always do so in a way that people like to say is "empowering". Sometimes it's messy. Sometimes it hurts. Sometimes it leads to clouded judgment, knee-jerk reactions, bad decisions, and the destruction of relationships. I'm not doing this to pass some sort of judgment or give anyone a roadmap for navigating this shit. I'm just showing how it can be.

However you're dealing with things, it's okay, and there are people who will love you and care for you through it all. Find those people. You *can* be okay. You're worthy of love, you're worthy of joy. You can find those things, I promise. I'm living proof.

As in pretty much all my books, there's mention of drug use, gun violence, death, psychosis, and people being generally horrible to one another.

Please take care of yourself.

CHAPTER ONE

Cope

Magdalene sat with her sweaty back against the cottonwood tree, watching the shadow of the western cliff creep over the canyon bottom. The silence of the desert pressed around her, broken only by the trickle of spring water. Not even the ravens would brave the suffocating heat.

She closed her eyes and let the other world slide into focus. Each stone and blade of sunbaked grass came to life, and the sky spread out above, hazy blue with silver thunderheads billowing silently to the south. She sighed as the weight of emotion lifted from her chest and the heat retreated.

With a fluttering of wings, a tiny bird landed in the dust at her feet, its rainbow-colored feathers gleaming. It hopped closer, tipping its head to peer at her with black bead of an eye, then fluttered onto her lap and dropped a tiny, jewel-like flower from its beak.

Leaves began to push through the dry ground, unfurling gracefully and reaching upward. Buds swelled and burst into tiny, delicate blooms, blanketing the rocky ground in color.

Magdalene opened her eyes and the bird and flowers disappeared, the mantle of pain and heat settling heavy on her shoulders again. Omar was striding toward her on the path from the Commune, heat ripples rising around him.

He smiled as he approached. His body had regained most of its strength since his coma, but his face was still haunted by a hollowness that made his eyes look bigger. He sat down next to Magdalene in the shade.

"You and your pretty little flowers," she muttered.

"Just thought I'd add to the scenery." He searched her face and sighed. "Magdalene, you're spending a lot of time out here in your own private Purgatory."

She snorted halfheartedly and traced a pattern in the dust with a twig. It wasn't that she was running away from Omar. She just didn't want to vent her anger on him and end up losing him for good.

Omar took her hand. Magdalene stared at her knees. She wanted to look at him—she knew she was being sulky and annoying—but it felt like her gaze weighed six tons.

"You have every right to be mad," he said. "But we can work this out. If you want to talk, I'm here."

Magdalene sighed and leaned her head on his shoulder. "I'm not mad at you. I'm just...mad." He put his arm around her. She could feel the rise and fall of his breathing, her sweaty skin against his. "I can't get over it," she said. "Especially when I'm around Helena, I can't stop seeing the expression on Stan's face when he fell...when he died. Over and over again." She took a harsh breath. "I see it every waking minute. I see it when I sleep. I *can't get over it.*"

Since Helena had announced her pregnancy, she'd asked Magdalene to help her with the farm work, but Magdalene could barely stand to be around her. Omar had stepped in to help, but Magdalene felt guilty and childish having him do it all. Besides, she didn't want to invite questions about why she was avoiding Helena and her duties. There was no good way to tell someone their fetus was the reincarnation of a greasy, murdering shitstain. So, Magdalene had been getting her extra chores done as quickly as possible and retreating out to the cottonwood.

"I just can't be okay with what happened." Magdalene wrapped her arms around her knees. "I can't be at peace with a universe that would let Stan get away with killing Morris, and everything else he did."

Omar gazed at her, a furrow in his brow. "Justice is a dangerous concept, in this world and the next."

"Life isn't fair, and death isn't, either."

Omar leaned his head back against the cottonwood trunk and a brittle smile etched itself onto his lips. "If I hadn't lost control, none of this would be an issue. Stan would still be alive."

"He'd still be alive, and he'd still be after me. If you hadn't done what you did, who knows if I'd even have been able to get away." She massaged the spot between her eyes.

Omar absentmindedly twirled his fingers, and the gravel flowed in complicated patterns beneath them. "I talked to Andy and Helena and I'm going to take over all the extra farm work."

She blinked, then groaned. "You didn't tell them..."

"Of course I didn't tell them *that*. I just said I'd do all of it so you can go back with Lynn. It's much fairer that way, anyhow. Besides, it'll help me get my strength back." He flexed his biceps, pinching them sadly.

"But you're busy teaching Lynn and James and working with Bridgett."

He smiled grimly. "It's not like Bridgett and I are making much progress." They still hadn't been able to reach the skyscraper in Purgatory or discover much about who built it. Meanwhile, the Dead were getting restless. The Tower seemed to upset them, too. Omar raised his eyebrows. "You should be with us, looking for these people."

She wrinkled her nose and tossed a pebble into the stream. It hit harder than she intended and ricochetted into the scrub, sending a chipmunk streaking out across the wash. The little creature scrambled to the top of a nearby boulder and sat chipping at them and twitching his tail in indignation.

Omar ran a soothing fingertip down the inside of Magdalene's arm. "Close your eyes."

She let herself relax against him, and her eyes fluttered shut. The other world melted into place and her feelings lifted their boot from her neck again. She smiled at Omar. He still looked different here, his eyes and hair giving off blue-black glints like raven's wings. "Better?" he asked.

She nodded.

"I really am sorry, Magdalene."

"I know. So am I."

He kept stroking her arm, and she surrendered to the feeling of it. "Please come with Bridgett and me to Purgatory."

She stared out over the horizon. The landscape looked almost identical to the Waking World, the red rock desert stretched out beneath the searing sun, except here a clown floated above them, held aloft by a single balloon with *Death* written on it in looping script. He had long, black, greasy hair and tattered black clothes. His crimson lipstick dripped from the corners of his mouth like blood.

"Whoever built the Tower, what do they want with me?" Magdalene mused.

Omar smiled, but there was a furrow between his brows. "That's what you're worried about, isn't it? Why you're not coming with us? The Tower."

Magdalene chewed the inside of her cheek. She had the unsettling feeling that the dark doors of the Tower were just waiting to materialize behind her eyelids, as if part of her was already there. She watched the clown drift by, and he stared back at her, then pulled a kazoo from his front pocket. It was sleek, black and metallic and reminded her of the barrel of a gun. He gave her an unsettling smile, then brought the kazoo to his lips. The full orchestral version of *Ride of the Valkyries* blasted from it, echoing from the canyon walls. The clown's gaze never left Magdalene's until he disappeared behind the cottonwood and the music faded into the distance.

Omar cast Magdalene a sidelong smirk, but she ignored it. "I could get to the Tower again, if I wanted," she said suddenly. "I could go in and just ask them what they want."

Omar's eyes widened. "Are you crazy? *No.*"

She dug her fingernails into her knees. "I don't think they'd hurt me."

He frowned. "What makes you think that? Tower Guy had you *arrested.*"

Magdalene avoided his gaze. "It's just a feeling I have."

"Feelings can be wrong."

Omar was studying her far too closely for her liking. She tried to smile, but she felt it go askew on her face. "What's the point of me helping you, then? I'm not seeing what I bring to the table here." She tossed another rock into the stream. It bounced off the surface like rubber and soared in a high arc, growing flat and floppy and splatting back to earth as a slice of bologna.

Omar snickered, then his smile faded. "I feel like you need to be there. These people went after you for a reason. We don't know what the reason is, but you're a part of this somehow. And I don't want you out of my sight."

Magdalene was silent, staring into the distance and chewing on her lip. Finally, she sighed. "I'll come."

They found Bridgett sitting in a brightly patterned club chair in an open-air market, tapping her foot on the cobblestones and staring at the Tower. A miniature school bus drove round and round her seat, and an elephant the size of a puppy slithered between her ankles, blowing blasts out its trumpetlike ears and caressing her legs with its trunk. Bridgett didn't seem to notice.

"Why do the villains always hide in a tower?" Omar asked as they walked up. "It's cliché."

"That's probably why you see it as a tower," Bridget said curtly. "It's an effect of the storytelling culture on the collective unconscious."

"I think it looks like a tower because that's what it is," Magdalene mused. "It's a skyscraper. I think they're some sort of business."

Bridgett looked up and broke into a grin. "Magdalene! You came!"

Omar regarded Magdalene thoughtfully. "Why do you say that?"

She shrugged. She just knew, but she wasn't about to admit that out loud. The Tower was steely finger jabbing into the silvery sky. She could still feel the pulse of its door handle under her fingertips, and a strange longing nagged deep in her guts, the sense she was missing out on something, that she needed to be somewhere.

Magdalene tore her gaze from the building. "Things here look like what the creators want them to look like. What they're thinking about, what they want, or how they feel. Like my tree that fruited meatballs when I was hungry. And it looks like an office building to me." Magdalene squatted down to pet the elephant. It wrapped its trunk around her leg and honked lovingly.

Bridgett and Omar exchanged a look. "What business does a business have in Purgatory?" Omar wondered. "You can't sell anything to the Dead. They don't have money, and they don't need anything." He glanced around, a glimmer of amusement in his dark eyes. A woman in overalls and a top hat perused the displays of misshapen fruit, tossing pieces of it onto the ground. A naked person, armless and with barbie crotch, inched around like a caterpillar, gulping it down.

Bridgett raised her chin. "The Dead aren't the only ones here, and selling goods isn't the only thing a business does." She crossed her arms and glared up at the skyscraper. "The Guardians don't seem to be around as much lately. Have you noticed?"

Omar leaned back as a man stretched his neck into an elongated u-bend and shoved his face in his as he passed. "The Guardians tend to stay away from me, but you're right, I haven't seen many lately." The man whipped his head back and disappeared into an alley.

"I've tried talking to them," Bridgett said. "I can't get much information, of course—we're not the best of friends, the Guardians and I—but lately they seem confused and weak."

Omar raised his eyebrows. "Do you think the Tower is affecting them somehow? Draining them of power?" The tiny school bus tried to drive up his leg and he nudged it away.

Bridgett frowned. "I don't know how it would be done. It seems impossible. Perhaps I'm just imagining it."

Magdalene sat down cross-legged on the ground and the elephant crawled into her lap. "What are the Guardians?"

Omar and Bridgett looked at her, confused. "What do you mean?" Bridgett asked.

"I mean, are they Dead people that just got hired for the job or something?"

Bridgett rested her chin on her hand. "No. They're manifestations of a force that protects the integrity of this place, keeps it from being overrun by the living."

"They're like a force field?" Magdalene asked.

"More like a police force, I think," Omar said.

"Yes, they're individual beings, so to speak," Bridgett concurred, "not just different parts of a single power."

"So, who's the police chief?" Magdalene asked.

Omar and Bridgett exchanged a glance. "Good question," Omar said. Bridgett shifted in her seat, her forehead wrinkling. The woman in overalls was now playing badminton with a man in dirty cutoffs while the caterpillar person rolled back and forth between them, trying to catch the shuttlecock with their rubbery, elongated lips.

"That man, Jeffrey, what was it he said about the people who built the Tower?" Magdalene asked. "They're hoarders and manipulators or something?"

"Builders and destroyers, hoarders and manipulators," Omar said gruffly, imitating Jeffrey's voice.

Magdalene smiled dryly. "Do you know what that means?"

Omar shrugged. "Jeffrey is fairly lucid, but who knows? I've been talking to others of the Dead, some of them more coherent than Jeffrey, but none of them can tell me anything useful."

Magdalene poked the elephant's belly and it honked happily. She took a breath, not meeting her friends' eyes. "I don't think you guys take the Dead seriously enough sometimes." The little elephant wiggled, and its eyes turned into flashing red stars. She poked it again and it honked contentedly. "You're too used to it here, I think. You have too much power. You're living, and they're not, and you're too aware of the difference." She ducked her head and concentrated on petting the elephant.

Omar sat down beside her. "Maybe you're right. Maybe I am a little condescending to them."

"I don't know if I'd go that far," said Bridgett. "I think the gist of what Magdalene is saying is that most of the Dead may not have fully-formed consciousness at this point—they usually just have just the rubble left behind from their life on Earth—but the majority of them are still fully formed *souls*."

"We're treating them like children, when they want to be treated like adults," Omar said.

"Perhaps an apt analogy." Bridgett drew her legs up onto the chair and sat cross-legged, gazing thoughtfully at the Tower.

"Have you seen Morris lately?" Magdalene asked. She hadn't had the guts to see him again, and the guilt was eating at her.

Bridgett cast her a compassionate look. "He comes to my spot sometimes. He likes it there. But I haven't seen him in about two days."

They fell into silence, gazing at the Tower.

Bridgett's shoulders sagged. "I'm just so tired of getting nowhere." She stood and stomped her foot. "What gives them the right to come in here and tear up my neighborhood? And without even introducing themselves!" She stalked off down the lane, the tiny school bus trailing after her.

Magdalene and Omar exchanged a look.

They wandered back to the Commune as the sun slanted westward. Omar went to shower, and Magdalene went into the kitchen to help Lynn with dinner.

Lynn grinned when she saw her. "I get you back!" She danced across the floor as she pulled mixing bowls out of the cupboards. "Omar said some claptrap about needing more fresh air, so he's helping Helena." She stopped mid-waggle and looked askance at Magdalene. "You're not pregnant, too, are you?"

Magdalene glared at Lynn over her shoulder as she sliced zucchini.

"Good," Lynn said. "Though that would be one good-looking baby."

Magdalene scoffed and turned her gaze back on the squash, trying to banish the vision of the evil, slimy thing coiled up in Helena's womb.

After dinner, Helana called another of her famous meetings. Andy stood before the tall windows as the rest of them took their seats in the sitting room. Helena sat beside him, her feet propped on an ottoman. Her pregnancy wasn't showing yet, but she wore a flowy, pink maternity shirt anyhow. Magdalene slid onto the couch between Omar and Bridgett, who was bent over her ankles, pulling her long socks up and down, up and down.

"Good afternoon, friends," Andy began as they settled in. "I received a phone call yesterday evening from Frederick. You may all recall that he mentioned a friend of his might be interested in living with us. Well, in two days, Frederick will be bringing not only one but *two* people. Their names are Ingrid and Matthew. I know we'll all do our best to welcome them and ease them into our lifestyle so they don't get frightened off."

Bridgett froze, and her dreamy gaze focused on an invisible horizon. She raised her hand slowly, her pointer and middle fingers forming a V, her other fingers gently curled inward. "*Omne genu flectatur cælestium, terrestrium et infernorum,*" she said.

As everyone stared at her, she went back to her socks.

CHAPTER TWO

Death Will Not Stop the Party

Magdalene and Omar sat under the cottonwood, the heat pounding them with dry fists. Magdalene was practicing her manipulation of the dreamscape by giving Omar a halo of butterflies, but his t-shirt also kept melting away, exposing his broad chest.

Heat rose to Magdalene's cheeks as she opened her eyes on the Waking World. "I think *you're* the one who's imagining your shirt off, actually."

A corner of Omar's lips curled up. "Sure. It's hot out here, that's probably why."

Magdalene huffed. "Why do I have to be able to form a perfect landscape, anyway? Purgatory is chaos, and I'd have to fight with a thousand souls about what things look like."

He shrugged. "You don't have to form a perfect landscape. But you're getting an idea what it feels like to confront someone else's will, right?

Magdalene hugged her knees and nodded. "Your will feels like electricity, but in a good way. It sort of reminds me of sitting in one of those vibrating massage chairs in the mall."

Omar nodded slowly. "Interesting."

Magalene rested her chin on her knees. "What does mine feel like?"

Omar looked thoughtful. "When it rains here in the spring and everything smells like sweet, new sage, and the little flowers start poking out of the sand."

Magdalene snorted. "Really?"

"That's how I'd describe it."

She scooted closer to him and put her head on his shoulder. "That's a lot more poetic than a mall massage chair."

He put his arm around her. "Your will's just prettier than mine, I guess."

Magdalene watched the thunderheads billowing against the deep blue of the southern sky. They seemed closer today and she wondered if they'd finally get rain. "That elephant yesterday, and the school bus, were they human? Living people that were dreaming, or Dead people? Or were they just projections of someone's will?"

"Those were just pieces of life force. The Dead and the living are coherent units of it, but there are loose bits of it that aren't as organized and are more easily shaped by outside will."

"What makes someone a coherent unit? What makes us different than the loose bits?"

Omar plucked a twig from a nearby rabbitbrush and twirled it between his fingers. "That's an interesting question. All I can say is, the more life force that gathers together, the more powerful or luminous it gets. I guess that's consciousness. Some living things—or Dead things—have more of it than others. If you squished fifteen of those little elephants together, you'd probably have enough consciousness for a person." He took his arm from around her shoulders. "Close your eyes."

Magdalene obeyed, the scene reforming. Omar wore a black t-shirt now and had a hint of lightning in his dark eyes. He brought his hands together and when he drew them apart again, a tiny, colorful bird sat perched on his palm, like the one he'd formed the day before. It hopped around, peering at Magdalene with its bright eyes. "We can use our will to shape life force," he said. "We can draw it to us if we have force of will. If we lack will, however, we can disintegrate into less coherent bits when we die, or even sometimes while we're still alive."

The bird let out two musical chirps, dipping its tail, then fluttered back up the canyon. Magdalene watched it go, her scalp prickling. "What is will, then? Where does it come from? What gives one creature more of it than another?"

"That," Omar said, his gaze following the bird, "is one of the great mysteries of the universe."

That night they went to visit Jeffery again. The street he lived on looked completely different than it had on their last visit, and Omar let Magdalene practice her navigation skills by guiding them. She tried not to overthink it, letting the faint tug of her instinct pull her through streets cobbled with colorful, half-buried rubber balls. They went through a gigantic nylon tunnel and found a round hobbit door at the end. Opening it, they found a familiar cluttered apartment. Magalene tried not to let Omar see her relief as he gave her a fist bump.

The television was still on, showing a smiling man in a hairpiece pulling disturbing faces to the accompaniment of a laugh track. The little white dog, Matey, came jogging into the room, his long body writhing with pleasure as he greeted Magdalene with a human-toothed smile. Jeffrey ambled in after him, his dingy bathrobe swishing around his bare, bony ankles. He regarded Magdalene beadily as he flopped down in his armchair. She and Omar sat on the floor, and Matey coiled in Magdalene's lap.

"How have you been, Jeffrey?" Magdalene asked.

He stared at her. "It's a house of shit cards. A straight flush of turds, and here I am, holding the queen." His lips puckered into a fleshy smile.

Magdalene petted the long spiral of Matey's body, fighting her instinct to look away from the Dead man. "The people who built the Tower, have you seen them?"

Jeffrey's face wavered, briefly turning into something infantile, scared and furious. "They've blocked the roads out!"

Magdalene and Omar jumped and exchanged startled looks.

Jeffrey turned bland eyes to the television and his face melted back to normal.

"Do you want to leave here, Jeffrey?" Omar asked. "Are they keeping you from leaving?"

Jeffrey glanced at Magdalene. "Abnormally good-looking girl."

Omar tried not to smile. "Indeed."

Magdalene ignored them. "Why have they blocked the roads?"

Jeffrey squinted at the TV. "Toll booth," he grunted. "Passport. Hundred questions." He scratched his belly with hands that were surprisingly delicate, the fingernails immaculately clean. "Waste of time," he concluded.

Omar's brow furrowed, and he stood. Magdalene coaxed the reluctant dog out of her lap and stood as well, glancing at Omar for some clue as to why they were leaving, but getting none.

"Thank you for the information, Jeffrey," Omar said.

Magdalene smiled at the old man. "It was nice seeing you. We'll come back soon."

"I'll bake a cake," Jeffrey drawled. Matey snaked back up into his lap and Jeffrey caressed him, his eyes lost on the television screen again.

Omar and Magdalene ducked out the door of the apartment and into a crowded restaurant. In one booth, a man yelled at a huge, complicated copy machine that was spitting paper airplanes out of a slot. In another, a family of four gobbled cherry tomatoes from a large bowl. The walls were plastered with dried starfish whose googly eyes followed Magdalene and Omar as they passed.

They went out the door and the din of the restaurant faded. They were in a street lined with small, ranch style houses. "Where are we going?" Magalene asked.

"To try to get more information." Omar frowned. "From what Jeffery said, I'm worried these people are trying to take control of the dark portals."

"What?"

A crow wearing a baseball hat swooped down out of the silvery sky. "Chicken butt," it said, then alighted in a tree, pulled a tiny pack of cigarettes from under its wing, and lit one up.

"What does that mean, they're taking control of the dark portals?" Magdalene asked.

Omar's brow furrowed. "They might be trying to control who gets out of here, who goes through the portals to…whatever awaits them on the other side."

A hand suddenly thrust out of the ground at Omar's feet, grabbing his leg with grey-green fingers. Omar kicked free and jumped back, pulling Magdalene with him.

Magdalene's heart pounded as the hand groped at the empty air and pawed at the dirt. Omar put his arm around her and guided her around it. She glanced back and shuddered. The hand threw clods of dirt at them as they walked away. "Did we wander into someone's nightmare?"

Omar grimaced. "Maybe just my own."

Magdalene studied him. His father had disappeared into one of the dark portals. Was he afraid of what was on the other side, worried about what had happened to his father? Were his fears affecting the landscape?

Omar ran a hand through his dark curls, and Magdalene laughed. "Oh, my God, Omar. Look at your nails."

He blinked at them and broke into a grin. They were painted glossy black. "Metal." He flipped her the devil horns.

The path had turned into a paved street and houses began to appear on either side. A man stood beside a mound of dirt on an eye-meltingly green lawn, arguing with a little mole, who snuffled at him and continued to dig.

"Why do you think someone wants to control the portals?" Magdalene asked. "And how?"

"I'm hoping we can figure that out."

"Wouldn't you and Bridgett have noticed if they were messing with the portals?"

Omar gave her a grim smile. "We don't get near those places if we can help it. They're terrifying. And besides, it's not like regular navigation. You have to travel with intent to get to them, so it's not like we wander by them on accident."

The sun sank behind the distant, flat horizon, the sky staining pink and gold. Darkness fell quickly as they walked, and Magdalene watched in wonder as a huge, green planet with orange rings rose in the east. As they approached an intersection, they came upon a crowd of creatures waiting at a bus stop. A bus rumbled up to it, its motor chugging like a steam engine's. The creatures all climbed aboard and the door shut.

The bus's engine began to rumble, low at first, then louder, growing to a deafening roar until it blasted off into the twilit sky, trailing a plume of fire from its exhaust pipe. It streaked toward the ringed planet, growing smaller until it looked like a distant comet.

Magdalene watched the comet dwindle until it was just another star among the thousands that had begun to twinkle above. "Are we going to one of the portals now?"

Omar shook his head. "I wouldn't take you anywhere near one. Bridgett and I will try that later. Now, we're going to see more Dead people."

Magdalene scowled. "You don't think I could handle a portal? I've been through enough, and I'm still alive."

Omar stopped walking and sighed. "Magdalene, getting near a death portal is horrible. It's like..." He watched bemusedly as a mailbox lurched across the road on three tiny legs, waving its red flag forlornly. "At first, it feels like walking into the sickroom of someone you love who's dying. You get a dread and blackness in the pit of your stomach, thinking about death."

Memories of her grandmother's long illness lurched to the surface of Magdalene's mind. Omar took her hand and they continued down the path. "The dread gets stronger the closer you get. You want to run, but you also have the feeling that there's nowhere to run to, nowhere safe, no one in the world that cares about you at all." He frowned, the light from the strange planet reflecting in his dark eyes. "They're lonesome places, and I'm not looking forward to getting close to one of them again."

"If I go with you, you won't feel alone," Magdalene said.

Omar shook his head. "I can't put you through that—especially not now, when you've been going through so much."

Magdalene didn't want to argue about it, but it still annoyed her. She wasn't a child, or some sort of emotional invalid. If Omar and Bridgett could handle it, why couldn't she?

They turned down a side street and the small houses were replaced by huge mansions. They passed one with onion-shaped domes painted in a swirling blue and gold pattern that spiraled slowly upward. Another was surrounded by a moat, with a portcullis over the heavy, wooden gate.

"Is this where the Dead rich people live?" Magdalene asked.

Omar snickered. "There's no currency here, except in imagination and will. If we came back tomorrow, it would look different."

Twilight deepened around them. Omar led her through an iron kissing gate and down a lane flanked by ancient, twisted oaks with white and blue fairy lights twinkling amongst their waxy leaves. An assortment of bells dangled from the branches of one, and they tinkled and clanked as Magdalene and Omar passed. Another was hung with expensive-looking shoes, and another was covered in butterflies who milled about, gently fluttering their neon blue wings.

The path opened up and a manor house came into view, its many windows glowing. A peacock strutted across the lane in front of them, the murmur of a radio sports commentator issuing from his open beak. They crossed a circular drive and approached the tall mahogany doors, which stood ajar. As they passed through, Magdalene ran her fingers along their carvings of Egyptian-style figures in complicated sexual poses.

They stepped into an anteroom and Magdalene blinked. Sunlight fell through a skylight onto a stone fountain in the shape of a fish, which gushed water from its mouth into a wide stone basin. Golden and silver koi jumped from the basin, against the flow of water and into the fish's mouth, glittering like disco balls.

"It's beautiful," Magdalene breathed.

Voices emanated from an archway beyond the fountain, mingling with the musical burble of water. The marble statues lining the walls watched Magdalene and Omar as they headed for the noise.

They ducked into a large, crowded room, and a chaotic jumble of music and conversation engulfed them. A man sat on a tall table staring intently at a vase of flowers as they slowly changed color and shape. Another man drew designs on the wall with his finger, which flared up in bright lines of flame before dying out. Onlookers hooted and applauded his efforts.

Magdalene and Omar waded deeper into the room. The Dead watched them as they passed; Magdalene recognized the clown dressed in black who she'd seen floating over the cottonwood before. His mouth curved in a slow smile, showing pointed teeth.

"Omar!" A man strode through the crowd, grinning. He wore a purple velvet smoking jacket and a thick green tie. Perched on his sleek brown hair was a party hat with "Wow!" written on it in glitter, and a martini glass filled with violently purple liquid was balanced between his fingers. He leaned in conspiratorially. "I'm so glad you came. Charles and Elmore are going to give a short dramatic performance later. The only problem being, Charles must have thought this was an ugly sweater party. It hurts to look at him. I'll have to knit him something presentable when I have time." He turned his smile onto Magdalene. "Who's your lovely friend?"

"Nathan, this is Magdalene," Omar said.

Nathan looked Magdalene up and down. "Fabulous. Skin like an apple blossom, and those eyes! I should paint my bedroom that color." He shook Magdalene's hand. His face was a rapid succession of eloquent expressions, and yet it didn't seem to change at all. It made her dizzy.

Another man approached, and Omar had to back up several steps to include him in the circle. He was suspended in an adult-sized infant swing on a rolling frame, his legs dangling from the harness' leg holes. He was wearing overalls with bright fabric flowers sewn to the shoulder straps, and his lips drooped in an exaggerated frown. "Hello, you guys," he said in a slow, dejected voice.

"Magdalene, Omar, this is David." Nathan sipped his poisonous-looking drink. "My goodness, your costume certainly is inventive, isn't it?" His party hat now read ??!?!

Magdalene shook David's hand, and he gave her a wan smile, then rolled off again, the wheels of his contraption squeaking shrilly.

The characters on Nathan's hat morphed to spell out *Sigh* as he turned back to Omar. "Don't tell me you've come to talk to me about those *people* again. I've told you I don't know anything."

Omar smiled dryly. "What sort of party would it be without gossip?

Nathan rolled his eyes over the rim of his martini glass. "You *would* say that."

"I wanted to ask you about the roads out of this place," Omar said. "Have you heard about people having trouble leaving?"

Nathan frowned thoughtfully and took a huge sip of his drink, which seemed perennially full. His hat went blank. "Barry, the poor thing, felt ready to travel, and he went the long way, but they turned him back." A look of distress passed over Nathan's face, chased off by a teasing smile. "But we don't know what we'd do without Barry here. With him gone, who would slump around with that painful hairstyle, complaining about his mother?" *Bon temps roule!* appeared on his hat. "He should just stay here and enjoy the fun. I don't understand the hurry to leave."

"What did Barry say happened when they turned him back?" Omar asked.

Nathan's eyes wandered over the crowd and fixed on a group across the room that was playing a particularly limber game of

Twister. A smile flitted across his face, then he sighed. "Let's just ask him. Barry!" His gaze fixed on someone behind Magdalene, and he waved the hand that wasn't holding the drink. "Come join our little clique!"

A man in jeans and an off-white crew neck slid carefully toward them through the crowd, trying not to spill a clear plastic cup containing amber liquid and ice cubes. He had to dodge a group of rowdy boys slapping each other with large salmon, and a flailing, mouthless man with swirling kaleidoscopes where his eyes should be, before finally reaching their side. He had a friendly, freckled face, and his massively curly blond hair was parted on one side so that it looked like he had a leaning pyramid of frizz on his head.

He smiled and gave them a jerky wave. "Hey."

"Barry, dear, these are my friends Omar and Magdalene," Nathan said.

"Live ones," Barry remarked with a shy smile. "You always have a novelty act, Nathan."

Nathan scoffed. "I'd find a more exciting act than Omar. He wants to ask you questions about your little trip."

Barry blinked at Omar, his expression hesitant. "It was a disappointing experience."

"What happened?" Omar asked.

Barry shrugged. "They had this guy at the gate, face like a slice of ham and about half as much personality. He wanted me to fill out *paperwork*." He grimaced, slurping his drink.

"Was the guy living?" Omar asked.

Barry shook his head. "Dead as a doornail. I don't know who made him queen of security, but I filled the forms out anyway because, you know, it's not like I had anything else to do with my afterlife at the time." He looked around at the crowd, spinning his drink between his hands. "You should have seen some of the other poor things there trying to get through. They couldn't even hold a pencil. I filled out the papers and gave them back to Queen Hamface, and he told me I wasn't appropriate or something. They had some force field, like the jail on the Starship Enterprise, that kept me out." Barry gave Omar a morose look over the rim of his cup as he gulped his drink. "And the worst of it is, some of those other globs that can't keep their rear ends from turning into a cheese chimichanga, they got a pass. It was so unfair."

Nathan laid a consoling hand on Barry's shoulder. "At least you didn't miss my party. Later Charles and his sweater are going to star in a short drama." Both men snorted into their drinks.

"I'm sorry that happened to you, Barry," Omar said, "and thank you for the information. You, too Nathan, you've been a lot of help."

"You two aren't leaving, are you?" Nathan complained. "Oh, Omar, you never stay for the fun." He glanced at Magdalene. "But it looks like you have all the fun you need right there. Oh look, she's blushing!" Nathan turned to Barry. "Isn't she darling? She's like one of those paintings by a horny Victorian artist."

Omar exchanged a smirk with Magdalene. "It was nice to meet you guys," she said.

"You two come back soon," Nathan said. He and Barry turned away just as Magdalene woke up in her bed.

After trying for about fifteen minutes, she knew she wouldn't be able to get back to sleep, so she padded down to Omar's room in her pajamas. She was glad when he answered the door to her soft knock.

He stepped aside to let her in, and they sat on his bed, settling back on the pillows. "What just happened?" Magdalene stretched out, her leg touching his. "The Tower people are making the Dead fill out paperwork in order to go through the portals?"

"Not literally, I think, at least not in the strictest sense." His bare foot waggled. "Everyone and everything who lives in Purgatory is constantly shaped by the wills of all present. Perception there is even less absolute than in the waking world. Barry is an extremely coherent Dead man who has managed to retain a lot of imagery and memory of his past life. He may have seen the obstruction of the portal as a guard requiring him to fill out paperwork, but not all beings would have seen it that way."

Magdalene chewed her lip. "But, no matter how people are seeing it, the portal is being blocked."

Omar frowned. "Yeah, and they have a list of criteria or something to pass through, because some souls were allowed to pass while others weren't. It's disturbing. All of it. I don't know whether to be more or less worried by the fact that the guard was Dead."

"Why?"

"If the guard had been living, it'd mean Tower Guy has a whole army of people from the Waking World able to exercise their wills to a disturbing degree there. As it is, I'm worried that they're able to recruit the Dead to do their work for them."

Magdalene fidgeted with the frayed hem of her pajama shirt. "So, they're using their powers to get the Dead on their side."

Omar chuckled. "I'd like to know how they're managing that."

"What I want to know is why the Dead want to go through the portals, if they're as horrible as you say."

He shrugged. "All I know is, sooner or later the Dead in Purgatory seem to be called to the portals, either for rebirth or for whatever is down the dark road. It is almost as inevitable as death is on this side. Whether the other portals lead them simply into nonexistence or into some other life, or maybe into something I can't even conceive, I don't know." He fell silent, his fingers distractedly tracing the embroidered pattern on his blanket. Magdalene knew he must be thinking about his father.

She didn't like to think about nonexistence. What if Morris was called to that path? "There are other portals, though, right? Not just one? Why doesn't Barry take another?"

Omar seemed to come back himself. "It's complicated with the portals. The Dead are generally only called by one of them. Dead people don't, as a rule, travel much. They end up somewhere in Purgatory and they stay there." He scrubbed his hand over his face. "And, to tell you the truth, I don't know how serious Barry was about wanting to leave. Other people that I've seen called, it's an obsession. They can't think about anything else. They retreat into themselves until one day they start walking and they're never seen again. I think Barry was just bored and wanted to take a trip." Omar shrugged. "I don't know, though. I've never seen them turned away. Maybe if they meet an obstruction, the obsession leaves."

Magdalene yawned. "That was a fun party." She laid down, stretching out on the bed. "Why are some dead people so coherent, and other people not?"

"That's a good question." He glanced at her, a smile curling his lips. He reached over to turn off his bedside lamp then stretched out beside her.

Moonlight streamed through a gap in his curtains, casting a silvery stripe across the ceiling. Magdalene cuddled closer to Omar, pressing her forehead against his chest, and he slid his arm around her. Her heart skipped a beat.

"Some people are just more together to begin with," he said, his breath stirring her hair. "Maybe that translates into more lucidity in the other world. Others, if they stay there a while, become more lucid with time. Those people can be weird, though. Purgatory is all they know, it's like they've grown up there."

Magdalene lay there, feeling the rise and fall of Omar's breathing. "It's like if a kid grew up in the circus, they might act like a clown."

He snickered. "A little like that."

He fell silent and his breathing became deep and even. Magdalene was comfortable in Omar's arms and liked the feeling of being next to him. Eventually, she fell into normal, muddled dreams.

CHAPTER THREE

Disney Princess and Fuckboy

Magdalene awoke with a jolt. Pearly light shone through the window. Omar was asleep beside her, one arm draped over the pillow above his head and a faint smile on his lips. She stirred, and he turned over, throwing an arm around her and pulling her closer. "Good morning," he muttered sleepily. His fingertips traced the curve of her waist, teasing the bare skin between her shirt and pajama bottoms.

Warmth poured through her and her heartbeat accelerated. Slowly, shyly, his touch ran over her hip, down her leg toward her knee, and Magdalene was overwhelmed by the heat of his body, his breathing, his closeness.

Out of nowhere, fear surged through her. Her body tensed and her chest constricted around her lungs.

Omar pulled away. "I'm sorry."

Magdalene shook her head. She wanted to tell him it was okay, but the words wouldn't come. A feeling oozed in, like a rivulet of sewer in a churning stream: Stan's hands on her breasts, the smell of his rancid breath.

Magdalene squeezed her eyes shut and concentrated on steadying her breathing. She wanted to pull Omar close again and make those feelings go away, but she couldn't. Her head swam.

"I'm sorry," Omar repeated.

She couldn't look at his face. She was sure it would be full of pity and contempt and disappointment.

I'm a tease.

I'm a coward.

I'm a crazy bitch.

She could feel Omar's gaze on her, but he didn't say anything, and he didn't try to touch her again. She wanted him to understand what she was feeling, but if she opened up like that, it would just be awkward and scare him away.

If he really cared about her, he'd understand, right?

No one will ever care about you like that.

Magdalene pressed her palms into her eyes and forced herself to breathe slowly through her nose.

"I'm not being fair to you," Omar said. "You've had a pretty hard life..."

She huffed.

"Magdalene—"

"I just..." She pressed her fists to both temples, as if she could squish her brain back into shape. "I don't want to talk about it. I'm fine. I'm sorry." She jumped out of bed, mumbling another apology as she went out the door. She just couldn't deal with this right now.

She passed by James in the sitting room on her way to her own room. He watched after her with his eyebrows raised, but she ignored him.

Magdalene stood in the shower for a long time, barely feeling the water running down her body. She cursed herself out loud as she shampooed her hair and scrubbed herself. Then she sat in the tub, pressing her forehead into her knees as the water cascaded over her neck. By the time she got out she felt numb, except for a dull shame pounding behind her eyelids.

She found Lynn in the kitchen, putting sheets of miniature scones in the oven. Omar, his hair still wet, was pouring himself a cup of coffee while James leaned against the dishwasher, drinking from his own cup. They all looked up when Magdalene walked in, and she froze.

Lynn and James both broke into broad smirks. Lynn started dancing as she put the next pan of scones in to bake, singing "Let's spend the night together."

Magdalene's cheeks burned red hot. She'd worried about so many things, and yet somehow forgot to worry about *this*. She made herself meet Omar's gaze.

He gave her a sheepish grimace and gestured toward James. "Don't blame me, it was this guy with the big mouth. I told them we were just talking and you fell asleep."

Lynn snorted. "Way to make sure you have your stories straight."

"Stop." Omar's voice was quiet, but it banished the smirks from Lynn and James' faces. His gaze never left Magdalene's. "We've got to have a chat with Andy about what the Dead told us."

Magdalene nodded.

Lynn and James watched them with furrowed brows. "He's in his office," Lynn said. She started tossing baked scones into a basket. "Take him some breakfast. He rarely eats lately unless you remind him."

Omar took the basket. As he and Magdalene turned to leave, Lynn shot her a look and mouthed, *What's going on?*

Later, Magdalene mouthed back. She and Omar went out the doorway. Lynn and James started talking in low voices as soon as they were out of sight.

Omar glanced at her as they went down the hallway. He opened his mouth, and Magdalene tensed, anticipating some sort of Serious Talk. But he didn't say anything. Instead, he took her hand. Warmth flowed into her where his skin touched hers, and her shoulders relaxed.

Andy looked up from his computer and uttered a grunt of surprise as they walked in. They cleared the paperwork and other debris off the chairs and sat down. Omar perched the basket of scones on top of a pile of notebooks on the desk, and Andy took one. He frowned as he examined their faces. "What's up?"

Omar recounted what they'd learned the night before about the blocking of the portals while Andy nibbled his breakfast with a perturbed expression.

"They're gaining power," he remarked. "They're trying to control who gets out. How and why?"

Omar glanced at Magdalene, his foot tapping the carpet. "Magdalene has a theory they're a business."

Andy spat a curse. "Profit! The worst of reasons. How would they even make that work? I'd love to see their business model." He scoffed, spraying his computer screen with crumbs. "If they start building golf courses in the afterlife, I'll be sure to take the first portal into a dog's womb when I die." He threw down his pencil and it skidded across his desk, clinking to rest against a dirty coffee cup. "I thought I was a pioneer in this field, and now some halfwit lump with an MBA got the jump on me? How are they doing it?"

Omar chuckled dryly. "You're too much of an academic, Andy. I'll put it out there for your consideration that the desire for profit isn't limited to halfwit lumps. They may have another motive, but I wouldn't rule out money."

Andy considered him thoughtfully for a moment, then turned back to his computer, his fingers tapping over the keyboard. "I've been calculating how much energy it might take to build a control center like theirs with an adequate system for keeping out intruders." He spun his chair to face Omar again.

"Probably not that much to construct it," Omar said. "It's *maintaining* it that seems ridiculous. It would take up all your time and energy."

"Precisely," Andy said. "And now they're also sealing the portals, apparently manipulating the Dead into working security for the venture. We don't know how effective this scheme is yet, but at any rate they seem to be vertically integrating, as it were." He looked down his nose at Omar, as if he were a teacher posing a particularly difficult question to his favorite student. "What do you think? Is it just a group of them, working in shifts to perpetuate the project? Or is it something else?"

Omar gave him his little smile, his gaze distant. "Or they've somehow built a machine to channel the energy for them. But that's your area of expertise, professor. I've never tried to channel more energy than I can with my own hands. It seems like a dangerous game to play."

"Dangerous, indeed," Andy mumbled, his expression sobering.

Omar gazed at the older man. "Their objective has always been different than yours, Andy. You've concentrated on exploration and investigation, while they're focused on conquest. They haven't outwitted you. You haven't even matched wits until now."

Andy grimaced. "What's bugging me most is that I *must* know them. Anyone else working on projects that could relate to Purgatory, I've approached them about collaboration. They've *all turned me down*. And yet..."

"Here they are, capitalizing on Purgatory without involving you at all," Omar said.

"I have no idea which one of those bastards would do this to me." Andy took his head in his hands, his hair poking out like tufts of bleached wheat between his long, thick-jointed fingers. He sent Omar a sidelong glance. "In terms of sheer power, you could likely overcome them and demolish their little edifice, correct?"

Omar shrugged. "Maybe. But what good would it do? They'd just build it again. I won't fight what I can't see. All it would do is bring more attention to us and give them more insight into our capabilities."

Andy grunted. "Like I've told you, I suspect they've found a way to divert energy from the Waking World to fuel their projects. So, it's possible that any solution on our end will have to be four-dimensional, so to speak. We'll have to find their center of operations in the Waking World and go from there."

Magdalene sat listening to them talk, chewing on her lip. She finally spoke up. "And I'd like to know what they want with me."

The two men exchanged an anxious glance, and Omar took her hand, lacing his fingers with hers.

Frederick arrived just before noon with his two friends, Matthew and Ingrid. The Commune gathered in the front room to meet them—all save Bridgett.

In contrast with the gregarious Frederick, the two newcomers seemed reserved. Magdalene caught Matthew's gaze skimming her body, but he looked her in the eyes as he shook her hand—firmly, like a man interviewing for a job.

Ingrid was willowy, with a heart-shaped face, stunning hazel eyes, and a thick, black braid that fell to the middle of her back. Magdalene shifted on her feet as this elegant creature shook Omar's hand, giving him a smile that lit up her face and showed perfect, even teeth.

The sitting room seemed crowded with all of them there. Helena had moved in more chairs, but the newcomers and Frederick took up all the space on the couch. Omar sat in one of the club chairs and Magdalene settled with her back against his knees.

Frederick told James about a prank one of his friends had pulled on their data structures professor while Andy and Helena made small talk with Matthew and Ingrid. Lynn was uncharacteristically silent, tapping her fingers on the arm of her chair. Magdalene didn't feel like talking much, either. She was glad when the smell of baking lasagna wafted in, signaling that it was time for her and Lynn to get lunch on the table. They went into the kitchen.

The friends exchanged a look as they worked together, getting the lasagna, garlic bread, and salad ready. "Do the new guys make your nervous?" Lynn whispered.

Magdalene pursed her lips. "I thought it was just me."

Lynn studied her, then broke into a grin. "You're worried about Omar and Disney Princess out there, aren't you?"

Magdalene scowled and grabbed a handful of silverware from the drawer. She was a bit too rough, and a fork clattered to the floor. She huffed as she picked it up.

Lynn laughed. "Girl, you have nothing to worry about. She may be a Disney princess but you're a Victoria's Secret model. There's no competition."

Magdalene grunted as she set the table. Maybe Omar preferred the princess type. Maybe he was only with her because, before now, she'd been his only option, unless you counted Bridgett, who didn't spend enough time in the Waking World to make a good girlfriend.

Lynn cocked an eyebrow as they chopped lettuce and cucumbers. "What was up with you and Omar this morning, anyway? Why were you so upset?"

"It was nothing big. We're not fighting. And we *didn't* bang."

Lynn's eyebrow crept higher. "Why not?"

Magdalene rolled her eyes as she carried the pan of lasagna to the table.

When everything was ready, she and Lynn called everyone in to eat. The crowd took their seats, and Magdalene found herself wedged between Omar and Matthew. Ingrid sat on Omar's other side, and Magdalene could've sworn she was sitting with her chest thrust out. Her boobs strained against her blouse and peeked above her neckline like twin pearls.

Matthew smiled at Magdalene, his freckled nose wrinkling. His dark hair was moussed to stick out in all directions. It was what Magdalene's friend Adelaide would've called fuckboy hair, and an unexpected pang of homesickness hit her. Would she ever see Adelaide again?

"This lasagna is really good," Matthew said. "You helped make it, right?"

She nodded, swallowing her mouthful. "Me and Lynn." She cast a glance at Lynn, who looked annoyed; she was stuck between Frederick and James, who were talking across her about video games.

"Why did you decide to come here?" Omar asked Matthew.

Matthew wiped his mouth with his napkin. "I left school and worked at a friend's gaming startup for about a year. It was fun and all, but I wasn't really into it." He leaned back in his chair, his immaculate sneaker tapping the tile floor. "I want something more, you know? Then Frederick told me about this place. I was interested mostly because of the lucid dreaming thing. I have those all the time."

Magdalene and Omar exchanged a look. "Really?" Magdalene asked.

Matthew nodded. "Ingrid too. We were at school together and we used to talk about our dreams and wonder about, like, that other world. We were both looking for something that had a little more meaning than writing code, making money—we didn't want to end up these boring people commuting three hours a day and working seventy-hour weeks." He shrugged. "So, we came here to check it out."

Magdalene studied him, wondering what it would be like to have a life like Matthew and Ingrid. Fancy college, good jobs...and they'd left them to come here. Would she ever have a good life, or would she get flushed back down the dark hole of poverty and end up like her mom?

James asked Matthew if he'd ever seen some band from Austin that he liked, and Magdalene turned back to her lasagna.

"So, how did *you* end up here?" Ingrid asked, and Magdalene glanced up to see her giving Omar her perfect smile.

Every muscle in Magdalene's body went taut. She stabbed a piece of lasagna with her fork and made herself eat it, even though what she'd already eaten was creeping back up again.

Omar shrugged. "I met Andy's sister Bridgett and when she told me about this place, it seemed like where I should be."

"Like a premonition?" Ingrid giggled, and Magdalene's eye twitched. "I kind of felt like that when I heard about this place. It felt like fate."

Magdalene barely kept herself from snorting tomato sauce all over herself.

Ingrid asked Omar if he he'd gone to college (he hadn't) and if he planned on going. He told her he'd thought about getting a degree in ancient history, and Magdalene felt suddenly hollow;

she hadn't known he had an interest in history. She wasn't even smart enough to ask him about stuff like that.

He and Ingrid started talking about the history department at Ingrid's college, and Magdalene stared so hard at her lasagna that it took her a moment to realize Matthew had asked her a question. She glanced up at him, blinking. "Huh?"

He gave her a lopsided smile. "I asked how you like living here."

Magdalene tried to tune out Omar and Ingrid's chatter and smiled at Matthew. "I love it. The food's good, the beds are comfortable, and the people are nice."

Matthew laughed. So did Ingrid, at something Omar was saying, and a bolt of irrational anger seared through Magdalene. Is this what love was like? Being jealous all the time? It hardly seemed worth it. She turned in her chair so that she couldn't see Omar and gave Matthew her best smile. "So, what do you do for fun?"

Magdalene was glad when everyone was done eating and she could get up from the table and help Lynn clear away the dishes. She was exhausted, her neck ached, and the sound of Omar and Ingrid's continued talk as she sprayed the dishes made her want to puke.

She turned to fetch another load of dishes almost fell backward. "Ohmygod."

Omar stood before her with an armload of leftovers, smiling sheepishly. "Sorry. Should have said I was behind you."

Some of the tension drained from her. "You don't have to help."

"I wanted to."

Then Ingrid pranced up behind him, carrying a stack of dirty dishes. "Where do you want these?"

Magdalene sounded unnaturally cheerful as she showed Ingrid how to load the dishes into the rack.

CHAPTER FOUR
Love is Literally the Worst

After lunch, Frederick left, shaking his friends' hands and wishing them luck. He took a long look at Magdalene before he went out the door and shook his head. "Take care of her, Omar, you lucky bastard."

Magdalene glanced over to find Ingrid's dark eyes on her. The other girl quickly looked away, a faint smirk on her full lips.

When Frederick was gone, Helena called another meeting. Magdalene made sure to get a seat next to Omar on the couch. Ingrid settled into one of the club chairs, her long arms draped gracefully over the armrests.

Andy stood before them and welcomed the newcomers into the group, then gave them a short introduction to his theory that human beings could enter another dimension during lucid dreaming and act with purpose while there. Afterward, Matthew and Ingrid were assigned a rotating chore schedule similar to Magdalene's when she first arrived, except (to Magdalene's relief) Omar didn't volunteer to tutor either of them.

When the meeting broke up, Andy and Helena took the two newcomers for a tour, and Magdalene and Omar walked out to their spot under the cottonwood. They tramped silently through the dust under the fierce afternoon sun, Magdalene twisting the hem of her tank top between her fingers until she stretched it out of shape. Omar frowned at his feet, and Magdalene experienced a wild fear he was gathering the courage to break up with her.

Finally, Omar glanced at her. "What do you think of the new kids?"

Magdalene wiped the sweat from the back of her neck. "I don't know. They're not kids, though, they're older than us."

Omar shrugged. "Not by much. Ingrid's twenty and Matthew can't be much older."

Magdalene clutched her hands together so she'd stop twisting her shirt. "Well, older than me, anyway."

He smiled. "I always forget you're only sixteen."

Magdalene's feelings scrabbled at the inside of her chest like trapped rodents. She really wanted to be alone to try to get her head straight, but she fought the desire to run away. *You'll deal with this like an adult. Just because he was talking to her doesn't mean he likes her.* She sighed. "I think they're okay. What do you think?"

Omar's brow furrowed. "I don't know them well enough yet."

Magdalene studied him. Had she misread the situation? Had he just been trying to assess the newcomers? "They don't seem...like us."

Omar broke into a lopsided smile. "Too normal, you mean?"

Magdalene nodded. "I don't know why someone like them would be here. They had everything going for them on the outside, and it's not like Bridgett found them in Purgatory and told them to come here, like she did with you. So why would they leave it all behind to live in the middle of nowhere with us?"

"We're not that bad." Omar's smile faded and the crease returned to his brow.

"I didn't mean to insult the Commune," Magdalene said quickly. She was twisting her shirt again, and she made herself stop.

"It's not that." Omar sighed. "What's really worrying me is Bridgett."

Magdalene's heart stumbled. Had she been worrying about stupid teenage shit while Bridgett was in trouble? "What's going on with her?"

"I haven't seen her since the meeting a couple days ago. Not even in Purgatory. She's giving her body just enough attention to keep it alive, but she's just...gone."

Magdalene's mouth went dry. She'd lain in Omar's bed with his vacant body for seven days when he disappeared into the afterlife. Was something similar happening to Bridgett? "Why didn't you tell me?"

"I didn't want to worry you. I don't think it's that bad yet."

"Is she doing something important in Purgatory?"

"Not that I know of." He ran his hand over his hair. "Bridgett lives with one foot in the other world all the time. It's weird I can't find her, but I'm sure she's fine."

They finally reached their spot under the cottonwood and Magdalene splashed cool spring water onto her face. They settled with their backs against the trunk. Omar sat close, his leg touching hers, and warmth rushed through her. It felt so *right* to be close to him. Maybe she was worrying for no reason. She gazed out over the shimmering desert at the thunderclouds that billowed on the horizon, tantalizingly close but still too far away to break the oppressive heat. "What was that symbol Bridgett threw at the meeting the other day?" Magdalene held her fingers up in a V. "And she said that stuff...was it Latin?"

Omar chuckled, rolling his eyes. "I do believe it was."

"Do you think it was some sort of warning? Maybe a clue as to where she is?"

He shrugged. "Who knows? A lot of what Bridgett says and does only makes sense in retrospect. She's really annoying that way."

Magdalene fidgeted with the gravel. "You don't think Tower Guy could be keeping her hostage in Purgatory or something, right?"

Omar frowned. "Tower Guy would have to play a pretty fierce game to beat Bridgett on her home turf, and I don't think he's up to it. I'm sure she could come back if she wanted to." He smiled reassuringly. "Bridgett will be okay, she always is."

Magdalene nodded. Bridgett was one of the most powerful people she'd ever met, and she was sure Omar was right. "What are we working on today?"

Omar smiled and leaned back against tree, stretching out his legs. "It's too hot to work." He made a swooping gesture with his hand and the cottonwood leaves began to rustle in the still air, dancing, folding in on themselves.

The breeze they produced stirred Magdalane's hair and cooled the sweat on her face. "Nice."

The corners of Omar's lips curled. He made another small, graceful gesture and a handful of leaves plucked themselves from their branches. Hovering against the blue sky, they folded themselves, forming little triangular heads and beaks. Soon a flock of origami cranes of green and faded yellow fluttered around Magdalene's head, fanning her with their wings.

She giggled and plucked one out of the air. The delicate leaf was creased into tight and perfect corners.

Omar waved toward the open desert and the little cranes shot away like rockets. The one in Magdalene's hand struggled like a trapped bug until she set it free.

The little flock swooped in a graceful arc, forming kaleido-scopic silhouettes against the deep blue sky. A lopsided grin grew on Omar's face as he aimed at them with his finger guns. "Pew! Pew, pew!" Little flowers of white flame bloomed and streaked toward the earth. Soon, all that was left was a sprinkling of ash floating on the sluggish breeze.

Magdalene huffed. "Rude!"

Omar blew imaginary smoke from his finger gun and settled his arm around her shoulders. "Destruction is the purest act of creation."

"Whatever, brute." She relaxed against him with her head on his shoulder. All her worries about Ingrid seemed far away. Even anxiety over Bridgett and the man behind the Tower evaporated in the muggy summer air. She was content, here in the shade of the cottonwood with the gurgle of the spring over the sunbaked stones and the boy she loved beside her.

"We probably should do some sort of training." She raised her head and glanced up at him. "Why don't you do your magical junk and I'll try to copy you in Purgatory?"

A sly grin grew on his face. "You're on."

Omar took his arm from her shoulders and stood. He grew still, his brow furrowing with a look of concentration, then he raised his hands.

Silvery, undulating droplets of water began to rise from the creek, dozens of them, about the size of marbles. They drew together and, with a *plip*, fused into a jiggling orb that caught the sunlight and threw watery reflections around the canyon like a psychedelic disco ball. He moved his fingers as if playing an invisible piano, and more water flowed up from the creek to join the orb. A snout formed, and a torso, then two powerful legs ending in long, narrow feet, the toes tipped with curved talons. Tiny arms grew, and clawed hands bloomed from the ends of them. Finally, a long tail sprouted and snaked along the ground. The creature turned toward Magdalene, opening its jaws to display teeth like glittering shards of crystal.

Magdalene laughed as the transparent t-rex lumbered toward them, its feet slapping the pebbled bank with little splashes. "No fair! I'll never be able to copy that."

The dinosaur stomped closer. "That's not true," Omar said. "You just have to—"

The sound of voices cut through the slosh of the dinosaur's footsteps. Omar quickly dropped his hands and his creation splashed to the ground, becoming a puddle on the rocky bank.

Matthew and Ingrid appeared around a clump of willows at the mouth of the canyon. Ingrid was talking animatedly, gesturing with her hands. Then Matthew spotted Magdalene and Omar and waved, and Ingrid fell silent.

Omar smiled as the two approached, but Magdalene's contentment disintegrated into a dirty puddle to rival the erstwhile t-rex. Ingrid stepped carefully around shrubs and rocks in her ballet flats. She and Matthew looked out of place in their clean Abercrombie clothes and perfectly styled hair.

Matthew glanced around. "Nice spot."

Magdalene settled back against the cottonwood. "Yeah, we come out here to enjoy the solitude."

Omar shot her a faint smirk as he sat down beside her. "You guys out exploring?"

"Yep." Matthew plopped down and wiped the sweat from the back of his neck.

Ingrid swept pebbles and debris aside before she sat, spreading her skirt over her knees. "I wanted to get a look around at this gorgeous area before we start work tomorrow." She aimed a sparkling smile at Magdalene, whose eye gave another twitch.

"You start out with Helena tomorrow, right?" Omar asked.

Ingrid turned that smile on him. "I'm looking forward to milking the goats. I used to help with that as a girl."

"You grew up on a farm?" Magdalene glanced at Ingrid's delicate, long fingers with their perfect nails. She looked like she'd never done manual labor in her life.

Maybe she'd get a blister.

Ingrid's silver earrings jingled as she shook her head. "I grew up in Sacramento, but we went back to visit family a lot, and my grandparents had a farm."

"I'm with Lynn tomorrow," Matthew said. "I'm sure I won't be able to make food as good as yours, though, Magdalene. I'm not much around the kitchen."

Magdalene felt the skin of her cheeks stretch as she smiled.

Ingrid turned her luminous hazel eyes back on Omar. "How about you, Omar, do you cook?"

Omar sifted pebbles through his fingers. "I'm not much of a cook, no."

Matthew asked a question about something Andy had said in his lecture involving consciousness particles as the vehicle for navigating Purgatory, which Magdalene had only half listened to. Omar tried to explain it while Magdalene watched the cottonwood leaves stirring in the sluggish breeze, her thoughts scurrying like agitated ants. She had been so happy here, just starting to get comfortable and trust people, and in one day everything had changed.

She suddenly realized that everyone was staring at her. "Huh?"

Matthew grinned. "I asked whether you believe time travel is possible."

Magdalene blinked, coming back to herself. She vaguely remembered Andy talking about time travel during the meeting. Something about the consciousness particle being able to slip through dimensions and time being nonlinear.

Omar was smirking at her again, and Magdalene shrugged. "I don't know whether to believe half the crap Andy says, but maybe."

Matthew pulled a vape from his pocket. He didn't hit it, but just twirled it between his fingers idly. "If you could go back in time, when and where would you guys go to? I think I'd want to meet Galileo. Wouldn't that be sick? I'll bet he was fun to hang out with. He probably had ADHD, like me."

Ingrid stared dreamily into the distance. "I'd want to see the Indus Valley Civilization. How about you, Omar?"

Omar's brow creased in thought. "There's a lot of things I'd love to see, but if I had to choose..." He drummed his fingers against his knees. "I think I'd just stay right here, but go back about three thousand years so I could meet the Ancestral Puebloans." He gave Magdalene his little smile. "Your turn."

Magdalene chewed the inside of her cheek. All three pairs of eyes were on her. Ingrid's lips curled in the faintest of sneers, no doubt waiting for her to say something dull and uneducated. Magdalene realized what she'd really want to do is go back and keep Morris from getting killed, but there was no way she was going to say that out loud right now. She shrugged. "I'd travel back to the Mesozoic era and ride a dinosaur. Or maybe I'd go back and fuck Napoleon or something."

Omar quirked an eyebrow, holding back a grin. Matthew and Ingrid laughed, but Ingrid's sounded false and grated on Magdelene's nerves.

Magdalene stood, dusting off the seat of her shorts. "I've got to help start dinner." Omar stood, too, and laced his fingers with hers. Her shoulders relaxed, and she smiled up at him.

The other two got to their feet and Ingrid smoothed her skirt. "We should all go back, it's hot." Not a single bead of sweat dewed her flawless skin. Her gaze darted to Magdalene and Omar's clasped hands, and a strange look crossed her face, but it was gone so quickly that Magdalene wondered if her jealousy was making her see things that weren't there.

Magdalene stood at the kitchen counter, kneading pizza dough and listening to the musical rise and fall of Ingrid's voice from the sitting room, punctuated by Omar's laughter.

"You're going to leave bruises on that dough," Lynn said. "That's domestic violence. I should call the sheriff."

Magdalene scowled.

Lynn studied her as she grated cheese into a bowl. "What's up?"

Another peal of laughter came from the sitting room and Magdalene socked her knuckles into the dough. "Ingrid is all up on Omar."

Lynn's eyebrows slowly crept aloft. "You can't blame her for trying but she hasn't got a chance in hell. That boy is sprung on you."

Magdalene scoffed halfheartedly. Ingrid was beautiful. She'd been to college, had a career, and probably wasn't an emotional train wreck with baggage strewn far and wide.

Lynn stepped over and gave Magdalene an awkward squeeze around the waist, holding her hands at a weird angle so as not to get mozzarella brine on her. "Don't worry about it," she muttered. "He'd be idiotic to leave you, especially for that poptart." She pressed her lips to the crown of Magdalene's head before going back to the cheese.

Magdalene looked away so Lynn wouldn't see the tears in her eyes. If she lost Omar, could she stand to live here? But if she left, she'd lose Lynn, too, not to mention Bridgett, James—she even was growing fond of Andy, and she'd probably like Helena better if it weren't for the beast growing in her belly.

She wiped her nose on her shoulder, biting back a surge of frustration. *Why did that bitch have to come and ruin everything?*

During dinner, Ingrid sat on Omar's other side again and prattled on about her experience as an exchange student in France and the three months she'd spent on a humanitarian mission to Haiti. Magdalene, whose only travel experience was fleeing drug deals gone wrong, chewed on the inside of her cheek until it started to swell. When Ingrid discussed her plans to open a school in the slums of Mumbai teaching poor children how to code, Lynn caught Magdalene's eye, pretending to gag.

No one else noticed. Not even Omar. His knee touched Magdalene's under the table, but all his attention was on Ingrid. Magdalene was sure he was relieved to finally have someone to talk to who was on his intellectual and social level.

The meal dragged on. Andy and Helena felt the need to talk about everything under the sun with the newcomers, probably trying to make them feel comfortable and happy. By the time Magdalene and Lynn cleared the table, the red flare of the setting sun was fading from the clifftops outside.

The others went into the sitting room to continue their conversation while Lynn and Magdalene did the dishes. Yet another burst of Ingrid and Omar's laughter rolled through the archway, and Magdalene dropped a plate, which shattered noisily on the floor tile.

Magdalene cursed under her breath and started picking up the pieces. She felt like she was going to puke.

"Hey," Lynn said, putting a hand on Magdalene's shoulder. "It's okay. It really is."

Magdalene's throat closed up. "How could he forget about me this quickly?"

Lynn frowned. "He isn't forgetting about you. He's just being polite."

"That isn't *being polite*. Seriously, he *should* choose her over me. She's hot, and I'm a fucking hot mess."

Lynn grasped her shoulders and pressed her forehead against Magdalene's. "You've been through a lot. These emotions are all normal. You're going to be okay, and this is going to be okay."

Magdalene sighed and closed her eyes, her shoulders sagging. She wished she could believe that.

"You guys breaking stuff in here?"

It was Omar's voice. Lynn squeezed Magdalene's shoulder and went back to the dishes.

Omar sauntered in from the dining room. His brow furrowed when his gaze fell on Magdalene. "Everything okay?"

Magdalene smiled, but her face felt tight. "It's fine. I just dropped a plate. Ouch!" She winced as blood welled from a cut on her finger. She'd forgotten she was holding broken shards of porcelain.

Omar gently took the bloody shards from her and placed them on the ground next to the others. "Let me take care of it." He studied her face. "You sure you're okay?"

Magdalene nodded, swallowing. "Why wouldn't I be?"

He examined her for another moment, then took her hand, inspecting the cut. Blood was dripping from the pad of her middle finger onto the floor. He grabbed a piece of paper towel and wiped it away, then pressed his lips to the wound. When he pulled away, Magdalene watched with a creeping sense of unreality as the cut sealed itself and disappeared. She stared up at him, her heart squeezing. He was so amazing. The thought of losing him opened up a howling black hole in her chest. She turned away and grabbed the broom from the corner and started sweeping up the shards of plate, mostly so he wouldn't be able to read her thoughts in her eyes.

"Put that broom away," Omar said. His gaze flicked to the doorway to the sitting room, where the others were still laughing and chatting. He smiled and pointed his finger at the shards on the floor. "Fix your shit."

The broken pieces scraped across the tile and jumped back together with a musical clink. Lynn startled and squeaked as the plate wobbled to a rest on the floor.

Magdalene shook her head. "Nerd."

Lynn bent to pick up the plate and turned it over in her hands, then rinsed a smear of Magdalene's blood from it with the spray nozzle and examined it again. "Not a scratch. That is just fucked up."

Omar pulled Magdalene into his arms, and she pressed her cheek against his chest, letting herself sink into the comfort of him. *Maybe I am just being anxious for no reason.*

"You guys are cute," Lynn said. "Cute, but gross. Get out of my kitchen." She picked up the broom and swept at their feet. "Seriously. Go."

"I have to finish the dishes," Magdalene protested halfheartedly.

Lynn gave her a knowing smile. "I've got it. They're almost done anyway. *Go.* Take a night off for once."

"Okay, we're going," Omar said. "Calm down." He took Magdalene's hand and they went out the back door to the garden.

Magdalene's feet led her to the orchard, and they sat together on a bench beside Morris' grave. Magdalene stared at the mound of fresh earth, a pang of guilt hitting her. She missed Morris, but the thought of visiting him was just too overwhelming. She had so many emotions that she barely had time for them all.

A soft breeze rustled through the leaves, the silhouettes of them fluttering over the first stars in the indigo sky. Magdalene put her head on Omar's shoulder. "Are you going to the portal tonight?"

"I'm going to wait one more day to see if Bridgett shows up so that we can go together."

Magdalene chewed her lip. "I wish you'd just let me go with you."

Omar put his arm around her shoulders, a furrow between his brows. "It would be selfish of me to take you along. Going near a portal isn't fun at all."

Magdalene sat listening to the crickets and the hiss of the wind, all the day's worries and questions poised on the end of her tongue. She wanted to talk to him, to tell him how jealous she was of him and Ingrid. She wanted him to comfort her, tell her she was being silly and had nothing to worry about. But what if he didn't tell her that? What if he got annoyed with her for being jealous and hysterical? What if he confessed that he was actually into Ingrid?

Images of Stan's leering face rose into her mind, and for a sickening second, she swore she caught the reek of beer breath on the wind.

"Are you okay?" Omar asked.

Magdalene's muscles were vibrating like untuned guitar strings. She let out a quiet breath. "Yeah, I'm fine."

The starlight showed Omar's frown as he brushed a lock of hair from her cheek.

Magdalene cuddled closer to him, cursing her own cowardice.

CHAPTER FIVE
Plop, the Shoe Drops

Omar and Magdalene spent the night searching for Bridgett in Purgatory, but didn't find her. They even checked her spot under the willows, but it was empty, the stream gurgling its way between its solitary banks. Morris was gone, too.

Magdalene awoke with the first glimmer of dawn stealing into her room and guilt picking the scabs on her heart. Had Morris already moved on, taken a portal to the next plane or been reborn? If so, she'd let her discomfort stop her from seeing her friend one last time and saying goodbye. She prayed that wasn't the case. Maybe he and Bridgett had gone somewhere together.

That morning Ingrid was working with Helena and Matthew with Lynn, so Omar and Magdalene didn't have duties. They headed back out to their spot in the canyon. The air was still cool as they settled with their backs against the cottonwood tree, munching toast and listening to the birds squabbling in the upper branches. Omar gazed at Magdalene as she tossed pieces of toast at a chipmunk. "Are you sure you're okay?"

Magdalene wrinkled her nose. "I just…" Her tongue reached for the words to tell him how she'd been feeling, but fell short. She picked one of the other many things that were bugging her, instead. "How am I going to feel when the baby is born? How am I going to look at his little face and know that he killed Morris?"

Omar gazed at her with a sad smile. "The baby won't be Stan."

Magdalene clutched her head in her hands and fought the urge to smack that smile off his face. "The world is just…" She huffed. "You never know when someone is going to fuck you over." She winced. "You never know if some asshole is going to take someone you love from you and get away with it. That shit happens *all the time*." She tossed her last piece of crust toward the chipmunk, sending it ricochetting off the rocks, and the little rodent scurried to hide under its log. "How can you live like that?"

Omar gazed dully at the horizon and shrugged. "Life is uncertainty. We can't control everything. All we can do is deal with what happens." He reached out and took her hand, twining his fingers with hers. "You've been through some horrible stuff."

Magdalene sniffed. Everyone had been saying that to her and she didn't know how to respond without sounding like a self-obsessed whiner.

Omar gave her his little smile and traced a graceful circle in the air above their heads with his free hand. A sudden breeze kicked up, caressing her face and tossing Omar's curls. The gusts gained in power, circling around them, picking up dead leaves and dust until they were encased in a whirling, whistling dust devil, isolated from the outside world in a small circle of clear air. Magdalene's gaze followed the walls of the maelstrom into the blue sky. The leaves of the cottonwood danced and hissed above them, and their hair floated on rogue air currents, but the flying debris didn't touch them.

Omar caught Magdalene's gaze, and she smiled. The wind seemed to whisk some of the heaviness from her chest. He leaned forward and brought his lips to hers.

Magdalene's heart raced. Around them, the wind whirled slower, the dry leaves falling back to the ground with a dry rattle.

Omar broke the kiss and gave her a challenging grin. "Now you try."

Magdalene grinned back, then closed her eyes and concentrated.

The sun was blazing hot overhead. Omar and Magdalene huddled in the shrunken shade of the cottonwood. "I'm too hungry to concentrate," she said, taking a chug from her water bottle. "We need to take a break or I'll just be creating a tornado of cheeseburgers."

Omar snickered as he opened the sack of food they'd pilfered from the kitchen and handed her a sandwich. They leaned against the trunk and unwrapped their lunches.

"Are you going to the portal tonight, or are you going to wait longer for Bridgett?"

"I need to go soon, Bridgett or no."

Magdalene picked the crust of her sandwich apart. She'd already made a fool of herself begging him to take her along, and she wouldn't keep nagging. If he didn't want to take her or didn't think she was strong enough to handle a portal, there was nothing she could do about it.

Omar studied her for a long moment, then sighed. "We could go to the closest portal right now. It sounds like they've got it blocked at a distance, so it might just be unpleasant instead of horrible."

Magdalene stopped picking at her sandwich. "Either way, I can handle it."

Omar ran his hand over his curls, frowning. "It might also bring you into contact with the people behind the Tower."

Magdalene's heart skipped a beat, and a wave of adrenaline coursed through her. "I'm willing to risk it. We've faced him before."

Omar nodded, though he was still frowning. He settled back again against the tree and closed his eyes. Magdalene leaned against him, took a breath, and did the same.

Purgatory melted into place behind her eyelids, different than she'd been expecting—not the reformed cottonwood tree on the streambank they'd been practicing in all day, but a small copse of oak trees amidst rolling hills. Omar sat beside her, wreathed in the strange halo of darkness and electricity that always enveloped him in that world.

Magdalene looked him up and down, smirking at his tight black t-shirt and black leather pants. "You look like a metal guitarist cosplaying the god of lightning."

A slow grin spread over his face. He jumped to his feet and punched his fist in the air. "I am Zeus, God of Thunder!"

A pillar of blue fire exploded from his fist into the silvery sky with a crack that split Magdalene's bones. She sat gasping for a moment, then began to laugh. "You are such a dork." She got to her feet, still shaking her head at him.

He grinned, but then his gaze was drawn by something over her shoulder and he sobered. Magdalene followed his gaze to the Tower, which rose in the distance like a fissure through the fabric of reality. She could feel it tugging at her, tugging at the whole landscape, like gravity dragging them in.

Omar put his hands in his pockets. "Let's go."

They started down a dirt footpath that led through the rolling hills, away from the Tower. They wound around the curve of a knoll and into a gully, then up the opposite slope through a stand of oaks. A fuzzy creature wearing galoshes peeked from behind a trunk as they passed by.

"Why can't we just navigate straight to the portal?" Magdalene watched the creature as he clumped away.

"Portals are different. Distances are always weird here, but when you're trying to get to a portal, you always have to journey a bit. There must be some kind of rule about having to work at it."

"Who makes the rules?" Magdalane asked.

Omar shrugged. "Who wrote the laws of gravity? Who knows? I let Andy worry about the math, the hows and whys. I just work here."

As they crested the hill, Magdalene eyed he path ahead, which stretched out straight and long. She gave Omar a challenging grin. "I'll race you."

With no warning, Omar took off running. Magdalene chased after him, cursing. Her feet pounded the dirt. She felt light as a bubble, her lungs not having to strain for oxygen like they would in the Waking World.

With a giggle, Magdalene pushed off from the ground, launching herself into the air. She waved at Omar as she soared over him. A man with a round, bald head, wearing nothing but a red vinyl belt, stepped out of a stand of oaks and craned his neck to watch her.

Omar leapt, shooting up straight like a rocket. As he passed Magdalene, he tickled her armpits.

"Aarrgh!" Magdalene fell back toward the earth, her concentration broken. Omar caught her around the waist, and they drifted down together like leaves. A huge skateboard materialized beneath them as they neared the ground. They landed on it and began barreling down the path, the landscape around them a blur.

"We'll see how *you* like it." Magdalene tickled his armpits, but he just smiled his little smile, completely unperturbed. "Figures," she grumbled. "One of the major signs of evil is not being ticklish."

Omar laughed. A corona of lightning wreathed his head, and his hair and eyes glinted blue-black.

Magdalene concentrated and pointed a finger at the path ahead. A wooden jump appeared. They giggled and held onto each other as they swooped up it and arced into the sky. The skateboard reached its apex and stayed aloft, flying over the undulating parkland, the odd creatures of Purgatory ogling them as they passed over.

Then Omar's smile faded. The skateboard descended and landed, and they rolled to a halt.

The path ahead was blocked by a gate. A tall chain link fence stretched on either side of it, continuing over the rocky hills in both directions until it faded into the far distance.

Omar hopped off the skateboard and strode forward. Magdalene followed him.

Two guards in khaki uniforms stood inside the gate, watching the small crowd of Dead that milled about outside it. One Dead man had his green face pressed against the fence. He looked up as Omar and Magdalene approached, the pattern of the chain link sunk into his flesh.

"This is the portal?" Magdalene asked. "I feel fine."

"This is just where they've blocked the road in." He pointed past the guards. "The portal is there."

In the distance beyond the fence, the rolling hills flattened into a wide plain. The path ran under the gate and bisected the landscape, a tan line which ran perfectly straight until it disappeared abruptly into a dark haze in the distance, as if night had suddenly fallen over that spot.

A shiver seeped through Magdalene's skin and engulfed her insides in a vague, soupy dread. "Oh." She swallowed.

Omar studied her. "You feeling okay?

She smiled dryly. "I'm fine. It's not even as bad as the best day I had living with Stan and Charla."

Omar grunted, his dark eyes flashing, but let the subject lie and continued toward the gate. Magdalene followed him. There were around fifteen people and creatures gathered in front of it, and Magdalene recognized a leaning pyramid of curly, blond hair. "Is that Barry?"

"It sure looks like it." Omar waved, and Barry spotted them and smiled. He made his way toward them through the crowd, wrinkling his nose as he stepped around a man who was burping multicolored bubbles from his wide mouth. "How are our little reverse ghosts doing?" Barry asked.

Omar cocked an eyebrow. "Reverse ghosts, are we?"

"The living are haunting us. It's creepy." Barry grinned coyly. He reached into a pocket of his baggy jeans and pulled out a tall boy. "You two want a beer?"

Magdalene wondered briefly what Purgatory beer would taste like, but she shook her head, as did Omar. "Did you come back to try to get through the portal again?" Omar asked.

Barry made a face. "No way. I'm not wasting my afterlife on that jazz." He cast a weary glance at the guards. "I just came to, you know, stage a protest, because this," he waved a hand around at the fence and the gate, "is totally unacceptable. I mean, who do these people think they are?"

Omar surveyed the scene. "It is unbelievable that someone thinks they can take over the portals. We're trying to figure out who they are so we can fix this."

Barry glanced around discreetly, then leaned toward him and whispered, "I'm going to go to the Chieftain."

Omar nodded. "That could work, if you can get him interested."

Barry cast a scowl at the guards, who were staring at the crowd and pulling at their fleshy lips. "Oh, I think this is just the sort of thing the Chieftain would be interested in, because I'm not the only person pissed off about it."

"Who's the Chieftain?" Magdalene asked, being careful to keep her voice down, but wondering why it was necessary.

"If there were a leader of this part of Purgatory, it would be him," Omar said. "He's been here longer than anyone else, I think."

Barry nodded. "Big, beefy guy, hair everywhere."

Omar's gaze drifted beyond the gate to the darkness of the portal. "Do you know of anybody who *has* gotten through?"

Barry shook his head, his tower of hair wobbling slightly. "That dorkus Felipe thought he would try it, but he was back home again last night. They bounced him like a rubber ball. Natalie and Amira, too. I've seen a couple people allowed in, but I didn't know them, they were just some big nobodies." His forlorn gaze settled on the bubble-blowing man. "There's going to be a backlog."

Omar nodded. "If you talk to the Chieftain, will you tell me how that goes?"

"You bet." Barry glanced toward the gate and cringed. "Oh, that is so gross." Magdalene looked over and saw that one of the guards had a stubby finger rooting in his nostril.

Magdalene and Omar snickered. Then Omar's smile faded. "We'd better go. Even being this close to the portal is making me a little antsy."

Magdalene nodded. She mostly felt fine, but a dreariness had settled over her and a nagging sense that something bad was about to happen. They waved goodbye to Barry, then opened their eyes back in the waking world.

Magdalene stretched her stiff legs. She was still leaning against Omar underneath the cottonwood tree and she stayed there. The sky seemed a deeper blue than usual, and the thunderclouds hovered closer than ever.

"So, we have to walk there, but we don't have to walk back," Magdalene mused.

A smile flitted over Omar's face, but there was a furrow in his brow. "There's another portal that's a little bit further, but not too far to walk. I'm going to go there tonight to see if these people are interfering there, too."

Magdalene looked up at him. "I felt fine at this one."

His brow furrowed deeper. "Let me go first alone, then I'll take you next time. I want to try to get closer tonight to try to figure out how they have them blocked."

"With a fence," Magdalene said, and he laughed.

"Sure, but building a fence in Purgatory isn't the same as building one here. There's no hardware store in the afterlife."

Magdalene picked at a fray on her shorts, fighting the knot in her throat. "You shouldn't go alone."

"I'd rather go alone than risk you getting hurt."

Sudden anger made Magdalene's ears ring. She sat up and crossed her arms. "Do you really think I'm so weak and help-less?"

Omar blinked. "No. I—"

She huffed. "Why do you even like me, Omar? You're like this all-powerful being, and I'm just this little girl that you'll always have to protect."

His face stilled. "I'm not an all-powerful being." Magdalene sniffed, and Omar sighed, rubbing a hand over his face. "It's not that I think you're weak, Magdalene. It's just, being near a portal can make you relive the worst moments of your life, the worst feelings of your life, and haven't you been through enough already? You don't have anything to prove."

Nausea bloomed in the pit of her stomach and she got to her feet. "You think I'm trying to *prove* something?" She glared down at him, his pained expression blurred through her tears.

"I didn't mean it that way," he murmured.

"Whatever." Magdalene spun on her heel and stalked back toward the commune. Omar called after her, but she didn't stop.

She was only a few yards away when she started to feel bad for how she was acting. She couldn't keep herself from listening for his footsteps following her, but the only sound was the rattle of june bugs in the mesquite. She had too much pride to look back, to turn around, to apologize.

Her heels kicked up itchy dust on the trail. Her tears evaporated in the burning heat, leaving salty deposits on her cheeks. She could never be Omar's equal. She had nothing to offer him but her body, and she was too scared to give him that. How long could he continue protecting her, slaying her enemies with lightning bolts and getting nothing in return, before he got bored and moved on?

She was hoping to get to her room without being seen, but Matthew came into the kitchen just as she slipped through the back door. She gave him a half-wave and fake smile before darting down the hallway.

She shut herself in her room. Sitting on the edge of her bed, she swiped away her tears and took a deep breath. The tide of her anger had already started retreat, leaving behind a refuse of broken and ugly feelings.

She hid her face in her hands. *I'm being a bitch and I'm going to end up losing him.*

A knock sounded on her door and Magdalene's heart leapt. She dried her eyes on her sleeve and smoothed her hair, then got up to answer it.

When she opened the door, though, it was Matthew that stood in the hall, holding a plate full of powered donuts.

Magdalene's shoulders slumped. "Hey."

Mathew smiled. "Lynn says donuts cheer you up. She wanted to come, but I didn't know how to do the egg roll things she was doing, so I said I'd come instead."

"Thanks." Magdalene forced a smile.

Matthew came in and set the plate down on her table. Steam curled up from the donuts, and the confectioner's sugar was melting on top. "Lynn just made donuts from tomorrow's bread dough, really quick. She can do anything with food." He studied her face. "Are you okay?"

Heat rose to her cheeks. "I'm fine." There was absolutely no privacy in this damn place.

He blew out a sigh. "Listen. I know you don't know me from anyone but, I mean, you're pretty new here, too, right?" He snickered. "And this place, I can already tell, it's kinda weird."

"You have no idea." Magdalene sat down again on the edge of her bed. Matthew hesitated, then sat next to her. He smelled like hair products and body spray. He frowned. "I mean, this place is okay, right? They treat you okay?"

Magdalene nodded. "Yeah, everyone here is really nice." Matthew shifted his position, and his knee was almost touching hers. She resisted the urge to scoot away.

"It's probably none of my business what's bothering you," he said.

Magdalene chewed on her cheek. *You'd be right.* Why was he here?

There was a knock on the doorjamb and Omar came in the open door. He stopped when he saw the two of them sitting on the bed, and stood there, looking taller than usual. His eyes took on a steely glint that reminded Magdalene of how he looked in Purgatory. "Sorry to bug you," he said. "I'll come back later."

Magdalene jumped up, but Omar turned and was gone before she could get a word out.

Matthew stood also, grinning sheepishly. "I think I just got you in trouble. I'm really sorry. I'll talk to you later." He scooted out, shutting the door behind him, leaving Magdalene alone and in silence.

Magdalene cursed, her feelings moshing in her chest. She wanted to run after Omar and explain, but stopped herself. Did Omar really think that she'd invite Matthew to come to her room? Did he think so little of her that the first place his head would go when seeing her with another guy was that she was flirting?

But a burst of satisfaction flared in another part of her heart. She'd made Omar jealous, which he deserved for laughing and talking with Ingrid so much.

Magdalene fell face-down on her bed and screamed into her pillow.

She stayed in her room all evening, reading. Omar didn't come back. For once, no one bothered her, and Magdalene wondered if they'd all finally had enough of her bullshit.

It was almost two in the morning before her mind settled enough that she thought she could sleep. As she hugged her pillow in the darkness, though, her aching heart kept her awake. She missed Omar. She wanted to go to his room and talk to him, to try to work this out. But he was probably at the portal and it would be rude to disturb him now.

Finally, in the cool hours before dawn when even the crickets had quit for the night, Magdalene managed to drift off to sleep.

She was standing in Bridgett's field in Purgatory. The bleached summer grass hissed in the wind, undulating like golden fabric. In front of her, under the shade of the willows, a figure sat with his back to her.

Magdalene's heart leapt. "Morris!"

She hurried toward him, and he turned as she approached. He smiled, and Magdalene felt like her heart would burst. She'd missed his big, hairy smile so much.

"Hey, Little One! I'm just watching the mountains. You know, in case they try something sneaky."

She sat beside him. "How have you been?"

"Oh, I've been doing just fine in my retirement." His gaze wandered over the far landscape. "It's a pretty intense scene out there." He gestured vaguely. "Lotsa weird people. I prefer to just sit here, thinking."

Magdalene wondered what Dead people thought about and decided she didn't want to know. "Have you seen Bridgett lately?"

His brow furrowed, then cleared. "You mean the little girl?" He thought for a moment. "I don't think I've seen her for a while, but I don't know. Time is running a little weird lately."

Magdalene watched the willow branches dancing in the breeze, each leaf as distinct, intricate and real as in the Waking World. But Morris was right—no matter how real the landscape looked, Purgatory was still different. Time seemed to spread out in all directions, an eternal, singing moment instead of a series of moments slipping through your fingers quicker than you could grasp them. What would it be like, living always in this place? Did nighttime ever fall here, or did the sun shine down endlessly over the waving grass? Maybe Morris' will now sustained the landscape, since Bridgett was elsewhere. Maybe it was up to him. It was so complicated in Purgatory.

The sound of voices and laughter floated on the breeze, cutting through the serene hiss of the grass. Magdalene turned.

Omar and Ingrid were strolling toward them, too engrossed in conversation to notice they weren't alone. Omar smiled as Ingrid talked, gesturing animatedly with her graceful arms. She evidently said something really funny, because Omar doubled over in laughter.

Ice pierced Magdalene's heart. She'd never been able to make him laugh like that. And hadn't he said he was going to the portal tonight?

They stopped in the middle of the field, facing one another. Omar, still smiling, brushed an escaped lock of Ingrid's dark hair from her cheek. He bent toward her, and their lips met.

Magdalene sprang to her feet, breathless. Omar startled and backed away from Ingrid. Ingrid's eyes flew wide, and for a moment they all stood frozen.

Morris gazed up at Magdalene with a furrow in his brow. "Are you okay, Little One?"

Magdalene woke up in her bed, clutching her sheets.

CHapTer SIX
Party at Heaven's Vista

The clock read four a.m. and Magdalene lay in bed, curled around the tight knot in her stomach. She kept trying to tell herself that what she'd seen had been some sort of trick, but as much as she dodged it, the cold truth continued to stare her down. People could manipulate the landscape of Purgatory, but she'd never heard of anyone being able to create hallucinations there. And why would anyone want to make her see Omar kissing Ingrid, anyway, even if they somehow figured out how to produce an image that detailed and realistic?

The simplest answer, the true answer, was that Omar had betrayed her, lied to her. No wonder he hadn't wanted her to go along with him to the other portal. She'd been stupid to think he was different. In the end, people only cared about themselves.

Magdalene couldn't even blame him for wanting to be with Ingrid after the freaky way she'd been acting lately, though. A wildfire of pain roared through her, and she gritted her teeth. *Don't be weak.* She made herself get up. She made herself take a shower and brush her hair. *Just keep moving.* Trying not to think, she left the safe solitude of her room.

Wandering through the dark, silent house and into the kitchen, she made some coffee. She was sitting alone at the dining table, drinking her second syrupy-sweet cup, when Lynn came in to start breakfast.

"You're up earlier than morning wood," Lynn quipped, but then glanced at Magdalene's face and stopped, her smile fading. "Oh my God, what happened?"

Magdalene's shell cracked, and she took a shaky breath. Lynn swooped into the seat next to her and gathered her in her arms, hugging her tightly. Magdalene pressed her face into Lynn's bony shoulder, battling the searing lump in her throat.

Magdalene caught a whiff of jasmine and glanced up to see Ingrid standing in the doorway. She was clutching her hands in front of her and couldn't quite meet Magdalene's gaze. "Magdalene, can I talk to you? I can explain—"

Magdalene jerked herself from Lynn's embrace and sprung to her feet. She pushed past Ingrid, heading back to the safety of her room.

She locked the door behind her. Her chest hurt, her stomach was full of boiling acid. She climbed under her blanket, shivering and gasping. For some reason, images of Stan kept flashing through her mind. He sneered at her for being so weak and stupid. A wave of nausea hit her, that Stan could still berate her, even though he was dead.

Except he wasn't. He was curled in Helena's womb, slowly ripening.

Magdalene pressed her face into her pillow. She had no one. Morris was dead, and now Omar had left her, too. Where would she go?

She squeezed her head between her hands, trying to stop her thoughts. Her body shook. Her mouth tasted like blood and stomach acid, and she kept seeing Stan's face, smelling his stale beer breath and sour body odor.

There was a knock on her door. Magdalene stayed frozen on her bed and ignored it. Whoever it was, they didn't knock again.

She couldn't breathe. She was going to die. She wished it would happen quickly. But it didn't, and eventually her thoughts screamed a little more quietly, the pain in her chest eased. She was able to take a deep breath. Her heart was an empty husk, but feeling empty was a relief.

Wrapped in a humid cave of blankets, Magdalene's body finally gave up and she fell asleep.

She felt like she was being squeezed through a tube of toothpaste, and when she was squirted out the other end, she was at a fancy party.

She was sitting at a small, round table set with a white cloth and red cotton napkins folded into lotus flowers. The mellow lighting flashed off silverware and cocktail glasses, and a jazz band played on a stage in the corner. Groups of people stood chatting on a wide dance floor, all of them dressed elegantly.

Magdalene squinted around at the scene. She knew she must be dreaming, but it all looked so normal and mature for Purgatory. Nobody was turning into something else. Nobody had feathers or a six-foot-long neck. They weren't jumping around bizarrely, and they all had their clothes on.

A man sat beside her at the table. He was maybe in his mid thirties, wearing an expensive-looking grey suit with a thin blue tie, his thick, red hair falling over his forehead. He reclined in his chair with his legs crossed, showing the red soles of his loafers and studying Magdalene with sharp blue eyes. He looked familiar somehow, but she couldn't place him.

There was a man sitting across from her, but her head buzzed and the scene faded in and out like a television with poor signal. Magdalene struggled to focus on him. The buzz faltered and the scene cleared again, and Magdalene blinked. It was Morris. He was wearing a tuxedo and staring at the crowd with a vague frown.

Magdalene looked unsteadily down at herself and realized she was wearing a formal dress of minty green silk that ended just above her knee. "Where are we, Morris?" Her words came out thick as if her lips were numb from the dentist. Dizziness washed over her, and a heavy sleepiness dragged her into the earth.

Morris glanced in her direction for a moment, then went back to frowning at the crowd.

"Thank you for coming, Miss Richards," the redheaded man said.

Magdalene turned toward him, and the world swooped and tumbled around itself. She took a deep breath and tried not to fall out of her chair.

The man held out his hand. "My name is Gavin Cavanaugh."

Magdalene shook his hand. Her arm weighed fifty pounds and felt like someone else was trying to pull it in the opposite direction. Whatever was going on here, it was almost, but not quite, like facing down a Guardian.

But Gavin Cavanaugh didn't look like a Guardian. *Fight it,* she told herself. *This is Purgatory, and you can do whatever you want.*

Magdalene concentrated, relaxing her muscles and focusing on seeing from the spot between her eyes. Gradually, the buzzing in her head diminished and control seeped back into her limbs. It was like forcing herself to walk when her legs had gone to sleep.

Mr. Cavanaugh raised his eyebrows. "You have amazing control." He drummed his fingers idly on his knees. "I apologize for my security measures, which are probably the only reason you're having trouble."

"Security measures?"

"We can't have just anyone showing up here. I tried to enter you into our system to allow you in, but since we've never actually met, that proved difficult."

All around, people talked and laughed. A man glanced Magdalene's direction and she froze: his right eye was glowing an electric blue. She looked around and realized many of the guests had glowing eyes. "The glowing eye people. That's *you.*"

Mr. Cavanaugh nodded. "A side effect of the consciousness stabilization device I've created. Some of my friends and clients require it to stay awake here, although I've designed this room to be easy to travel to." He smiled. "It took me a while to master it myself, but as you can see," he indicated his normal eyes, "I managed it eventually. You, however…" He raised his eyebrows. "Your abilities are amazing."

Another wave of dizziness rolled over her, and she fought it off. The air seemed to thrum, like a giant, barely audible heartbeat. "Where the hell am I?"

Gavin gestured at the room that surrounded them—a lazy, elegant gesture. "In the most amazing place in the universe. It's been my life's work to build it." He stood. "May I show you?"

Magdalene chewed her lip, then nodded and stood. Her legs felt odd, but she didn't fall. She glanced at Morris—he was still frowning distantly at the crowd.

"I believe your friend is adjusting to our security measures, as well," Gavin said. "He'll be happy enough where he is."

They wove through the laughing crowd. Gavin Cavanaugh was short for a man, only about half a foot taller than her, but she never would have noticed from the way he carried himself. He was confident, poised, smiling at the guests.

A woman in a glittering red dress put her manicured hand on Gavin's shoulder as they passed. Magdalene tensed, thinking she was a Guardian until she saw the glowing blue eye. "Mr. Cavanaugh," the woman gushed. "Thank you so much for this opportunity."

He smiled. "I'm privileged to be able to provide it, Mrs. Selvers. I trust you're having a good time?"

Mrs. Selvers exchanged a teary-eyed look with her companion, a woman who resembled her with curly brown hair and wideset eyes—though both of hers were brown, neither of them glowing. "A wonderful time, thank you."

Gavin squeezed the woman's shoulder and he and Magdalene moved on. Several more people greeted him, and he responded politely but didn't stay to talk.

The crowd thinned as they approached a wall of tinted glass. Gavin stopped and gazed out. "I'll never get tired of this view."

Magdalene approached the windows hesitantly. Far below, the landscape spread out like a complicated quilt, small buildings and curving streets glowing in the fading light of evening. As she watched, the streets seemed to writhe, changing shape, and a new building popped up like a bubble in the middle of the town.

Magdalene's ears rang. Her head cleared, and realization doused her with a bucket of ice. "We're in the Tower." She gazed at Gavin Cavanaugh with renewed interest, her heart hammering. She was finally meeting him.

Gavin smiled, his sharp eyes on her. "Welcome to Heaven's Vista, Miss Richards. It took many years to build, but we finally have a base from which we can safely operate here in the afterlife."

Magdalene stared out the windows, barely seeing the view, trying to gather her thoughts. "What are you doing here? What am *I* doing here?" She squinted at him. "And what is Morris doing here?"

Gavin nodded. "I hope you'll give me a little of your time so that I can answer those questions. I believe it would be to the benefit of both of us."

Magdalene chewed her lip. The strange town below glowed in the falling darkness. "I'm here," she said, shrugging. "So, talk."

Gavin leaned against the windows and put his hands in the pockets of his slacks. "Your friend is here because I invited him. I thought his presence might make you more comfortable. He's having more trouble with our security measures than you are, I'm afraid, but will be fine once he acclimates."

Magdalene nodded, still chewing her lip.

"Why you're here is a longer story." Gavin's gaze wandered over the crowd and his smile grew sad. "I won't tell you all of it. Not tonight. I wouldn't want to scare you off." His gaze found hers again. "I hope you'll forgive me, Miss Richards, but I've been searching for you for a very long time, and I'm glad to finally have a chance to speak with you. I've seen you in the Land of the Dead. You have unnatural power to affect events there, and I've been hoping to recruit you for my project. You can't imagine my distress when, right before I could contact you, you fell into the hands of those...charlatans."

Magdalene frowned. "Who, Andy?"

His expression darkened. "And Omar, yes."

Nausea rolled through her. She'd managed to forget about Omar for a whole fifteen minutes, but her luck had just run out.

"Andy Clayborn's group is a cult," Gavin continued, not seeming to notice her discomfort. "They lure people in and take their money. They aren't without talent, it's true, and if their principles weren't broken I'd want to collaborate with them."

Magdalene pressed her palm into her stomach, trying to focus. "Andy's a good person. They're not a cult." She swallowed as her half-buried doubts about Andy and Helena clawed their way back into the light. After all, she'd trusted Omar. How did she know they weren't all lying to her? She huffed. "*You're* the one who had me arrested."

He winced. "I can only beg your forgiveness. As sinister as my actions must have seemed from your end, I was doing the best I could to keep you safe."

Magdalene blinked. She'd expected him to deny it. "You had me *arrested* to keep me safe from *Andy*?"

"Yes, Miss Richards."

Magdalene scoffed, turning back to the window. Her mind was churning, her stomach twisted. She closed her eyes and took steadying breaths.

"When I realized you were with Andy Clayborn and his gang, it was terrifying," Gavin continued, and Magdalene opened her eyes again and forced herself to face him. "But I knew Andy would eventually arrange for a new bank account to be opened for you as part of his usual extortion operation. So, I watched the credit union for new account activity and acted as quickly as I could to rescue you when you showed up." He gave her a searching look. "However, I appear to have underestimated Omar's powers in the living world."

Magdalene tried to remain impassive as a tidal wave of emotions passed over her. Omar, saving her from juvie…saving her over and over again, just to abandon her in the end.

"I truly do apologize for my tactics, Ms. Richards," Gavin said, his voice quiet and sincere. "You would never have been harmed. Not with me. I was only acting in your best interests."

Magdalene massaged her temples. "Why didn't you just introduce yourself if you wanted to meet me so badly? Doesn't kidnapping seem a little, you know, dramatic and nonconsensual?"

He flashed a dry grin but quickly sobered. "Andy and Omar would never have allowed me to contact you directly out at the compound. And I *have* been trying to make contact with you here in the Land of the Dead. I haven't been successful until now."

Magdalene tore her eyes from him and gazed out at the view. It was fully dark outside now. Down in the city of the Dead, strange lights glimmered and flashed. She thought of Jeffrey, down there somewhere, sitting in front of his television, and Barry with his tower of hair. "Why are you sealing the portals?"

Gavin's blue eyes shone. "I am bringing order to the chaos of life and death, Miss Richards." His quiet voice cut as easily through the background chatter as if he were the only one speaking. "An end to the injustice on a universal level."

Magdalene blinked again. She didn't know what kind of answer she'd expected, but it hadn't been that one. "What do you mean?"

He fixed her with his sharp gaze. "Have you ever wondered why the world of the living is so miserable? Why there's so much violence, sadness, and rage? Human beings have been given the gift of life, and yet they spend the entirety of it hurting each other and wallowing in self-pity. And the truly evil ones—murderers, robbers, abusers and rapists—are not only allowed to keep living, they're allowed to pass into the afterlife and beyond without judgment."

Magdalene's heart pounded in her ears. Bullets and blood. Stan's face as he collapsed, dead. Stan's face as he disappeared into the rebirthing portal. And Morris...

"I've been gifted with the ability and guidance to effect great works here in the afterlife," Gavin continued. "What I'm doing is bringing justice to both worlds, to the living and to the Dead. Only when there is justice can there be peace. Only those who respect the life they've been given, respect themselves and love their fellow human beings, will be allowed to set foot upon the earth and to pass into what awaits us beyond. Those who inflict pain, cause death and destruction and misery, will be made to stay in the Land of the Dead until they realize the error of their ways. Their souls will be allowed to grow, to gain knowledge and compassion before they pass through into a new life or a new plane."

Magdalene stood frozen. "You're sealing the portals to restrict who enters them?"

Gavin nodded.

"How do you decide who gets through and who stays behind?"

Gavin smiled. "A fair question. Not me, if that's what worries you. No one person has the power to effectively judge another. But I have been blessed with insight into how it can be done justly and correctly."

"How's that?" The question came out sounding snider and more disbelieving than she'd intended, and Gavin flashed a sheepish grin.

"Every soul has a certain resonance, a signature—we all give off a cluster of frequencies that can be detected if you know how. The signal that a soul gives off has distinct and well-defined characteristics, not subject to human misinterpretation, which can be analyzed in order to gain insight into that soul's capabilities, fallibilities, and potential. This signal can change as the soul grows and develops. Acts of violence will change it, for instance. Acts of kindness and generosity will also. All this can be known, so that the person can be truly known with no room for trickery or error. To sum it up, I've built a machine. A computational system that can see into a person's being as clearly as God can."

Magdalene sniffed. He reminded her a little of Andy, but she wouldn't say so since he seemed to hate him so much. "So, you believe in God, but you think you've built a machine that can do better than God?"

Gavin laughed, and Magdalene blinked once more. It was a warm laugh, a little nerdy. Everything else about Gavin Cavanaugh seemed so composed, so polished. But that laugh sounded like he meant it, like he saw the irony in the situation, and it pushed faint dimples into his cheeks that made him look boyish. "My works have led me to believe strongly in God," he said, his sincere gaze meeting hers. "But God doesn't work directly, Miss Richards—that would defeat His purpose, which is to teach us to act for ourselves. He wants us to rely on our own free will, like a good parent.

"God does work *through* us, however. He's working through me, and through you. Sometimes it takes us a long time to learn from Him and understand what He's saying: we are children, stubbornly and petulantly asserting our free will. However, I've been able to lay aside my ego enough to hear His voice clearly. My system is the ultimate expression of His hopes for us. It is a way for humankind, once and for all, to weed out our baser instincts. To evolve into the loving creatures we were meant to be. My program is God's children helping themselves, solving the problems they themselves have created."

Magdalene raised her eyebrows. "Your machine denied my friend Barry, and he's a good person."

Gavin leaned on the windows, crossing his arms. "Few people are truly bad. Some will be denied because they aren't ready. They need time to prepare—to ripen, you might say—before passing into their next life. They, and all of us, will be richer for their growth." He shrugged. "I have faith in my program. I believe you would, too, if you saw it in action."

Magdalene stared out the window. Gavin had a machine that would keep people like Stan from ever being born. He had a way of making sure that people were punished when they inflicted pain upon others. It seemed farfetched. But Gavin Cavanaugh was powerful: he had built this Tower and could seal the portals, so he might be capable of amazing things. Was he, or his machine, qualified to play God, though? To judge people's souls?

She looked askance at him. "The Dead don't want you here, and this is their place. If your program is so beneficial, why are they so angry about it?"

Gavin nodded faintly. "You can't build anything without breaking ground first. The foundations have to be laid, and the structure built, girder by girder, brick by brick. Only then, after the structure is complete, may the work begin inside. The Dead may fear me now. I wouldn't blame them if they did. Great projects are intimidating to those who don't understand them. But understanding will come. The Dead will learn to love me, in time."

Magdalene studied him. Was this man's program truly the answer to creating a better world? It seemed risky to mess with the fabric of life and death.

What was the alternative, though? The status quo. A universe where people like Stan lived and Morris died, where people suffered needlessly and hurt each other in a million ways. A world that Magdalene herself couldn't make sense of or bring herself to accept. She straightened her shoulders. "What do you want with me, then?"

The corners of his lips curled up in a faint smile. "I can't do all this alone. I *need* you, Miss Richards. You're a remarkable girl, and we could do great things together."

Magdalene scowled. People kept saying things like that about her, and it made her bullshit meter swing into the critical zone.

He chuckled. "I sense you have doubts." He stood upright again and turned to gaze at the view with her. "You're young and haven't realized all your talents yet. I believe I can help you develop them. Give me a chance, Miss Richards. Come with me in the living world and let me show you the work we're doing so that you can judge for yourself. You don't have to give me an answer until you've been able to assess the situation firsthand."

Magdalene stood very still, the music and laughter of the party washing over her. Didn't she owe it to herself, to the world, to at least see if this system worked?

Her heart sank thinking about the people back at the hotel who she'd have to leave behind if she went with this man. Lynn, James, Andy, Bridgett...

Helena with the beast in her belly.

Omar.

Pain knifed through her guts, and it fully dawned on her what it would mean to go back to the Commune. It would mean watching Omar and Ingrid as they started their new relationship, watching them go out to the cottonwood tree without her, as they exchanged looks and fleeting touches and private jokes.

Her heart gave a hard wrench and she had to close her eyes to let the pain pass through her.

There was no way she could do that. She couldn't live there anymore, and here was the perfect opportunity presenting itself just when she needed it.

Sure, she still had doubts about Gavin Cavinaugh's grand system. But hadn't she had doubts about the Commune when she first arrived? Didn't she still have some of those doubts, in fact? All Gavin was asking was that she give him a chance. Where was the harm?

Magdalene nodded. "Okay. I'll come check it out."

Gavin smiled, showing his dimples again. He held out his hand, and Magdalene shook it with as much conviction as she could muster. "You won't regret this, Ms. Richards," he said.

She hoped that was true.

CHAPTER SEVEN

The Midnight Limousine

Magdalene woke in her bed and stared grimly at the ceiling of her dark room. The clock said 12:14 a.m. Somehow, she'd been asleep nearly sixteen hours.

She heaved herself out of bed, dressed quickly, and packed her few belongings. She refused to think or feel. She'd made her decision.

The hallway was dark and silent as she crept out of her room, her lumpy, overstuffed backpack jouncing on her shoulder. Even Andy's office was empty, and she heaved a sigh of relief when she made it to the front door without meeting anyone. Dully, she wondered what she would've said if she had. She didn't know.

Magdalene stepped out into the cool night and softly closed the door behind her. The sound of crickets mingled with the crunch of her shoes on the white gravel. She didn't look back as she started down the long driveway toward the road.

She stumbled over stones and tufts of grass in the starlight until she'd rounded the stone outcropping, which blocked her from view of the hotel, and felt comfortable turning on her phone's flashlight. Then she trudged on through the cool night, alone in the wide desert save for the occasional yipping of coyotes and the ghostly shrieks of barn owls. Lightning flashed far off on the horizon, but it was too far away to hear the rumble of thunder. Every so often a soft gust of wind would swirl around her, bringing the scent of distant rain.

It took her over half an hour to reach the highway. Then she waited, as Gavin had instructed. The moon rose over the ridges to the east, a few days past full. Moths divebombed her cellphone, so she turned the flashlight off. The shadowy desert whispered and sighed around her.

Every so often, a dull pang of uncertainty hit her, but then bitterness would flare in her core, drowning it out. Omar had betrayed her with Ingrid, and he'd betrayed her by pushing Stan into that portal. She apparently hadn't forgiven him for that, after all.

If Gavin truly could bring order and justice to the workings of the universe, then he was the good guy, and she was better off with him.

Headlights appeared around a far curve of the highway and the whoosh of an engine cut through the silence. The car sped closer until the headlights engulfed her, blinding her to the outside world but leaving her harshly exposed. The car slowed, then stopped. Magdalene was again in gloom, the beams cast over the sagebrush on the shoulder.

She blinked the spots out of her eyes and saw the vehicle was a white limousine, just like he'd sent for her at juvie. *A bit overdone, isn't it, Gavin?*

The driver's door opened, and a figure emerged, their footsteps crunching on the gravel as they came around the front of the car. The headlights revealed a thin man in a suit and chauffer's hat. "Miss Richards?" he asked pleasantly.

Magdalene shifted on her feet. "Yeah."

"Let me take care of your bag for you."

Magdalene handed him her backpack, watching bemusedly as he carried the tattered, malformed monstrosity to the back of the sleek car and put it in the trunk. Then he opened the back door and gestured for her to climb aboard. Magdalene stood for a moment, her heart hammering, then climbed into the dim interior. As he closed the door behind her, Magdalene was forcefully reminded of the time she'd been shut into the back of the police car.

But she quickly realized this wasn't the same at all. White leather seats lined the long passenger cabin like a sectional sofa. There was a television and a mini fridge, and a woman, who sat in the far corner, smiling at her brightly with red-painted lips. She held out her hand. "Hi! I'm Suzette."

Magdalene shook her hand, which was dainty and soft with red acrylic nails to match her lipstick. "Nice to meet you." Magdalene was strangely disappointed that Gavin Cavanaugh hadn't come himself. She'd spent so much time wondering about the man behind the Tower and had wanted to talk to him more. But he seemed like sort of a big deal. He was probably too busy to come.

The limo's engine purred as it made a U-turn, heading back down the highway the way it had come. Suzette was still smiling. Magdalene guessed she was in her mid-twenties, but the smile was polished and mature in a way that made her look older. Her glossy dark brown hair was cut in a sleek bob with bangs, and she wore a white blouse tucked into skinny jeans. "I'm so glad you're with us," Suzette said. "We're going to have a ball."

Magdalene tried to smile. "I'm sorry you had to come in the middle of the night."

Suzette waved the comment way. "It was no problem. Totally worth it." Magdalene thought she saw pity in the other woman's large eyes. It occurred to her that Suzette probably thought she'd had to escape the cult in the middle of the night or else they wouldn't have let her go.

Magdalene licked her dry lips. "So, where are we going?"

Suzette leaned back, draping her willowy arms over the seatback. "First, we're going to Vegas, just to have a little fun for a day or two. You could probably use some fun in your life right now. Have you ever been there?"

Magdalene's guts gave a hollow pang. "Yeah, I've been there. Briefly." She pushed back the memories. It was like trying to move a pile of boulders with a plastic spork. "Where are we going after Vegas?"

"To take a tour of the business, which isn't far from there." Suzette smiled again. Magdalene could tell she was trying very hard to be nice, but she felt dead inside. *Just get through this. Going with Gavin is your best option at this point, so make the best of it.*

"Do you work for Gavin also?" Magdalene asked.

A fleeting furrow marked Suzette's smooth brow. "Yes, I work for Mr. Cavanaugh. You and I will be coworkers, if you decide to stay."

Magdalene glanced out the window, but saw nothing besides her own pale, tired reflection. The blackness behind it was complete. "What do you do?"

"I'm an ambassador. I reach out to people with an opportunity to travel to the Land of the Dead so they can see it for themselves." Her eyes shone with enthusiasm. "It's amazing work. I love exposing people to that world, illuminating their minds and giving them the answers they've been seeking all their lives."

Magdalene could feel her eyebrows creeping up. "People believe you when you tell them about Purgatory, and you're able to teach them how to be conscious there? That sounds like heavy lifting."

Suzette laughed. It was deep and sort of dorky, and Magdalene liked her better for it. "I'm not saying it's not a trial sometimes, but Mr. Cavanaugh has developed a way to make it easier for people to enter that world, and seeing is believing."

"How has this not been all over the news then? If you're able to take people there, show them the afterlife, and everyone knows?"

Suzette gave her a meaningful look. "Mr. Cavanaugh makes everyone—employees and clients—sign a nondisclosure agreement and lets it be known he'll enforce it *very* strictly. Also, a lot of his employees aren't in the know about what's really going on. The admin staff and even a chunk of the development departments aren't working on the project they think they are, if you know what I mean. Until the world is ready to accept that the afterlife exists, and until we're a bit more established, the Land of the Dead is on a need-to-know basis. Otherwise, stuff could get pretty complicated."

Magdalene snorted. "Yeah, I'll bet."

Suzette drummed her nails on the seatback. "Mr. Cavanaugh is really good at organizing and running things. He always knows the best way to get the job done." She regarded Magdalene curiously. "Recruiting you, for instance. I hear you don't need any help at all staying awake in the Land of the Dead."

Magdalene plucked at a fray on her shorts. "Yeah, I guess not."

Suzette squinted at her thoughtfully. "I think he'll probably put you in recruitment in the *other* world."

"He wants me to recruit the Dead?" She chewed on her lip. Omar and Bridget had wondered how Tower Guy had managed to recruit the Dead to work with him. Was she going to be part of that now?

Suzette shrugged. "Some of the Departed have been causing problems and he might need someone to be an ambassador for our cause."

Magdalene fought back a wave of nausea. Was she going to be put in charge of fighting people like Barry? *You haven't committed to anything yet. If that's what he wants you to do, you can leave.*

The bitter knot in her stomach pulled even tighter. *And where will you go if you do?*

"Are you okay?" Suzette asked.

Magdalene forced a smile. "I'm okay. Just tired."

Suzette's eyes filled with pity. Magdalene was so tired of pity. "I really am so sorry for what you've been going through," Suzette said. "They say that he's really worried about you, you know, Mr. Cavanaugh. He was furious when he found out that those people took advantage of you the way they did."

Magdalene cringed inwardly. "He told you all about me?"

Suzette gave a sheepish shrug. "Your recruitment has been a company priority since I signed on, so we know some things. I heard you ended up in that cult because your parents were fleeing some sort of drug deal gone wrong, then you ran way."

Magdalene's fingernails dug into the leather seat. *How did he know all that?*

Suzette grimaced. "I'm so sorry. I'm not being very sensitive."

"It's okay," Magdalene said quickly. She tried to smile again, but she knew it wasn't very convincing. She was suddenly incredibly tired. Everything had been so fucked up for so long, and now here she was. Homeless again, with no one in the world who cared about her, speeding through the middle of the desert night and heading toward God-knew-what.

Suzette laid a soft hand on her knee. "I know you've been through a lot. I want you to know—I mean, you don't know me. You don't know any of us. But you'll be safe with us. You'll see."

Magdalene smiled again, and this time, she meant it. She wanted so badly to believe Suzette was telling the truth. *She* at least seemed to believe what she was saying.

Magdalene took a steadying breath. She had nothing to lose. The only thing that Gavin had to offer her was his promise that he'd make the universe a better place. He had no other hold on her. So, if his scheme turned out to be a farse, she'd leave. She didn't know where she'd go, but she'd worry about that if and when the time came.

For now, her mission was clear: gather as much information as quickly as possible about Gavin's operation and decide whether to help him or get the hell out.

"We're going to have so much fun, you'll forget about the past," Suzette said. "Your future is with us, and it's going to be awesome. This is the best job in the world. It's more than a job, really." She gave Magdalene a sparkling smile. "When was the last time you had a girls' night out?"

Magdalene smiled awkwardly. "Uh, like two weeks before never."

Suzette's smile turned a bit wicked. "I can't wait to hit the Strip with you. But for now, you look exhausted." She scooted to the end of the seat and opened a compartment under it, pulling out a couple pillows and blankets. "Let's try to get some sleep. It's not even the crack of dawn, and we have a big freaky day ahead of us." She passed Magdalene a pillow.

Magdalene didn't argue. She stretched out on the long bench. She may have just finished sleeping a staggering number of hours, but she didn't feel like she had, and she didn't really feel like making small talk for the rest of the long drive.

Suzette covered her with a fuzzy blanket, tucking her in like a fussy mother. "Night night," she said.

Magdalene smiled. "Thank you." She was so lonely, and the gesture warmed her heart.

Suzette retreated to the far end of the cabin, where she kicked off her strappy platform sandals and lay down, as well.

Magdalene lay in the darkness, her mind spinning dizzily. Eventually, the hum of the motor and sway of the limo lulled her into a dreamless doze.

CHAPTER EIGHT
Spoiled

Magdalene awoke to the sun shining dully through a tinted window, the hum of the limo's engine surrounding her. It took her a moment to realize where she was and for the events of the last couple of days to drip back into her skull.

The guilt, pain, and dread hit her like a barrage of bricks. She took deep breaths, sealing her heart in a soundproof box so she couldn't hear it screaming. *You're doing the right thing. There's no point crying about it.*

Magdalene sat up, rubbing her eyes. Suzette was already up, curled in a corner of the bench seat fixing her lipstick in her compact mirror. She snapped it closed and smiled. "Good morning. Did you get some rest?"

Magdalene smoothed her hair back. Some of it was stuck to her face with drool and she had to peel it off. "Yes. You?"

"Yes, thank God." She tossed her compact in her gigantic, sea-green leather purse and got out a hairbrush. "These seats are actually pretty comfortable to sleep on."

Magdalene nodded, her gaze drifting out the window. The highway was packed with cars and the Vegas suburbs sprawled across the valley floor like a crust of dried soup in a bowl.

"After we get settled into our rooms and freshen up a bit, we should go shopping," Suzette said. "We're going to a little party tonight, and we might as well look fabulous."

Magdalene glanced down at her frayed shorts and stained t-shirt.

"And, of course, all of this is going to be on the company credit card, so we can go absolutely crazy bananas if we want. In fact, I was encouraged to spend money like a freak today." She grinned enthusiastically, her lips stunning with their fresh coat of lipstick.

"Cool," Magdalene said, trying to look anywhere near as excited as Suzette did. Internally, she felt like she'd been infested by a swarm of buzzing question marks. Once again, the man behind the Tower was surprising her. If she'd been asked to make a list of what she'd expected after accepting Gavin Cavanaugh's offer, shopping wouldn't have been on or anywhere near it.

Suzette chatted about how great Mr. Cavanaugh's parties were as the limo descended into the city. She dropped a few names of celebrities she'd met at them, and Magdalene, who hadn't watched many movies or shows, made little impressed noises as if she knew who the hell Suzette was talking about.

They pulled off onto the Strip. Magdalene's heart struggled as she watched the tourists wandering the sidewalks, the morning sun slanting through the palms and casting long shadows over them. The last time she'd been here, she'd been with Omar. He'd seemed like such a cool boyfriend. They'd laughed together, watching the tourists and performers, until cops had pulled them over and arrested her. Then, Omar had saved her from juvie.

Now, he'd betrayed her, and Magdalene had run off with the guy who'd had her arrested. It was a funny old world.

Magdalene pressed her forehead against the warm glass of the window. *It doesn't matter now. Forget the past and deal with the present.*

They pulled in front of a hotel entrance and a man in a grey suit rushed to open the limousine door. He was short and stocky with thinning strawberry hair brushed back from a broad forehead. He smiled at Magdalene, the skin around his blue eyes crinkling. He had a kind face. "Welcome to Las Vegas, Miss Richards. My name is Marcus. I'm here to welcome you on behalf of Mr. Cavanaugh, who is unfortunately tied up at the moment."

Magdalene smiled back as she climbed out, stretching her sore limbs. Suzette gave Marcus a little hug and greeted him like an old friend. The chauffer took Magdalene's backpack from the trunk. Magdalene reached to take it from him, but the chauffer just smiled politely and signaled to a porter by the entrance, who sprang forward to take charge of it. Magdalene watched as he toted it off, the toe of one of her socks flopping out a hole in the zipper.

"This way, ladies," Marcus sang. Magdalene and Suzette followed him through the front doors and into a noisy casino. Crystals dangled from the ceiling and slot machines flashed. The noise and color jangled through Magdalene's body. She'd been so long in the relative quiet and solitude of the Commune that she'd forgotten what society was like. They wove through slow old couples, leering groups of drunk men, tottering girls wearing wilted bachelorette crowns, then traversed a maze of gambling tables before finally reaching a door marked "Private".

The door shut behind them and the din of the gaming floor quieted. They were in a small lobby with two elevators. Marcus inserted a card into a slot and a set of doors slid open. He ushered Magdalene and Suzette inside.

"Wait until you see this condo," Suzette said in a singsong voice, checking her hair in the elevator's ceiling mirror. "It's fantastic."

"I thought this was a hotel," Magdalene said. "We're staying in a condo?"

"Mr. Cavanaugh has arranged for you to use one of his private condominiums while you're here," Marcus said. "They're located above the hotel floors."

"Oh." Magdalene plucked at the hem of her shirt, staring at her distorted reflection in the black enamel walls. Things were starting to fall into place. The limo. The shopping. Gavin Cavanaugh was, like, *rich* rich.

The elevator doors opened not on a hotel hallway but directly on an entryway. Magdalene and Suzette followed Marcus out of the elevator and into a large, sunny room.

Magdalene clamped her lips down against a moan of awe. The white marble floors were inlaid with geometric patterns in black which complimented the black marble wet bar. There was a seating area with an overstuffed white couch and chairs, and the dining area had a gleaming black table with room for six.

Magdalene wandered over to the floor-to-ceiling windows and gazed out at the Strip far below, watching the tiny people on the sidewalks, the cars jostling for position on the street. "We must be at least thirty floors up."

"Thirty-five," Marcus said. He gestured down a passage to the right. "There are two bedrooms, and we've arranged for you to take this one, Miss Richards." Magdalene tore herself from the window and followed him down the hall.

The bedroom had a low, king-sized bed and, down a few marble steps, a sunken hot tub in front of more huge windows. A doorway led to a private bathroom.

"Here you are," Marcus said, "and I believe I hear Brennen with your luggage."

Brennen, the porter, nodded to them as he entered the bedroom carrying her backpack. He put it in an armoire and closed the door on it so it couldn't sully the décor. Magdalene wondered if she should tip him, then realized she didn't have a dollar to her name...at least not that she had access to. He didn't show any sign of expecting money, however, and left as quietly as he'd come in.

Marcus clasped his hands behind his back and smiled. "I'll come back for you this evening at seven to take you to a dinner party. If you need absolutely anything in the meantime, Suzette knows how to reach me."

"Thank you," Magdalene muttered. Marcus dipped his head and left. He exchanged a few words and laughed with Suzette in the sitting room, then the elevator doors whooshed and all was silent.

Magdalene walked down the steps and sat on a white fainting couch next to the hot tub. The city beyond the Strip sprawled over the desert valley, ringed by bare, brown ridges of folded rock and dirt.

"Knock-knock," Suzette called. "May I come in?"

"Sure. I'm decent."

Suzette strolled in. "Well, that makes one of us. I'm going to take a quick shower, then we should go shopping."

Magdalene plucked at a button on the couch. "That's really okay. I don't need to go shopping."

Suzette lifted her chin, and Magdalene could practically taste her effort not to look at Magdalene's old clothes and dirty sneakers. "It's all on the company card. Besides, I'm guessing you don't have any fancy dresses in that little backpack of yours. You'll need something for the party tonight, not to mention work clothes."

"I..." Magdalene's cheeks heated. "I just..."

Suzette smiled and traipsed down to perch on the foot of the fainting couch. "Mr. Cavanaugh was really insistent that we buy you some things, and it's not like he can't afford it. Even if you decide not to take the job, you'll have something to show for it. Yeah?"

Magdalene glanced around at the marble floors and crystal chandeliers. Why shouldn't she have some nice things for once in her life? If there truly were no strings attached, why should she feel bad?

Magdalene shrugged. "Okay."

Suzette sprang to her feet. "Let's get cleaned up, and we'll go. Oh! I'll call for some breakfast, too. We haven't eaten." She trotted off down the hall.

Magdalene's head gave a little throb. She hoped there would be coffee. She rose with a sigh, opened the armoire and dug her toiletries bag and her nicest t-shirt and shorts from her backpack, then headed for the bathroom.

When Magdalene went back out into the sitting room, fluffing her wet hair, she found the bar groaning under a spread of food. Her stomach clenched, and she realized she hadn't eaten in almost two days. She grabbed a plate. The scones were still warm, and she slathered one with butter. Her fingers hovered over the sausage links. When was the last time she'd eaten meat?

She pushed away the memories of Lynn's cooking and took two sausages out of spite. Then she poured herself some coffee from the carafe and ate in front of the windows, watching the thickening crowds crawl around the sidewalks.

She was licking her fingers clean and thinking about more sausage when Suzette strode out of her room, completely dry and perfectly coiffed, wearing a sleeveless white cotton dress. Magdalene slid her sneakers, which were caked in red Utah dust, under her chair.

"Ooh, the food came." Suzette pranced over and loaded a plate with sliced fruit and toast, then came to lounge on the chair next to Magdalene's, daintily nibbling at her food without messing up her lipstick. "Nice view, right?"

Magdalene nodded. "Gavin owns this condo, then?"

Suzette gave her an odd look. "He owns the entire building."

Magdalene's eyebrows crept up. "He must be loaded."

Suzette rolled her eyes theatrically, spearing a strawberry with her fork. "Crazy rich. He pays well, too. This is an awesome company to work for."

Magdalene sipped her coffee. "How does he have so much money?"

Suzette shrugged. "I believe he started out as a software engineer and developed programs for gaming machines. Now he's expanded into other areas, including the Land of the Dead."

"Is he able to make money in Purgatory somehow?" Magdalene kept her tone light, her gaze out the window.

"It's weird how you call it Purgatory." Suzette's brow furrowed. "I don't think his work there is really for money, I think it goes much deeper than that. But I'm guessing he'll eventually make at least enough for the operation to be self-supporting."

"How? The Dead don't have any money."

Suzette shot her a meaningful look. "But the living do. He's been carefully selecting clients and investors and showing them the wonders of the afterlife. All the people that I've worked with so far are willing to pay to see it and visit their loved ones there. They also have a guarantee that they, and their loved ones, will have a nice place in the Land of the Dead—Purgatory—and an escort to Heaven when they're ready." Suzette jumped up and put her empty plate on the bar. "It's a wonderful thing that Mr. Cavanaugh is doing, but even he, as rich as he is, couldn't afford to implement that technology without making some money at it."

Magdalene pressed her hand into her belly. "That's where you think the dark portals go? To Heaven?"

Suzette checked her lipstick in the mirror over the bar. "Yes. Mr. Cavanaugh is certain, and he's a smart guy. Besides, where else could they possibly go?"

Magdalene chewed her lip and shrugged. "How does he select clients?"

Suzette looked at her watch—a shiny, dainty thing with a red strap—and grabbed her gigantic purse off the couch. "We should go meet the car."

Magdalene heaved herself up, putting her empty cup on the coffee table and following Suzette to the elevator. It opened immediately when Suzette punched the button.

"I'm not sure exactly how he selects clients," Suzette said as the elevator started down, "but I understand he wants them to have shown the virtues of charity, compassion, and faith."

Magdalene wondered if she herself would pass that test. "What about people who don't have enough money to pay, but have those virtues?"

"After the project is more established, I think he'll have a tiered system to allow people to visit their loved ones who have passed on, even if they don't have a ton of money." Suzette leaned toward Magdalene confidentially. "Don't tell my clients that, though. They like to feel special."

"And what about rebirth?" The elevator came to a stop and the doors opened. "What do people have to do to be reborn?"

"That's not my department, but I know he's developed a system for that, as well." They entered the noisy casino and conversation became impossible. Suzette moved confidently through the crowds as they crossed the gaming floor, her hips swaying in her tight white dress. Tourists clogged the aisles, clutching drinks and shopping bags. There was a woman dressed as Mrs. Claus pushing a normally dressed man in a wheelchair, and Magdalene smiled to herself. This place was more like Purgatory than any place in the Waking World she'd ever seen.

Her smile disappeared when she imagined how Omar would have laughed with her.

The limo was waiting for them outside, and it drove them a scant block down the Strip and left them off at a mall. Magdalene followed an almost-skipping Suzette to Neiman Marcus, where she seemed to know all the salespeople. They all gathered around Magdalene, fawning over her figure, her hair and her eyes, then brought her heaps of clothes to try on. Magdalene felt like a dress-up doll.

Despite her discomfort and mild protests, Magdalene somehow ended up with several business outfits, two evening dresses, three pairs of shoes, and even some lingerie. When the lot was rung up, Magdalene glanced at the total, and her breath stopped: it was well over ten thousand dollars.

Suzette showed no sign of concern about spending a gangster amount of money on a couple bags of clothes as she handed the clerk the company credit card. They left the bags with the saleslady with instructions that they be delivered back to the condo.

Magdalene, who had been looking forward to going back to soak her feet in the hot tub, was horrified when Suzette dragged her next to the Gucci store. Some sunglasses were added to the haul, and a handbag Magdalene suspected she'd be too embarrassed and terrified to ever be seen with in public.

And yet Suzette still wouldn't hear of quitting. She took Magdalene to Nordstrom where they got yet more clothes, then hit the makeup counter, where the salespeople gushed about Magdalene's skin and insisted on giving her a makeover.

By the time Suzette agreed to be done, it was almost two in the afternoon. Magdalene's feet felt like they'd been pounded with a hammer, but Suzette seemed unscathed even though she was wearing platform heels. "Let's get you changed into one of your new outfits and get some lunch."

Magdalene's feet immediately got into a heated argument with her stomach. Suzette must have misinterpreted her expression, because she laid a hand on Magdalene's arm. "Still on the company card. Please don't worry about anything. Mr. Cavanaugh gave me strict instructions to spoil you."

Magdalene shifted on her sore feet. *Why,* though? This seemed like a lot of money to spend on a prospective employee. Weren't workers supposed to *make* you money?

Magdalene decided she was too hungry to worry about it at the moment. *Don't look a gift horse in the mouth.* A few weeks ago, she was lucky to get regular meals. Now she apparently had a fucking Gucci handbag and meals out on a company credit card. She was sure her good luck would evaporate as quickly as it had come, so she should enjoy it while it lasted.

The car took them back to the condo, where the shopping haul was magically waiting in Magdalene's bedroom, everything neatly hung in the armoire or folded in the drawers. Suzette helped her pick out a black and white print bouse and black skirt then shooed her into the bathroom to change.

Magdalene put the new clothes on, folding her old ones and tucking them out of sight by the garbage can, then stared at her reflection in the mirror. She barely recognized herself. She looked years older with the winged eyeliner and raspberry lipstick they'd put on her at the makeup counter.

Maybe she could completely remake herself. Maybe, somehow, this could be her new life.

She tucked that thought away and went out to join Suzette.

They took the elevator back down to meet the car, Magdalene tottering in her new strappy heels, which did nothing for her throbbing feet.

"You look fabulous," Suzette said as they climbed into the air-conditioned limo. "You're probably, like, the most beautiful girl in the world. You give 2010 Scarlett Johannsen a run for her money."

Magdalene's cheeks heated. "Thank you for taking me shopping."

"Don't thank me, thank Mr. Cavanaugh. Just another example of why this company is so awesome to work for. I mean, who else gets paid for a girls' day on the town?"

Magdalene flexed her abused toes. "Is this always how Gavin treats new recruits?"

Suzette grinned. "You're definitely a special case. He's been trying to catch you for a while. And if you don't need help to stay awake in the Land of the Dead, even outside the Tower, I don't blame him."

Magdalene fidgeted with a button on her blouse.

Suzette's smile faded. "None of this can be easy for you. Hopefully we can make you happy and comfortable so you can get past the things you've been through."

Magdalene forced a smile. "I'm totally having fun." The real Magdalene, deep down inside, facepalmed, but she ignored her. Spending a shit-ton of some guy's money wasn't exactly torture. For fuck's sake, she now owned a *Gucci bag*. What would her mom think?

Magdalene shuddered, hoping she'd never find out.

Suzette grinned. "This is the start of your new life. It'll take time, but you'll forget the past."

Magdalene nodded, wondering if she'd ever forget Omar and Lynn.

The car pulled up in front of another casino, and they hopped out into the sweltering desert sun. "I'm crazy starving," Suzette said. "We must have walked at least five miles today. This restaurant is excellent, though, and they actually give you decent portions."

A group of men leered at them as they passed through the front doors and into the cool, dim casino. They got more stares and head turns as they dodged through the crowds. Magdalene pretended not to notice, longing for her threadbare pajamas and solitude. She winced. *You're living every girl's dream and all you want to do is crawl into bed and read?* She lifted her chin and walked tall, letting herself forget that she was trailer trash cosplaying hot girl summer.

Suzette's unerring instincts led them through the maze of dinging and flashing machines and into an elevator. They crowded in with a pair of men holding aluminum bottles of Bud Light. Suzette pushed the button for the top floor.

The two men stared. "Hello, ladies," one of them said in a New Zealand accent, smiling at Magdalene. "You having fun?" His friend snickered and rolled his eyes, taking a glug from his beer.

Magdalene and Suzette exchanged a glance. "We're here on business," Suzette said.

The two men laughed. "We wouldn't know anything about that." The elevator stopped, and the men got out.

"Room 23-164, loves, if you need company," the first man called as his friend tugged him away by his sleeve.

The elevator door closed, and they started up again. Suzette chuckled. "Vegas."

Magdalene couldn't help but grin.

The door opened again and they stepped out into a restaurant glittering with chrome and mirrors. Edison bulbs hung from the ceiling and there were windows all around with spectacular views. The host seemed to know Suzette; Magdalene was starting to think everyone did. He seated them at a window overlooking the Strip to the south.

Suzette ordered a grapefruit mimosa. When Magdalene asked for a 7-Up, Suzette scoffed. "I think not. Two mimosas, Charlie."

Magdalene hid behind her menu as Charlie bustled off. Did Suzette know how old she was? Should she tell her? Her brain began to whir. Was it even legal to work in Nevada when you were sixteen? If she accepted the job, what would the other employees think if they discovered her age?

Worse yet, Magdalene was starting to like Suzette. She felt like they might be able to be friends someday. But would Suzette be friends with her if she knew how much younger she was?

A pang of loneliness washed over her, and she decided to keep her mouth shut for now.

"Oh, they've changed the menu," Suzette said. "Do you like steak? They make excellent steak."

"Steak's good," Magdalene muttered. The menu didn't have prices, and a lot of the options had French names. What if she accidentally ordered goat testicles or some sort of hot buttered insect?

Charlie delivered their mimosas, frothy and pink in huge wine goblets, with a garnish of sugared grapefruit and mint. Suzette held hers up in a toast as the waiter trotted off again. "To your new life."

A grin grew on Magdalene's face as they clinked glasses. Suzette took a generous slurp, Magdalene a more conservative one. It was sweet and refreshing, but the aftertaste seeped through her nostrils, bringing a forceful memory of Stan. She quickly took a gulp of water to rinse out her mouth.

When the waiter came back, Magdalene ordered the eggplant. The sausage at breakfast hadn't really agreed with her, she reasoned, but deep down she suspected some stubborn part of her wasn't quite ready to let go of the Commune.

Suzette ordered something elaborate involving steak, then downed the rest of her mimosa and ordered another one. She snapped her fingers toward Magdalene's drink. "Keep up."

Magdalene smiled awkwardly. "I'm not big on alcohol."

"Well, no one's perfect." Suzette leaned in and whispered, "Mr. Cavanaugh doesn't like us to drink. He says it screws up our focus in the Land of the Dead." She grinned. "But it's Vegas, it's almost three p.m., and we're not working tonight."

Their salads arrived along with Suzette's new drink, which she wasted no time starting in on.

Magdalene speared a piece of Romaine. "How did you get this job, anyway?"

Suzette leaned back in her chair, the stem of her glass dangling between her fingers. "I worked in human resources in one of Mr. Cavanaugh's casinos, and he sent someone to meet with me to ask if I wanted a promotion." She popped a pear tomato into her mouth. "I really wanted the job, but when they first told me the job description I thought they were bananas."

Magdalene snickered, thinking of her first days at the Commune. "I know the feeling."

Suzette studied her over the rim of her glass as she took another sip. "You're some sort of prodigy there, though, right? How did you figure out how to get there and keep your human form? I mean, I always had lucid dreams, sort of, but I still need plenty of help staying conscious."

Magdalene swallowed her mouthful of lettuce and shrugged. "I've been going to Purgatory since I was a kid, but I just thought I was dreaming, that it was normal dreams until Omar showed me..." Magdalene's mouth suddenly went sour and she took another sip of water.

"Who's Omar?" Suzette asked. Magdalene's emotions must have shown on her face, because Suzette immediately looked sorry she'd asked. "I'm so sorry. Was he like...?"

Magdalene sat up straighter. "He was my boyfriend, back at the...at the cult. It ended badly."

Suzette shook her head, her expression darkening. "Dudes suck, am I right?"

Magdalene snorted into her water glass.

Suzette drummed the tabletop with her crimson nails. "We're gonna have a good time, put some distance between you and all the bad stuff." She guzzled more mimosa. "Whoever he was, you're worth fifteen of him. Maybe twenty-five. You can tell me all about how stupid he is when you feel up to it. I've got stories of my own in that department."

Magdalene grinned. When Suzette was drunk, she reminded her a little of Lynn.

"I dated this guy named Bradley once," Suzette continued between forkfuls of salad. "*Bradley*. Can you imagine? The name says it all."

Magdalene gave a sympathetic grunt.

"He was a real weenis," Suzette announced. "It's best to just move on. Hos before bros." She held up her glass for a toast, and Magdalene clinked her water against it. Just then, with the sun glinting off the expensive flatware, a free gourmet meal coming, and a potential new friend across the table, things didn't seem so bad. Maybe she'd be able to move on, start a new life—just her, her amazing job, and her Gucci purse.

CHAPTER NINE
The Boss

After lunch, they went back to the condo. Suzette headed to her room for a nap while Magdalene took off her stuffy clothes, cleaned the makeup off her face, and slipped into the hot tub with her book. She ended up gazing past the pages out the window to the busy Strip as the jets loosened the muscles in her back.

She could get used to this. But how long would it last? If she decided to take the job, she'd have to get her own place, and she'd probably have to use her fake ID to rent it. No one would rent to sixteen-year-old.

And what if she decided *not* to take the job? What would she do then?

Magdalene took a deep breath, her damp hair fluttering on the exhale. *Deal with the problems in front of you. Tomorrow's problems can wait their turn.*

It was about an hour later, and Magdalene had rinsed off and was sitting on her bed reading, when Suzette called down the hallway. "Are you decent?"

"Fairly." Magdalene was wearing the thick bathrobe she'd found in the armoire. She didn't remember buying it, so maybe it belonged to the hotel. Who knew at this point.

Suzette bustled in, looking perfect in a spaghetti-strap cocktail dress. "Your makeover team will be here in five. Have you decided which dress you're wearing?"

Magdalene blinked.

Suzette wrinkled her nose at her then threw open the doors to the armoire and began rifling through it. "I vote for the light green number with the flamenco skirt." She found it and hung it on a wall hook, smoothing it out. "It suits your coloring perfectly. And for shoes, definitely the cream heels." Magdalene sat mutely as Suzette found the shoes on the shoe rack and placed them under the dress. Then she whirled and fixed Magdalene with a wide-eyed look. "Well? Come on, then." She clicked out of the room on her spiky heels. Magdalene stared after her, wondering where she got all her energy. With a sigh, she heaved herself out of bed, then frowned at herself in the mirror as she brushed her teeth, idly wondering what a "makeover team" was.

She didn't have to wait long to find out. As she wandered out into the sitting room, the elevator doors opened and unleashed two women into the condo. One of them was plump, middle-aged and smiling, the other young, thin and severe. Suzette introduced the older woman as Kathryn, the makeup artist, and the younger one as Verbena, the hair stylist.

They both studied Magdalene with great interest as they shook her hand. "Gorgeous," Kathryn murmured.

"This is going to be fun," Verbena added with a twitchy smile as she pulled scissors and styling tools out of her bag.

They perched Magdalene in a tall, padded chair at the bar. Kathryn painted her face while Verbena trimmed and layered her hair (which now fell well past her shoulders, thanks to regular meals) then went at her with the large-barrel curling iron.

"I think simplicity is the key with Magdalene," Kathryn said, lightly brushing shadow around her eyes. "If you do too much, you just end up attracting attention away from her classic beauty."

"She'd look good no matter what you did to her," Verbena replied. "But I doubt she'd let me give her a high-fashion hair-wreck. Would you?" She grinned hopefully.

"Maybe another time," Magdalene said, and Verbena pouted.

When Kathryn finished with Magdalene's makeup, she talked her into a manicure and pedicure as well, then carefully shaped her chipped nails and painted them a glossy violet she thought would go well with the green dress.

When they were all done, they helped her into the dress, then led her to the full-length mirror in her room.

Although the makeup was much subtler than the eyeliner she'd had on earlier, she still didn't recognize herself. She had to admit she filled out the cocktail dress pretty well, though. *Maybe I should let people dress me more often.* She smiled. "I've never had a makeover before. It was really fun. Thank you."

"Anytime," Kathryn said. "Seriously."

"Can I take a photo of you for our website?" Verbena asked.

Magdalene's eye twitched. "Of course." There were another five minutes of them making her do weird poses, then finally they were gone.

But there was no time to rest. Suzette rummaged in Magdalene's new stash, picked out a small, beaded handbag for her and stuffed it with makeup. Next, she came at her with a perfume bottle.

"No," Magdalene insisted. "Enough. No perfume."

An evil grin grew on Suzette's face and she lunged, holding the bottle like a weapon. Magdalene ducked away, giggling and stumbling on her heels.

Suzette was chasing her through the dining area when the elevator door opened.

"What's going on?" Marcus asked. "Should I call the police?" He sidestepped as Suzette threatened him with the bottle. "Enough, you cretin. The party can't start without you two, so let's get going."

Suzette stuffed the bottle of perfume into her own small bag. Magdalene wondered if she really couldn't go a whole evening without it, or if she just used it like pepper spray if someone pissed her off.

"Is the party upstairs?" Suzette asked as they stepped into the elevator.

"Yes," Marcus said, inserting his key card into the slot before pushing the button marked *Penthouse*.

Suzette threw her hands in the air and hip-bumped him. "Yeah! Upstairs is awesome."

The elevator doors opened and they stepped into a room that gleamed in the late afternoon sunlight. Floor to ceiling windows framed a view of the town, which sprawled hundreds of feet below. Tables draped in black and white patterned linen were decorated with live orchids and candles flickering in cut crystal glasses.

Well-dressed guests posed and chatted, sunlight sparkling through their cocktails and setting off their jewelry. A buffet table stood against the far wall, groaning under a cacophony of hors d'oeuvres. In any other circumstances the food would have been the focus of Magdalene's attention for the whole evening but, at the moment, her imposter syndrome was cockblocking her stomach.

All these people looked incredibly rich and important, and the only one here that she knew was Suzette. Even Marcus seemed to have evaporated into thin air. Magdalene twisted her fingers together so that she wouldn't pick at the beads on her dress. "I don't see Gavin."

Suzette blinked at her, then grinned. "Mr. Cavanaugh always likes to make an entrance. I'm sure he'll be here soon. Come on, I'll introduce you to some people."

Magdalene wanted to pull her head inside her body like a snail. Instead, she straightened her shoulders and prayed she wouldn't trip in her heels as Suzette led her toward a trio of older women.

"Mrs. Lambert," Suzette cried, grasping the hands of one of the ladies. "I'm so glad you could make it."

Mrs. Lambert smiled. A stunning emerald pendant nestled in the hollow of her crepe-skinned throat. "Oh, Suzette, I can't tell you how happy I am to be here." She gestured at her two companions. "These are my sisters, Lilian and Deborah. Remember I told you about them? This is Suzette, Mr. Cavanaugh's outreach coordinator. Her kindness and patience are the reason we're here today."

Lilian and Deborah greeted Suzette warmly, their curious gazes darting to Magdalene.

"May I introduce Miss Magdalene Richards," Suzette said. "She's a special recruit of Mr. Cavanaugh's. You wouldn't believe the lengths we've gone to get her here today. She's a prodigy who has voyaged beyond where any others have dared to go in the Land of the Dead. We are *hoping*," Suzette winked at Magdalene, "that she will be an amazing addition to our team."

The women all grasped Magdalene's hand in turn, their eyes wide and wondering. Magdalene smiled, feeling as if she'd been yanked into some strange new dimension. Before she had time to process it all, Suzette promised the ladies they'd speak to them later and pulled Magdalene to another group.

It was more of the same, Suzette talking her up as if she were some interdimensional Marco Polo. "She will add *so much value* to the company if she joins us," Suzette told a man in a fabulous suit of peach silk.

"Well," the man said, drinking her in with his astute gaze, "I very much hope you decide to sign on with this little venture, then."

As they moved on to the next introduction, Magdalene chewed on the inside of her cheek. So much had happened in the last twenty-four hours that it hadn't had time to dawn on her until now the strangeness of this situation: Gavin Cavanaugh was selling tickets to Purgatory and beyond. This room was full of his customers. And he wanted her to help him. *How, though? And how does this goal tie in with his goal of universal justice?* Was it just a way to finance it, like Suzette had said?

Magdalene glanced around the room again, but still didn't spot him. Hopefully he'd appear soon. She had a lot of questions that needed good answers. Otherwise, she'd be homeless, penniless, and alone on the streets of Las Vegas.

After they escaped a long chat with a man who was far too friendly and invited them to his vacation house on Lake Tahoe, Magdalene shot Suzette a pleading look. "Can we go sit down for a bit? I'm sure we've met everyone in this room at least three times."

Suzette gave her a knowing smile. "Captain Hornytimes over there did count as about fifteen people. Let's grab something at the buffet and take a break."

Magdalene praised the god of parties that they made it across the room to the food without being pulled into another conversation. She and Suzette loaded plates up with sushi and dumplings. "Why do you keep introducing me like that?" Magdalene asked in a low voice.

Suzette looked askance at her as she heaped seaweed salad on her plate. "Like what?"

Magdalene wrinkled her nose. "Like some sort of prodigy."

Suzette gave her an incredulous look. "Because you *are?* It gives people even more confidence in the company knowing you might be on board. You and your skills will bring in *so* many new clients, you don't even know. The opportunities it opens up having a natural out in the wilds of the Land of the Dead—someone who can explore new territory and communicate with the Departed—it's amazing to think about."

Magdalene frowned at her plate. Is that why Gavin had had her dressed up like a doll and paraded around this party? To sell her as some sort of mystic conqueror of the afterlife? This was sounding less and less like what she'd signed up for.

She and Suzette grabbed a small table along the windows. Magdalene kicked her heels off and hid her sore feet under the tablecloth. "What do you mean a *natural*, anyway?"

Suzette bit enthusiastically into a dumpling and dabbed at her lips with a linen napkin. "You can stay lucid in the Land of the Dead without a beeper, even outside the Tower. Mr. Cavanaugh hasn't even mastered that, and he's been working at it for more than a decade."

"A beeper?"

Suzette nodded, swallowing another mouthful. "It's a device Mr. Cavanaugh developed that helps you stay lucid. It stabilizes your vibrational..." Suzette made a rocking motion with her palm, "vibrational thingy. It makes your eye glow blue, though, which makes it harder to approach and gain the trust of the Departed."

Magdalene curled her bare feet together. "That crap freaked me out, too. I had no idea what was happening."

Suzette snorted. "Mr. Cavanaugh had people trying to approach you for a long time, but you always ran. The Departed react the same way, so you can see why your skills are needed."

Magdalene polished off some more sushi as she wondered how Gavin had created a computer interface with Purgatory. It boggled the mind. She had a sudden urge to discuss it with Omar and Andy before memory stepped in, grinning cruelly, and the urge dwindled into a bitter knot in her throat. She pushed her plate away.

Suzette sighed as she glanced around the room. "This crowd is a bit ancient for my tastes." Then her gaze snagged on something over Magdalene's shoulder and she brightened. "Except for Armando. He's only slightly decrepit."

Magdalene turned to see a tall young man with dark hair strutting up to the table, and she froze. It was the guy who'd accosted her as she escaped from juvie. He was dressed in a black suit and tie with a black undershirt—everything black, like a ninja dressed up for business. He spotted Magdalene and paused, a grin growing on his face. "We finally got her. There she is." Magdalene watched him approach through narrowed eyes, and Armando's grin turned a little nervous. He glanced around. "You don't have that Omar guy with you, right?"

It was a kidney punch. Suzette sent Magdalene a worried look and pushed a chair out with her foot. "Sit your narrow butt down, Arnie, and stop being a jerk."

Armando raised his eyebrows as he plopped into the chair. "A jerk? Me?" He regarded Magdalene a little more seriously. "I was just doing my job."

Suzette glanced back and forth between them. "I feel like there's a story here."

Magdalene snorted, glaring at Armando. "The story is, he tried to kidnap me."

Suzette's gaze cut to Armando, who looked unfazed. "I think of it more as I was trying to save you from that cult. But then that Omar dude knocked us all out with some freaky kickboxing moves or something." His brow furrowed and he gazed at Magdalene distantly. "How did he do that, anyway?"

Magdalene studied him, tapping her bare foot against the cool tile. Is that how Armando really remembered it? He obviously knew about Purgatory, but his brain apparently couldn't grasp the concept of magic in the Waking World and was trying to rationalize it.

Suzette shot her another worried look. "She doesn't want to talk about Omar, dingwad."

Magdalene's foot stopped tapping as an unexpected surge of gratitude toward Suzette coursed through her.

Armando nodded. "Gotcha. Sorry."

"Anyway," Suzette said. "I guess I don't have to introduce you two, but Armando, Magdalene, Magdalene, Armando."

Armando gave her a lopsided smile as he shook her hand. "Nice to finally meet the famous Magdalene Richards in semi-normal circumstances. I'm glad you're here, and I hope we can start over."

Magdalene nodded curtly, the strangeness of the situation inundating her all over again. She was in the lair of the man who'd had her arrested and tried to kidnap her. But if Gavin truly thought that Andy's group was a cult, wouldn't that have been justified, maybe even heroic?

Was Andy's group a cult? Magdalene's heart squeezed, and she took a deep breath. *You don't need to figure all this weird shit out right now. You're here. What's done is done. Just deal with what's in front of you.*

"So, how you doing here so far?" Armando asked. His tone was light, but Magdalene could see the concern and curiosity in his eyes. Magdalene Richards, the poor little girl who had escaped a dangerous cult.

She smiled. "Having lots of fun. Suzette took me shopping today."

Armando laughed. "Of course. Suzy over here really doing the dirty jobs."

Suzette rolled her eyes and popped a grape into her mouth.

"What do you think of our project so far?" Armando asked.

Magdalene drummed her manicured nails against the table. She still couldn't get used to having them painted. "I haven't seen much of it yet, but honestly I didn't think I'd be involved with selling trips to the afterlife. I thought we'd be working toward bringing peace and justice to Earth."

Suzette and Armando exchanged a look. "That's exactly what we're doing. All these people here are investors in that project." Suzette gestured around the room. "But, in order to get people to invest, he has to give them something in return, and he has to show them that the Land of the Dead is *real*. That's why he's developed the beeper and everything else."

"It's an amazing project," Armando agreed. "And complex. I'm not sure we can even fathom the directions it will go. But Mr. Cavanaugh's prime goal is the betterment of all humanity."

Magdalene nodded. In the privacy of her mind she wasn't totally convinced. But that's why she was here: to investigate and vet Gavin's motives. "Why is that device called a beeper, anyway?"

Armando snickered. "Because it looks like one of those old-fashioned beepers—it clips to your belt. It also makes your ears ring in a rhythmic pattern, which sounds like beeping."

Magdalene raised her eyebrows. "You clip it to your physical body before you go to sleep?"

Armando nodded. "It helps you sleep, too. Turn it on, it puts you right out, transports you directly to the Land of the Dead. It's awesome."

A bustle of activity and a change in the atmosphere made them look up. Gavin Cavanaugh was stepping out of the elevator, flanked by two men in dark suits.

People migrated toward him like iron shavings to a magnet. He waded into the crowd, smiling and shaking hands, while the two men in suits hung back on either side of the elevator, surveying the scene and blending into the background like chameleons.

Suzette and Armando sat up a bit straighter, exchanging a look. "The Boss is here," Armando murmured.

Gavin was in an expensive-looking suit again, dove grey, with a thin, pale green tie the color of Magdalene's dress. His gaze found hers and he gave her a little smile.

Adrenaline surged through her, and she quickly looked away, studying the dry ridges that ringed the valley. *Everyone else acts like he's some super big deal, but that doesn't mean I have to. He's just a person.*

Except something about him seemed different than other people. She studied him out of the corner of her eye. He was talking to a couple that Suzette had introduced her to, Gabriel and Cindy Smith. Omar couldn't be the only one with powers in the Waking World, and hadn't Omar himself said he thought Tower Guy had some sort of magical powers of persuasion?

People did seem to respond to him, but couldn't that just be because he had so much money?

Suzette turned her back to Gavin and quickly drained her cocktail, placing the empty glass in front of Armando.

He placed it back in front of her. "Don't pin your alcoholism on me."

Suzette pushed it toward Magdalene. "Golden Girl can have all the drinks she wants without getting in trouble. She's not working yet."

Armando folded his arms and grinned wryly. "We should get her wasted, then."

Suzette scowled. "Be good, you man-whore."

A chiming caused the hum of conversation in the room to quiet. All eyes turned to a waiter who was tapping a crystal glass with a fork. "Ladies and gentlemen, please go ahead and be seated. Dinner orders will be taken momentarily. You will find your menus on your tables."

There was a murmuring and scraping of chairs as everyone sat. Gavin took a table at the other end of the room with the Smiths. "Wait, there's dinner, too?" she asked. "I thought it was just the buffet."

Suzette grinned. "There's always more food when Mr. Cavanaugh throws a party, silly girl." She slid a menu from beneath Magdalene's napkin and handed it to her. Magdalene looked it over, deciding that maybe her decision to come here hadn't been so bad. When a waiter came to take their orders, she chose the summer vegetable and goat cheese pasta.

Then she turned to smile at Armando. "So, what sort of work do you do here?"

"I work outside the Tower, in security and recruitment." He cocked his head. "I do believe the Boss wants you to work with my team."

"Oh?" She'd be working with *this* douche? "How long have you worked for Gavin?"

Armando blinked and exchanged a fleeting glance with Suzette. "About a month. I had a summer job working security in a casino when Mr. Cavanaugh sent someone to me about this job. I jumped on it. I'm a criminal justice major at UNLV and wanted to be in the FBI, but this gig is much better and I hope to stick with it."

Suzette snorted. "God help us, Arnie in the FBI. He'd lead a SWAT team to conduct panty raids."

Armando raised his eyebrows. "I don't need a SWAT team to help me with panty raids, Suzy. You wanna see why?"

She made a face. "I'd rather watch my mother do it with Christopher Walken."

Armando laughed. A waiter brought them colorful salads with candied pecans and crumbled feta, a little silver dish of dressing on the side. Suzette whispered for the waiter to bring her a vodka tonic on the rocks in a water glass.

Magdalene poured dressing on her salad. "What does security and recruitment involve?"

"Initially the idea was to try to win the Departed over to our side, so we tried to play ambassador." Armando picked a pecan from his salad and crunched it. "We didn't have much luck, honestly. The locals are getting really agitated about our project. So, the last few days we've mostly been doing crowd control."

Magdalene's guts twisted. "Crowd control?"

He nodded. "The Departed keep mobbing the fence, so we scare them off." He snickered and popped another pecan in his mouth. "My job is to scare ghosts."

Magdalene concentrated on her salad, thinking of Barry. If she had better luck with diplomacy, would there be less need for *crowd control*?

"So, we going to hit the clubs later?" Armando asked, pushing his plate away and leaning back in his chair.

Suzette wrinkled her nose. "If we do, you'd just be a drag on us." She grinned at Magdalene who did her best to grin back. She had her fake ID with her, so she could get into clubs, but if Suzette and Armando noticed the name Andrea Laird on the license, it would invite questions.

"You ladies need someone to look after you, make sure you don't get into trouble." Armando leaned toward Magdalene confidentially. "After a few more drinks, Suzy here will be dancing on tables for tips."

"I don't do it for tips." Suzette primly sipped her disguised drink.

Their dinners came, and they talked about movies and books (Suzette wasn't much of a reader, but Armando liked suspense novels). The sun buried itself behind the hills, leaving fading layers of red and green on the horizon. The dining room glowed, bathed in flickering candlelight and sparkling fairy lights.

Magdalene glanced over at Gavin, who was in deep conversation with his two tablemates. He shot her his mysterious smile, and she quickly glanced away, her heart pounding. Had he known she was looking at him? Or was it just coincidence?

The waiters glided through the dining room, carrying away dinner plates and bringing trays laden with desserts. There was cake covered in chocolate ganache and ice cream sundaes in tall, etched-crystal glasses. Magdalene chose the sundae while the other two got cake. She dug her long spoon through the scoops of coconut ice cream into pockets of dark hot fudge. The toasted coconut topping added crunch, and a chocolate-dipped strawberry on top made it perfection.

She glanced up to find Armando watching her, his fork poised in midair.

She paused in digging the last of the hot fudge from the corners of the glass. "May I help you?"

He grinned. "Nothing, just enjoying the show."

Suzette pursed her lips and smacked him across the shoulder.

Magdalene put her glass down, looking forlornly at the neglected fudge. What would he say if she told him she was sixteen? Would he even care?

"Don't pay attention to this knob," Suzette said. "I'll protect you from him, with a goddamn shotgun if need be."

Magdalene got a vision of her spraying him in the eyes with her bottle of perfume and bit her lip to keep from smiling.

There was another bout of cutlery tinging against crystal, and she looked up to see Gavin standing at the front of the room, tapping his wineglass with a fork. When the murmuring and laughter subsided, he set the glass and fork down.

"Welcome, friends." His quiet voice filled the room. "Thank you so much for coming, and a heartfelt thanks for your hard work and unerring support during these last months. In the case of some of you, years." He nodded at Gabriel and Cindy Smith, and they beamed. "It has been a long and illuminating road, and you've all been indispensable."

There was applause, and he waited for it to die down before continuing.

"I am not going to make a long and tiresome speech, as I know all of you want to dance and enjoy yourselves. I just want to announce that, finally, after all our hard work and struggle, Answers Industries is officially in business."

There was enthusiastic applause and cheering, including from Armando and Suzette.

Magdalene clapped dutifully, her gaze scanning the crowd. All gazes were fixed on Gavin, wide and shining, worshipful. In the eyes of these people, he might be something close to a god: he was giving them access to the afterlife.

The cheering died down and Gavin went on. "As all of you are old hats at business, you know the work doesn't stop here. We have many struggles ahead. This is a groundbreaking venture, and those often face a rocky rollout. Society has a hard time accepting that which is truly revolutionary. However—" There was a bustle; waiters were passing out goblets of champagne. Gavin took one and held it with the stem dangling between his fingers. "—the fact that we've arrived at this juncture should be a matter of great pride and lasting hope to all of us. So," he raised his glass just as Magdalene was served her own goblet, "I would like to propose a toast." There was a solemn silence as all raised their glasses, the bubbling liquid turning to shining gold in the candlelight.

Gavin glanced over and his gaze snagged Magdalene's. "To eternal life."

The crowd erupted in cheers as they toasted and drank. Magdalene clinked her glass against Suzette and Armando's, then pretended to take a sip, watching Gavin through narrowed eyes.

People swarmed up to shake the Boss' hand. Armando pulled his phone from his pocket and started scrolling. Suzette downed her champagne in one, plunked her glass down, and raised her eyebrows at Magdalene. "I think we can safely leave, if you want."

Magdalene nodded. She felt weird here: young, poor, and confused. *Eternal life.* The words still rang in her ears.

"If you take me with you, I promise I'll be good." Armando slid his phone back into his pocket and gave them puppy eyes.

Suzette gazed a question at Magdalene, but she was spared from responding when there was a disturbance in the Force. The people in the surrounding tables went suddenly quiet, and Magdalene looked up to see Gavin Cavanaugh approaching. Suzette and Armando sat up very straight, exchanging a wide-eyed glance.

Gavin smiled. "Please excuse the intrusion, but I'd hoped to borrow Miss Richards here." He looked down his straight nose at her, wearing his enigmatic smile. "May I have a moment?"

"Of course." Magdalene got her feet, her cheeks burning as she realized she had to slip her shoes back on.

"Really great party," Armando said with a wide smile as Magdalene worked her feet into the strappy heels. "Everyone seems really energized about the project."

Mr. Cavanaugh nodded. "As well they should be. We've been working hard, and we've built something amazing. Just wait until they see what we have in store next."

Armando let out a hearty laugh that made Magdalene and Suzette exchange a deadpan look. "I can't wait to see their faces," he said.

Magdalene, who had managed to get her shoes on, stood awkwardly, not knowing what to do with her arms. Gavin smiled. "Shall we?"

With one last glance at her tablemates, who were staring at her with frozen expressions, she let Gavin lead her off through the crowd.

People greeted them as they passed, and Magdalene felt their appraising glances. She was suddenly hyper-aware of all the skin showing above the neckline of her dress. Between that and the professional hair and makeup, she wouldn't blame people for thinking she was older and for getting the wrong idea.

Sourness crept into her mouth. Did *Gavin* have the wrong idea? He had to know her age. He'd had her put in juvie, after all. But some men didn't care. She glanced at him from the corner of her eye, and he gave her a sharp look.

Something about that look put her at ease, and her shoulders relaxed slightly.

The elevator doors opened as they approached. The two bodyguards still flanked them, and they stepped inside after Magdalene and Gavin had entered. Then the doors closed, shutting them off from the noise of the party. Magdalene stared at her hazy reflection in the elevator doors. She really was showing a lot of boob. Whose idea had that been? Not hers. She didn't think she'd had an idea of her own all day.

Gavin leaned against the elevator wall, studying her. "I suspect it's been a long day for you. You probably aren't used to this sort of lifestyle."

Magdalene blinked, and she smiled blandly. "It's like you read my mind."

He gave her a knowing look. "It doesn't take the skill of a great psychic to make that determination."

The doors opened again, and Gavin and Magdalene stepped out. The bodyguards didn't budge, and the elevator closed, taking them back to whatever warehouse or broom closet they were stored in when not needed.

They were in a wide, low-ceilinged room with mellow, recessed lighting, and the silence settled over her. They were alone. Magdalene clutched her hands together in front of her. "I haven't thanked you yet for all the stuff. You didn't—"

Gavin cut her off with a wave. "No need to thank me. It's not out of the goodness of my heart. I'm trying to recruit you." He gazed at her. Magdalene wasn't sure she'd ever seen eyes quite so sharp. They were bright blue and seemed to take in everything.

"It was still nice." She wondered if he even knew how much money he'd dumped on her. Maybe Suzette had been overenthusiastic. Maybe when he got the bill, he'd send his minions to empty out her closet.

Gavin's lips twitched in a smile. "I can afford it. Besides, it's the least of what you deserve after what you've been through." He beckoned to her as he strolled toward a bank of windows at the far end of the room. "I'd like to show you something."

Magdalene followed him. They stood at the windows, gazing down through a curtain of crystal beads onto the bustling casino floor. Streams of people wandered the sinuous walkways between the gaming machines and tables, like blood cells flowing through capillaries.

"If I can convince you to stay, you'll get used to this lifestyle," Gavin said. "You weren't meant to roll in the gutters with pigs, Magdalene."

She snorted. "Are you serious? I'm as white trash as it gets."

His little smile disappeared. "I'd like to hurt the people who made you believe that. I suppose I'll have to settle for making sure they receive their eternal justice."

Magdalene's heartbeat accelerated. She wanted to believe, but it was too complicated, too big of a thing for one man to accomplish. Though if anyone could singlehandedly change the world, maybe it was this man who apparently farted money and had a knack for making people think he was some sort of god.

Gavin nodded toward the windows. "Look at the people down there." He squinted down onto the casino floor with a furrow between his brows. "Humanity doesn't consist of individuals. All those people milling around my machines are part of a giant, living organism with patterns of behavior that can be quantified."

"And taken advantage of?" Magdalene clamped her lips shut, cursing her lack of filter, but Gavin just smiled, showing his dimples.

"It's better to direct the human organism than exploit it." He glanced at her. "Some would say my casinos serve no purpose, but we can certainly learn a lesson from them. I don't force people to come here, nor am I using any kind of subterfuge to take their money. They come to have a good time, and I provide that service." He twisted a thick, onyx ring on his left pinky. "However, through careful observation of human behavior, we've learned how to maximize our profits—without taking advantage, but with carful guidance." He gestured toward the windows. "Have you been down on the casino floor?"

Magdalene thought she knew where he was going with this. "It's a maze, easy to get turned around, easy to get distracted. There's no windows, no clocks, so it's easy to lose track of time, and it's hard to find the doors out."

He nodded. "Exactly. And who would want to leave when we have everything they want right here? No one could say we're compelling them to stay, but we are providing encouragement." He shot her a grin. "I'm an asshole, aren't I, darling?"

Magdalene snorted, then shrugged. "Maybe a little bit. But that's business, I guess?"

Gavin smiled—a sheepish, vaguely boyish smile. Magdalene chewed on the inside of her cheek. Gavin Cavanaugh was *likeable*. He was thoughtful and didn't talk down to her. He listened, paid attention to people. Was that his only trick? Was this the man they'd been so leery of?

Gavin's smile faded as he gazed down at the casino floor again. "This casino may be a vulgar example of it, but it's possible to provide humanity with direction, with purpose. That concept can be used to help human beings reach a higher form of existence."

Magdalene raised her eyebrows. "A higher form of existence?"

"A world where people are no longer at the mercy of their base instincts. No longer ruled by their need to conquer and control. I mean to create a world without violence, deceit, or envy, where humans don't hurt one another anymore."

Magdalene's heart pounded steadily into the silence. "You think you can do all that?"

He nodded. "It won't be easy, but yes." He twisted his pinky ring. "Many have tried to change the world, but they haven't had the tools I now have at my disposal and so they've only succeeded in creating more chaos and tragedy. Men throughout history have failed to realize that you don't need to use force to achieve your ends. All you need is careful manipulation of the parameters, of the environment in which we live and die, to cause people to *choose* a result that is more desirable, humane, and healthy." He caught her in his sharp gaze. "Together, Magdalene, we can build a better world."

Magdalene licked her dry lips. They tasted like lipstick. "I still don't understand why you need me."

"Relax, darling." He strolled to a cabinet against the back wall and opened it, pulling out two bottles of water. He handed one to her. "I believe you possess talents similar and complementary to mine." When she opened her mouth to protest, he pressed on. "You're young and don't appreciate your worth, of course. Your unfortunate upbringing hasn't helped." He gazed at her, his eyes glinting steel. "That's over, completely in the past."

Magdalene took a drink of her water, then frowned at the bottle, turning it around in her hands, and sent him a probing glance. "You think I have the ability to influence people, like you do?"

He raised his eyebrows. "I know you do."

"I certainly haven't noticed."

He shrugged. "I wouldn't have expected you to. But surely you recognize that people *like* you, Magdalene. And it's not just your looks. You have something that draws people in like moths to a flame."

Magdalene studied him from the corner of her eye, remembering how the people at the party had flocked to him, how they'd looked at him. People didn't act like that around her. She took another sip of water.

"You're still young," he repeated softly, "and your circumstances haven't afforded you many opportunities to recognize and weild the power you have. But you have it, and I can teach you to use it."

She turned to face him, leaning against the window, gathering her courage. "Are you talking about charisma? Or something else?"

He gave her his mysterious little smile. "I think you underestimate the power of charisma, especially when you know how to use it."

She regarded him for a few more moments, then turned again to gaze out the tinted windows. The ghostly reflection of her face was superimposed over the gamblers at their machines, the lights glinting off their glassy eyes.

"This is a lot to process, especially at the end of a long day," Gavin said. "I just hope you'll give me a chance to show you what you're capable of, and the *good* you'd be able to do in this world."

Magdalene watched a woman settle into an empty seat in front of a slot machine and feed her ticket in. "Would it be possible, with these abilities you're talking about—this charisma—to do evil?"

Magdalene watched Gavin's reflection in the window. He was gazing distantly down onto the casino floor. "I fell into that trap in my youth." A shadow passed over his face. "If I can save you from my own mistakes, I will." Magdalene studied him, wondering what mistakes he was talking about. He caught her looking and grinned. "I'm not going to tell you sordid tales of my youth. Not tonight. I'm sure you're exhausted, anyhow."

Magdalene shifted on her sore feet. She was exhausted. Her brain was crammed with thoughts, all of them wiggling and begging for attention, and fatigue pounded the back of her eyeballs.

The elevator doors slid open, revealing the two bodyguards, and Magdalene blinked. Did he have some secret call button?

Before she could start toward the elevator, Gavin put a hand on her shoulder. His palm was warm and dry against her bare skin. "Whatever happens, thank you for meeting with me and giving me this chance."

Magdalene smiled. "It's been very interesting."

Gavin smiled dryly. Then the dryness left his expression. "Tomorrow, I can show you how Answers Industries works."

A prickle of adrenaline threaded through Magdalene's veins. "I wouldn't miss it for anything."

He took his hand from her shoulder and nodded at the bodyguards. "Be ready at eight thirty. Oh, and Magdalene—" He gave her a wry smile. "When you meet with human resources tomorrow, don't be thrown off by the fact they're a bit hazy on your job description. We'll discuss that later."

Magdalene nodded. "Got you."

Gavin turned his gaze to his bodyguards. "Please escort Miss Richards back to her condominium."

They raised their chins in acknowledgment.

Magdalene stepped into the elevator and the doors closed, hiding her from Gavin's bright, blue eyes.

CHAPTER TEN
Answers Industries

Magdalene was in Bridgett's field.

The little girl sat under the willows with her back to her, her blonde hair blowing in the breeze. A dulled wave of anguish eddied around Magdalene's heart. She scanned the streambank and the wide field of grass, but there was no sign of Omar, Ingrid, or anyone else.

Magdalene had left the Commune, had left Bridgett and everyone else behind. Perhaps it could be said that she'd betrayed them. And yet she found herself here.

No matter what Omar had done, Bridgett had no part in it. And, despite what Gavin believed, Magdalene couldn't bring herself to mistrust the girl. She took a step forward, then another. When she was a few steps behind her, Bridgett turned.

Magdalene gasped and fell to her knees at the girl's side. Bridgett was gazing at her with the same calm, blue eyes as always, but where her mouth should have been was only a swath of blank, pale flesh.

Magdalene reached for Bridgett's face, then drew her hand back. "What happened?"

A sad smile shone in Bridgett's eyes. She touched Magdalene's cheek with her childlike fingers. She didn't look like she was frightened or in pain. There was no anger or accusation in those eyes. But when Magdalene had left, no one had seen Bridgett in days. It was entirely possible she just didn't *know* Magdalene had run off.

Magdalene winced. "Bridgett, I have to tell you something." She dug her fists into the grass and forced the words past the knot in her throat. "The man who built the Tower came to me—"

Bridgett's eyes flew open and she slapped her hand over Magdalene's mouth.

Magdalene frowned and pushed Bridgett's hand away. "But I left..." Bridgett shook her head sharply and pressed her palm more tightly into Magdalene's lips.

Magdalene fell silent, studying the girl.

Slowly, the sad smile took over Bridgett's eyes again. Magdalene had never fully appreciated how much people could communicate with their eyes alone. The little girl withdrew her hand, but Magdalene kept her silence. If Bridgett didn't want to hear about it, for whatever reason, she'd respect that.

And honestly, it wasn't like she really *wanted* to confess her crimes.

Magdalene leaned back on her elbows, staring at the distant mountains. Bridgett plucked long strands of grass and braided them together. The breeze lifted their hair. It was peaceful.

Magdalene had missed Bridgett. If she came here again, though, how did she know that Omar wouldn't be there with Ingrid?

The scene wavered as Magdalene's eyes filled with tears. Bridgett tossed the grass braid aside and took her hand, her little brow furrowed, her eyes now burning with anger.

The two sat side by side as the breeze hissed through the willow boughs. Eventually, Magdalene curled up in the grass and fell into a meaningless, restful dream.

She awoke in the quiet room, the king-sized mattress soft beneath her. Outside the tall windows, the first light of dawn had begun to push back the canopy of stars, the distant ridges creating a jagged margin. She sighed, swung her legs out of bed, and lowered her feet onto the cool marble floor.

The smell of coffee wafted in. Praying it wasn't a hallucination or coming from one of the surrounding condos, Magdalene padded out into the living room.

The lights over the bar cast a warm glow over a huge carafe and a tray of pastries and fruit. Magdalene took a cup of coffee and a cheese and tomato croissant and curled up in a chair by the windows.

The horizon grew rosy, dimming the lights of the city. Images marched through Magdalene's head as she sipped her strong coffee: Bridgett with no mouth. Gavin's mysterious little smile as his crowd of admirers vied for his attention. Whenever Omar tried to push his way in, she pushed him back out.

An orange glow touched the tops of the distant ridges and crept downward until the sun broke over the horizon with a flash. Today was a new day and all she could do was move forward. Hanging onto the past would just drag her to a standstill.

She took a shower and chose an outfit from her haul: a black skirt and suit jacket with a broad-collared white blouse. After she put them on, she stood in front of the full-length mirror on her armoire. She looked much older.

She looked good.

I guess not as good as Ingrid, though. Or maybe I'm just too fucked up for him.

Magdalene huffed a long breath through her nose. "Not today, Satan."

When she went back into the living room, Suzette was on the couch in her pajamas, drinking coffee and scrolling on her phone. She looked up and smiled brightly. She was wearing thick-framed cat eye glasses, which were cute as hell on her. "Good morning," she sang.

Magdalene smiled. "Morning."

Suzette's gaze followed her as Magdalene poured herself another cup of coffee and sat down in one of the club chairs. "Look at you, rocking the new clothes. You look *a-ma-zing.*"

"Aw, shucks." Suzette continued to stare at her, and Magdalene raised her eyebrows. "If you want to ask me what happened last night, just ask. It's not like I slept with him or anything."

"That's not what I thought," Suzette blurted. "I'm just curious, that's all."

Magdalene rested her coffee cup on her knees and tapped it with the tips of her manicured nails. "Does everyone think I'm some gold digger or whatever?"

Suzette gave her a look over the rims of her glasses. "Well, I certainly don't think that, nor will anyone who knows how hard the Boss worked to track you down and what kind of skills you have. But I certainly wasn't prepared for you to look like—" she gestured at Magdalene, "—this. You can't blame people for getting ideas." Suzette squinted at her. "Just out of curiosity, how old are you?"

Magdalene's cheeks burned, and she expelled a long sigh. "I'm sixteen."

"Whatthefuck." Suzette stared at her in mute horror. "You can't be fucking serious."

Magdalene shrugged and sipped her coffee. "Don't tell any-one, okay? I feel like people will be jerks if they know how young I am, especially if they know how much money he's throwing at me."

Suzette sputtered. "Well, I mean, they can go to hell if they're worried about that. None of *them* can stay lucid in the Land of the Dead without a beeper. But, Jesus, sixteen..." She winced and smacked herself on the forehead. "I ordered you a drink yesterday. I'm such a monster. Thank God you're a good little girl and didn't drink it."

Magdalene snorted.

"I thought you were at least twenty-one, which would still be ridiculously young, but...wow. Anyway, what *did* Mr. Cavanaugh want to talk to you about?"

Magdalene gazed out at the golden sun glinting off the windows of the surrounding hotels. "He just talked about his business."

Suzette squinted at her over the rim of her coffee mug as she took a sip. "Mr. Cavanaugh hardly talks to any of us, ever. He always sends his lackeys to give us messages if he needs to tell us something." She frowned. "Are you sure you don't want me to tell everyone how old you are? Because they *are* going to talk."

Magdalene grinned dryly. "The rumors would just be *worse* if you told people how old I am. He'd get deadass canceled."

Suzette's frown contorted into a look of disgust. "Ugh." She sent her a sidelong glance. "He really did just talk about business, right? He doesn't seem the type, but you never know with dudes."

"Yes," Magdalene said. "I do know. And no, he wasn't like that at all."

Suzette's shoulders relaxed visibly. "You're just his little pet prodigy, is all."

Magdalene snickered. "Oh, yeah, that sounds better."

Suzette gave her a wicked grin. "Meow, little kitten." She hopped to her feet, tossing a look over her shoulder as she refilled her coffee. "The rumor is Mr. Cavanaugh used to have a daughter, who died when she was a baby. So maybe you're sort of her replacement. Maybe he's even grooming you to take over the company."

The smile drained from Magdalene's face. His daughter had died? "That's sort of a stretch, don't you think? The guy's talked to me like twice."

Suzette shrugged as she plopped back onto the couch. "You never know."

"He never had any other kids?"

"Not that I've heard of." Suzette crossed her legs. Her toenails matched her crimson fingernails. "No wife, no girlfriends, no boyfriends. No one has even known him to go on a date. He's really solitary and works constantly."

Magdalene plucked at the hem of her skirt, her heart squeezing. Did he really have no one? "Well, I guess he has plenty of money to keep him company."

Suzette snorted into her cup.

Magdalene glanced at the clock and her nerves twinged. "I'm supposed to be ready in fifteen minutes." She jumped up and went into her bathroom, rummaging through the new makeup. She chose a shade of lip gloss that looked like a subtle stain of blackberry juice, and stared at herself in the mirror, trying to collect her thoughts as she applied it. *You're going to have a good day. You're going to find out everything about this company and you'll be so happy you came here.* She wiped the lip gloss smears with her pinky and fluffed her damp hair.

She wouldn't think about Omar. She wouldn't think about anyone in the commune.

She straightened her shoulders and flipped herself the peace sign in the mirror.

When Magdalene walked back into the sitting room, it was just in time to see Marcus step out of the elevator. "Morning, ladies. Do you have a client today, Suzette?"

"Nope." She curled around her coffee cup. "I have a day off."

"Magdalene isn't so lucky, though." He grinned at her. "Are you ready?"

Magdalene nodded.

They stepped into the elevator. "Have a good day," Suzette called. Magdalene waved to her as the doors closed.

Marcus smiled as they started down. "Are you nervous?"

"A little." She fidgeted with the buckle on her purse—not the Gucci, but a little black leather one with a long strap. She wasn't exactly sure what situation was appropriate for a Gucci purse, but she'd know it when she saw it. "Where are we going, anyway?"

"Oh, I'm just taking you to the car," Marcus said. "The driver will take you to the operations building of Answers Industries, which is about half an hour from here."

The elevator opened and they stepped out through the lobby doors and onto the busy casino floor. Magdalene glanced at the glazed-eyed patrons in front of the slot machines as she followed Marcus through the labyrinth of aisles. Were they really gambling at eight thirty on a weekday morning out of their own free will? Or would they have gone home by now without Gavin's *careful guidance*?

She snorted at herself. People had gambled their asses off since long before Gavin Cavanaugh was born. She was overthinking it.

The thick heat assaulted her as they stepped out the front doors. Marcus opened the back passenger door of a white Mercedes idling at the curb, and Magdalene climbed in. The air conditioning was going, and the buttery black leather of the back seat was cool on her legs.

Marcus bent down to smile at her through the open door. "I'm sorry I'm not going with you, but I was given less pleasant duties. I'll see you this evening, though."

"It's cool," she said, buckling her seatbelt. "I hope you have a good day."

He gave her a salute. "Always. You, too." He started to close the door, then stopped and opened it again. "You look wonderful, by the way."

She smiled. "Thank you."

He shut the car door. She watched him stride back into the casino, wondering if he thought she was banging his boss.

The Mercedes pulled out onto the Strip, then onto the freeway, heading south, out of town.

Magdalene's palms were sweating by the time they pulled off the freeway and into a parking lot. It was a huge complex, two taller towers ringed by clusters of three-story buildings that looked like apartments, all of it surrounded by rocky fields of Joshua trees. The sign at the entrance said Answers Industries.

Magdalene chewed on her lip as they pulled up in front of the towers. She had imagined a much smaller operation. How many of the employees here knew what they were really working on? All these people wouldn't keep their mouths shut about Purgatory if they knew, nondisclosure agreement or no.

Andy hadn't been able to figure out how Tower Guy had pulled off a project this complex. He'd thought he was up against one person, or a small group. This was hundreds—maybe thousands—of people. She had to give Gavin credit for his organizational skills, if nothing else.

The driver got out and opened her door. She thanked him as she stepped out into the furious heat, wondering if she'd be spared the grueling task of opening her own doors the whole time she was here. Her stomach gave a flutter as she looked up at the buildings. *Is this the first day of the rest of my life? Will I never have to open a door again?* She had a vision of herself in several years, stuck inside a burning building because she'd forgotten how to work a doorknob, and dried her palms on her skirt.

The doors of one of the towers opened and a man and a woman strode out to meet her, smiling. The woman held out her hand. "Miss Richards? My name is Lonnie Meyers."

Magdalene shook her hand. "Nice to meet you." Lonnie was thirty-something with curly brown hair loose over her shoulders. She wore a plaid skirt and sleeveless blouse, which showed off her athletic limbs.

The man introduced himself as Jessie French. He was maybe forty, Black, with a mustache. "Nice to meet you, Miss Richards. We're part of the executive human resources committee here at Answers, and we've come to get you started on your tour today, discuss our operations here, and outline a possible compensation package. Have you had breakfast yet?"

"Yes, thank you." The two shot her surreptitious glances as they strolled back toward the building. She got the feeling she wasn't what they'd expected.

Jessie held the glass door open, and they filed into a lobby. A receptionist smiled brightly from behind a long counter. The company logo was backlit on the wall behind her. They took the elevator to the third floor, Jessie and Lonnie chattering about the weather, her trip, and how she liked Las Vegas. "It's an interesting place," Magdalene said. "Really good shopping."

"You ride the roller coaster on the Stratosphere yet?" Jessie laughed. "You should check it out if you like being terrified."

They led her into a conference room, and they all settled in leather armchairs around a long wooden table. A duo of young women came in with paperwork and pitchers of water and coffee, then retreated. The doors clicked softly closed.

"We'd like to thank you for meeting with us today, Miss Richards," Lonnie said. "You come highly recommended by Mr. Cavanaugh himself. He'll actually be joining us later to participate in the tour." She and Jessie exchanged a darting glance.

"Thank you for having me," Magdalene said, her cheeks aching from smiling.

Lonnie shuffled through the pile of paperwork and handed Magdalene a leather folder embossed with the Answers Industries logo. It was full of papers and glossy brochures. Magdalene poured herself some water and took a sip.

"As Mr. Cavanaugh's executive assistant, you'd have a variety of duties," Lonnie continued. "Some of them are listed on the packet in the lefthand side of your folder, but Mr. Cavanaugh has indicated he'll cover your specific job duties with you personally."

Magdalene found the sheet in question and pulled it out. Under the heading entitled *Job Description* was a list with about two dozen bullet points. She skimmed it. *Transcribing dictation. Calendar maintenance. Drafting correspondence.* Magdalene's insides squirmed. If she really had to do these things she was fucked. She knew how to type, sort of, but that was the extent of her clerical skills.

"While we wait for Mr. Cavanaugh to join us, I thought we would fill you in on our general mission statement and talk about what we do here," Lonnie said.

"Sounds great." Magdalene took another sip of water.

Lonnie crossed her legs and folded her hands in her lap. Her foot waggled in her moccasin loafers. "Here at Answers Industries, we engineer and market software that interfaces with individuals' online user profiles in order to enhance their web experience and life experience as a whole."

Magdalene nodded. She'd never had a job interview before but figured it would be bad form to show surprise at the company's mission. "You gather information for direct-marketing purposes."

"Yes," Jessie said, "but we have a distinct purpose here, different from other companies in the business of Big Data." He leaned back in his chair. "Our mission is philanthropic, and we get much of our capital through private donations. The information we gather is used to suggest self-help, betterment, and self-actualization activities for people based upon their perceived needs. We reach out to those who might be at high risk for self-destructive, violent, or criminal behavior and connect them with people who can provide fellowship, with the goal of preventing folks from acting out and of getting them back on the right track."

Magdalene's cheek muscles were really getting a workout from all this smiling. "I love what I've heard about your program, and I've been wondering what your success rate is."

Jessie beamed. "We haven't been in business long yet, and so we don't have hard statistics, but our system is very impactful. We already have success stories." He gestured at her folder. "You'll find testimonials in one of the brochures." Magdalene flipped through the papers and found a colorful booklet with a blissful looking woman on the front and some quote about how Answers Industries had changed her life.

She resolved to read it later. What the hell was Gavin *really* doing here? This part of the business couldn't be complete bullshit, right? Lonnie, Jessie, and all the other employees would have noticed by now if it were. "It's an amazing project," Magdalene said. "I love what I've heard about it so far."

Lonnie nodded. "It's a great company, and great to work for."

The door to the conference room opened, and Gavin walked in, changing the atmosphere as abruptly as if he'd been a class five tornado instead of a rather short man. Jessie and Lonnie sprang to their feet. Magdalene got up, as well, smoothing her skirt.

Gavin glanced at Magdalene as he shook Lonnie and Jessie's hands, and the corners of his lips curled up ever so slightly. "Good to see you all," he said. "Please, have a seat."

They all settled back down, Gavin taking the seat at the head of the table. "I trust things are going well?" He leaned back easily in his chair and sent Magdalene another faint smile. He was still wearing the thick silver ring with the black stone on his pinky, and he tapped it lightly against the armrest.

"We were just explaining to Miss Richards what it is we do here at Answers Industries," Lonnie said.

"Well, that's a good start," Gavin said. "I think I can handle Miss Richards' tour of the facilities myself so that you can see to other concerns. Can you meet us back here at around one thirty this afternoon?"

Lonnie and Jessie blinked and exchanged a glance, but quickly smiled. "Of course." They popped right back up again and retreated, closing the door behind them.

Magdalene watched them go, wondering how long it would take for the rumor of Gavin Cavanaugh's new fuck doll to spread through the entire campus.

"Sorry about that," Gavin said. "It's unfortunate that we're not yet able to be completely forthright about what we're doing here, but I'm sure you can appreciate our difficulties."

"I can imagine."

Gavin stood. "Are you ready for your tour?"

Magdalene got up, smoothing her skirt again. When was the last time she'd worn a skirt? Probably at her grandma's funeral.

They exited the conference room and got back on the elevator. Gavin pressed the button for the basement, and they started down. "I'm still not sure how to integrate the rest of the workforce here with our mission when the time comes but I expect an idea will present itself eventually."

She smiled. "They'll all think you're nuts, unless you show them."

He nodded. "Eventually, I'll have the technology to do that. But now, if I had to take time to train them all individually on the beeper and have them practice long enough to stay lucid, when few if any of them have any aptitude for it, most of them would be gone before giving me a chance."

Magdalene imagined people lining up to crowd their way into Purgatory. The idea made her deeply uneasy for some reason.

The elevator came to a halt and the doors opened on a long, windowless corridor lined with steel doors. A security checkpoint manned by four personnel greeted them as they walked out, but they nodded them through, Magdalene attracting curious glances. A strange hum filled the hall, and their footsteps echoed strangely.

"Where are we?" she asked.

"The foundations of my stronghold." He halted at one of the doors and opened it, gesturing for her to enter. The hum flowed out to engulf her, making her teeth buzz.

They stepped into a huge warehouse. Rows and rows of racks marched in neat lines around her, running the entire length of the long, dark room. Each was stacked with columns of identical devices, thin and black like stereo receivers. The air moved around her in alternating puffs of hot and cold, agitated by huge fans and air conditioning units. It was considerably more humid than it had been out in the hallway.

She approached one of the racks. A young woman sat at a small desk on wheels further down the aisle, her face lit by the glow of a laptop. Other employees moved up and down other aisles like shadows, their features lost in the gloom. Magdalene glanced up at Gavin questioningly.

"This is our server farm, Magdalene, which, along with our computer cluster, makes up the roots of Answers Industries." He had to raise his voice to be heard over the noise of the fans. "This is where the information we gather about people is processed and stored."

Magdalene didn't know how to respond. All these machines were full of people's information? That was a lot of information.

"If you're an environmentalist," he continued, speaking close to her ear, "you'll be happy to know that much of the energy needed to run this place is generated by our solar panels, and I'm having a wind farm built as well in hopes of getting us completely off-grid. I believe I now have the most efficient server farm in existence."

Magdalene gestured at the rows of machines. "So, you gather information about people with the program Lonnie and Jessie were talking about? That information somehow tells you whether people are worthy of rebirth, or passage...beyond?"

"It's more complicated than that. The program you heard about this morning is directed toward outreach to the living. It can give us very little direct information about individuals' resonance signatures."

"That's the soul signal you were talking about before."

He nodded. "As it stands now, I'm not able to capture someone's resonance unless they're physically present. Well, I can enter it manually but—" he rolled his eyes "—that's tedious and I don't have time for it. That's why you felt so odd when you were my guest at Heaven's Vista. I hadn't programmed you into the system yet. Now I have, so you won't have that issue."

Magdalene hugged herself. It was cold, and then every so often she'd be hit with a gust of stifling air. "So, you're gathering massive amounts of information of all kinds about people.

Some of that information you're using to help guide them down a better path in life so they can be worthy of passage through the portals when their time comes. But the soul resonance information is what you use to actually judge a person's worthiness. It isn't based on how they acted in life."

"An individual's soul resonance is a better indicator of their deeds in life than anything else available to us," he insisted. "We can't rely on people to accurately self-report their deeds, and other people's interpretations of those deeds are filtered through their own perception, and so are equally unreliable. The soul resonance, however, will speak to not only a person's actions, but to their *intent*. People can perform deeds which look benevolent, but their intent is not benevolent. Conversely, people can do things that appear to be bad, but their intent was good."

The image of Stan's face as he disappeared into the rebirthing portal flashed through Magdalene's mind, followed by Omar's haunted eyes when he woke up from his coma. "Does it matter if people's intentions are good if they end up causing harm?"

He smiled gently. "The age-old question. I think the answer is yes. Of course, it doesn't mean people are always blameless in the harm they unintentionally cause, because even good intentions can be misguided or based on willful ignorance. But sometimes we're faced with nothing but bad choices—choices that all cause harm—and we have to choose the lesser of the evils in order to move forward and get to a better place. Not to mention, we can't always foresee all the results of our actions."

He spun the ring on his pinky, his gaze distant. "If a doctor tries to save someone's life, having no way to know that the patient is on a certain medication, and ends up causing a drug interaction that ultimately kills the patient, that patient is still dead. But the intent is incredibly important. The doctor's intent was to save a life, not to murder someone. The problem is, sometimes people *think* their intentions are good—they convince themselves of it—when the reality is more complicated than that. My program can sort that out better than any human."

Magdalene ran her fingers along the smooth plastic casing of one of the servers, careful not to touch any of the buttons. The plastic was warm and pulsating, like a living thing. "Isn't it dangerous to let a computer program decide all this? To allow machines to judge people?"

Gavin focused his bright gaze on her. "Computers aren't like you and me, Magdalene. They aren't blindfolded by overwhelming emotions or obstructed by their opinions and ego. They're able to process a great deal of information with a high level of accuracy and consistent results. And it's almost impossible to trick them."

"But, I mean, isn't it just hard to judge people, period? How do you draw a line between who's good and bad?"

He gave her a searching look, and Magdalene could almost feel his sadness, the lurking shadow of some past pain. "It *is* hard. There is no bright line between good and bad. Fortunately, we're not in the business of sorting out the villains from the heroes here. We're trying to help people and make the world a better place. We don't punish anyone. We just try to help them grow."

"It's still human beings writing the programs," Magdalene persisted. "With all our emotions and ego. Doesn't that affect the program?"

He nodded. "That's an astute point. All I can do is show you the results of our operation and hope that you will stay to help us identify and remedy any errors." He gestured toward the door. "Shall we continue the tour?"

Magdalene noticed the woman at the laptop watching them through her eyelashes as they headed back out.

The hallway was much warmer and quieter. Magdalene was glad to be out of that warehouse. "How do you gather information about people, anyway?"

Gavin led her further down the corridor. "Partially through internet and GPS usage, etcetera. But most of that information is used only to establish identity. The process of matching each online profile to a specific individual's vibrational signature is fairly complicated. I'll show you how it's done later this week."

Magdalene had a moment of relief that her phone had been destroyed and that she hadn't been on a computer since school ended. And yet, she was apparently thinking of working for a data farm. Was this one of those lesser-of-the-evils choices Gavin had been talking about?

He led her through another door and into a similar warehouse with more rows of devices. "And this is our computational cluster. It gives us a great deal of computing power, which is of course necessary for our operations."

Magdalene ran her thumb over her manicured nails. "Is this how you built the Tower in Purgatory? With these computers?"

"In a manner of speaking. Interfacing our program with the Land of the Dead is, of course, an elaborate process."

She gave a jerky smile. "This is really complicated."

Gavin grinned and held the door open. "Let's go visit the second floor, where the real action happens."

They headed back toward the elevators. "The first floor is where the administrative offices are located, but I won't bore you with that," Gavin said. "You'll never have to do a single page of paperwork working here."

"Oh, thank God. That job description gave me anxiety."

Gavin snickered. "Well, I had to give HR something." They got back in the elevator and headed up. "The second floor is where the engineering offices are, and it may be instructive to see that process."

It made Magdalene sort of proud that she, Omar and Andy had guessed correctly about so much to do with the Tower. But she didn't feel much closer to understanding what was really going on here than she had before she met Gavin.

They got off on the second floor and entered a large, open room with huge windows. It looked more like a coffee house or arcade than an office. People sat around tables or on couches, talking and working on laptops. Two young women were playing foosball in the corner, and another group stood cheering on a guy playing pinball.

Then a guy on one of the couches spotted Gavin and his eyes widened. He pulled out his phone and started texting. Before she and Gavin had taken ten more steps, the noise level had diminished, the game tables were abandoned, and everyone was magically busy on their laptops.

Gavin and Magdalene exchanged a smirk. "All these fine people are working hard designing my software," he murmured.

She narrowed her eyes at him, biting back a grin. "You enjoy terrifying them, don't you?"

"Maybe just a little. But in all honesty, they work hard and shouldn't be ashamed to let me see them play now and again." He paused next to a young man hunched over his laptop. "Good morning."

The young man looked up at Gavin like a prairie dog looks at a hawk.

Gavin smiled as if he hadn't noticed his employee's abject terror. "I'm sorry to disturb you, but I'm giving Miss Richards a tour of the facilities. Do you have a moment to say a few words about our praiseworthy company?"

The young man sprang up from his seat and shook Gavin's hand. "I'm pleased to meet you, Mr. Cavanaugh. I'm Peter Rodriguez. And, sure, I'd love to. This is a great place to work." He smiled at Magdalene. He had a nice smile, even when he was terrified. "I could show you what my team is working on, if you'd like."

"Miss Richards isn't a software engineer," Gavin said. "A detailed explanation of your work might be lost on her. I'm just trying to give her a sense of the atmosphere at Answers."

"Oh, the atmosphere here is excellent. Everyone is really nice, and we have a lot of fun even though we do work really hard." He laughed. "There's also great food in the cafeteria. You have to love that."

Magdalene's stomach growled, and she pressed her hands to her belly, hoping no one had heard.

Gavin shook Peter's hand again. "Thank you very much for your time, Mr. Rodriguez."

"It was nice to meet you," Peter said. "Both of you." Magdalene smiled at him as she and Gavin headed for the door.

Magdalene shook her head in mock disapproval as they went into the hallway. "That poor guy. You just shortened his life by five years."

Gavin sent her a dimpled smile. "Come now. It was *you* who was terrifying poor Mr. Rodriguez."

Magdalene scoffed. "You're the Boss. Everywhere you go, people suck up to you. Does it ever get old?"

He gave her an appraising look, then shrugged. "It's lonely at times. I've had to get used to it. Now, let's have some lunch. I'm sure you're starving."

Her cheeks burned. Her stomach was so loud that she hated to be seen with it in public. "It would be cool to see the cafeteria."

Gavin pressed the button and they got back in the elevator. "You can see the cafeteria another time. No need to further terrify my long-suffering employees during their break. I'll have lunch brought up to my office."

Magdalene studied Gavin Cavanaugh out of the corner of her eye as the elevator took them up to the top floor. She should be scared of this man, or at least uncomfortable around him, but she wasn't. He was interesting and easy to talk to.

Omar believed the man behind the Tower had an ability to control people, and he'd probably say that Magdalene was in his thrall right now. Magdalene kicked that idea from her head and flipped it off before slamming the door in its face. She hadn't figured Gavin out entirely, but from what she could see, he was powerful, brilliant, and good with people. There was nothing magical about it.

It was Omar who had the ability to magically manipulate people, and Magdalene wondered with a hollow pang if maybe she'd been more in *his* thrall than she'd realized.

CHAPTER ELEVEN

Negotiations

Gavin took Magdalene to his office, where a small table was set for them by the windows, which looked out over the flat, rocky desert to the cliffs in the distance.

They sat. "What do you think of my project so far, Miss Richards?"

Magdalene tapped her nails on the dove-gray tablecloth. "It's really interesting, but I still need to see the results."

He nodded. "I would expect nothing less from you."

A woman came in and set glasses of ice water before them, then stood smiling down at Magdalene. "What can I get you?"

Magdalene frowned at the table, looking under the butter-colored linen napkins, next to the crystal vase of roses. There was no menu anywhere. "What are my choices?"

"We have a well-stocked kitchen and an excellent staff," the woman replied. "They can make just about anything."

"Ah..." She said the first thing that came to mind. "How about linguini alfredo?"

"Got it," said the smiling waitress.

Gavin ordered ginger prawns, then the waitress left. Gavin regarded Magdalene with his sharp gaze. "I'm so glad you're finally here."

Magdalene leaned back in her chair, her foot waggling, trying not to forget that this man had her put in jail and had tried to abduct her. Maybe he was right about Andy and Helena and Omar. Maybe they were a cult. She wasn't ready to think about that quite yet. And maybe his tactics would have been justified under those circumstances. Regardless, he had put a lot of time and effort and money into getting her here, into meeting her face-to-face.

Gavin leaned his chin on his hand and regarded her over the table. "I sense you're still wondering why I put so much effort into recruiting you." Magdalene's foot stopped waggling, and he shrugged. "You wear your thoughts on your sleeve. But just look how much effort I've had to put into developing beepers and secure rooms in the Land of the Dead, just to give people a taste of what it's like to be there. How could you doubt how much I would value someone who doesn't need all that assistance?"

She tucked a lock of hair behind her ear. "I've heard you're charging people to get through the portals when they die."

She knew him too well by now to think he'd deny it. He smiled. "It says in the book of Matthew that it's easier for a camel to go through the eye of a needle than for a rich man to enter into the kingdom of God."

Magdalene raised her eyebrows. "You're the expert. So, you're just building all this to increase your own chances?"

Gavin laughed. "I know I have my work cut out for me in that regard. But, no, that's not why. No matter how rich I am, I can't run an operation this complex without an infusion of capital. In order for the portals to be regulated and the information processed, for the system to function as planned, the business has to be self-supporting. The income from our self-help and betterment classes isn't enough. Even that branch relies on a substantial income from private donations and fundraising. I do have hopes to land some government contracts soon, but those haven't materialized yet."

Magdalene thought of the basement crammed full of expensive-looking electronics, the hundreds of employees running around, and nodded.

"Please be assured that I won't charge the poor for passage through the portals," he said. "That would not only be unjust, it would be ineffective, as it would keep all the poor trapped in the Land of the Dead, allowing only the rich to be reborn or to move on. And forgive me, but I'm well acquainted with the rich and I don't want to live in a world composed entirely of them. Even *that's* assuming enough of them are qualified to pass through the eye of that needle in the first place. In all honesty, if only the rich could traverse the portals, the earth's population would collapse in one generation."

Magdalene grinned reluctantly.

"The rich, however," he continued, "can afford to pay. They can afford to make the system function for the benefit of all. I'm competent to testify to the fact that the rich also have more to atone for than the poor, as is suggested in Matthew. We're a bunch of greedy, ungenerous bastards, whether we like to admit it or not. Thus, my rich clients perform good works in providing support for the betterment of the world, which can make up for their other shortcomings and better prepare them for entry into Heaven."

"So, you're not making a profit off Answers Industries?"

He winced. "No. In fact, I'm still losing money on it. Luckily my other businesses are profitable enough to make up for it." He gestured vaguely around the room. "You might not have gotten this impression from what you know of me so far, but profit isn't the most important thing to me." He paused, spinning the ring round and round on his pinky. "Long ago, I had a wife and daughter, and I still remember what it is to have something better than money."

Grief's icy tendrils crept into Magdalene's heart. She knew all too well what it felt like to lose someone you loved, and Gavin had that pain in his eyes. It was a tangible connection between them, a dark bubble that enclosed their table.

"The man who killed them," Gavin continued, "had just been released from prison. He shouldn't have been set free, should never have had a chance to do what he did. After he killed Melissa and Ann, he disappeared. He was never caught, never paid for what he did to them." Gavin's eyes had gone from bright blue to a cold gray. "That's why I've built this project. Because I need there to be justice, some sort of order and meaning in the world."

Gavin paused, tapping his ring on the table, his gaze lost in the far reaches of the desert. Eventually, he came back into himself, his gaze meeting Magdalene's again. "I've never been powerful in the Land of the Dead like you are. But I have my own talents. Everything I have, I've given to this mission. When my program is complete, people like the man who murdered my family won't have the chance to be reborn into this world, and they won't achieve peace in the next. Not until they've learned their lesson, if they're capable of it. I do all this for Melissa and Ann, and for all the others like them, and all those left behind who carry the same pain I do."

Gavin's pain was Magdalene's own. Her anger, her grief and frustration were his, the ice in his eyes pierced her heart. Their souls were laid bare together, a cold lunch on the table before them.

"I can't bring Melissa and Ann back," Gavin murmured, spinning his ring. "Even rebirth can't give us back what we've lost. But, if I can spare others the pain I've gone through, I will."

Magdalene gazed out the window and blinked back the tears in her eyes.

"My daughter would be just a little older than you are now," Gavin said. "I'm sure she'd be just as beautiful as you, and just as smart."

Magdalene glanced back at him, chewing on the inside of her cheek. Each beat of her heart sent emotion coursing through her veins. His feelings, her feelings, it was all the same, their hearts beating with one purpose. She could sense the sentiment coursing through him, feel the touch of his thoughts on her skin.

Dizziness engulfed her and she squeezed her eyes shut. In the darkness behind her eyelids the scene reformed. She saw Gavin, herself, the people in the offices around them. Their thoughts murmured and whispered in her own head. Dozens of people, hundreds, all of them connected by a gossamer network of power.

Gavin's power.

Magdalene's eyes flew open, her heart pounding.

Gavin scrubbed a hand across his face. "I'm sorry. I haven't talked about these matters for a long time, and I don't know why it's pouring out now. I've upset you. Please forgive me."

"No, that's not it. I'm..." She searched his face but saw only concern. She took a breath. "I'm okay. I'm just dizzy."

He grinned wryly. "I should remember to feed you more often. I'm used to keeping company with other old men, and we can survive on crackers and broth. Ah, here are our salads, at least."

A droplet of sweat ran down Magdalene's spine as the waitress came in and delivered their salads. The woman quickly retreated, closing the door behind her once more. The whispering in Magdalene's mind had quieted and her heartbeat was settling, her pain diminished to the normal dull ache in her chest, easily ignored. She dug into her salad. Maybe Gavin was right and she was just hungry.

Gavin spent the rest of lunch telling jokes and funny stories about famous people he'd met. She didn't recognize all the names, but she did recognize the President of the United States, whom Gavin had known since before his term in office. "This one time, we were having lunch," Gavin said. "He ordered pasta, just like you, except with a rich, red Bolognese sauce. He was wearing a white golf shirt and, knowing him well, his staff had brought extras for him. By the end of the meal, he'd had to go into the bathroom to change *four times.*"

Magdalene laughed, covering her mouth, which was full of linguini.

"That's not the worst of it," Gavin continued. "After dinner, he fell asleep at the table. The man is an overgrown toddler."

Magdalene snickered, studying the man across the table with new eyes. *This guy is a big fucking deal. And here he is having lunch with* me *for some reason.*

After a dessert of raspberry sorbet, Gavin sighed and said it was time for another meeting with Lonnie and Jessie. He told more jokes as they made their way back to the conference room, and they came through the doors laughing at an anecdote about George Clooney's iguana.

Lonnie and Jessie blinked at them wide eyed. As they stood to shake their hands, their gazes kept darting to Magdalene.

She remembered what Suzette had said about Gavin. *He's really solitary and works constantly.*

For a split second, she saw Gavin through their eyes: not the approachable man that she knew, but a mysterious figure, loaded with cash, notoriously reclusive, who had suddenly latched onto a strange young girl out of nowhere.

Another wave of dizziness washed over her, and she settled in her seat to hide it.

Gavin took the seat at the head of the table again, and the other two sat across from Magdalene. "Thank you for taking the time out of your busy schedules to meet with us again," Gavin said.

"Not at all," Jessie said.

"It's a pleasure," Lonnie said.

The leather folder containing the brochures, which she'd forgotten about when Gavin had appeared, was still there in front of Magdalene's chair. Lonnie placed more paperwork on top of it. "Here is your proposed employment contract, along with your compensation package. As Mr. Cavanaugh has likely informed you, we're offering a signing bonus of two hundred ninety-nine thousand, three hundred dollars, and a salary of three hundred thousand dollars a year. This is on top of housing and transportation, which we can also provide if you wish. It's a three-year employment contract, with opportunity for renewal but a noncompete clause if it is not."

Magdalene sat frozen. Lonnie and Jessie had very fixed smiles, and she assumed that the compensation sounded a little steep to them, as well. Behind them, Gavin leaned back in his chair with his little smile.

The signing bonus was exactly the amount she had left behind with Andy and Helena. He knew that, and he knew that *she* knew that.

Magdalene clutched her hands together in her lap. *He really wants me to stay.* Somehow the limo, the Vegas condo, the Gucci purse—none of that had driven home that fact the way the replacement of the money she'd lost, on top of three hundred grand a year—*and did she say housing and transportation?*—did.

Magdalene imagined all that money piling up in her bank account. She could travel. She could buy whatever she wanted. She could eat out three meals a day and never have the electricity shut off. As long as she worked for Gavin, she'd be fine. She'd be safe. Her life would be perfect.

Her pulse thundered like a herd of horses. He *really* wanted her to work there. She fixed the powerful man at the head of the table with a challenging grin. "Make it four hundred thousand a year."

Gavin laughed. "Three fifty."

"Three seventy-five, or I walk." It was a bluff, and they both knew it, but he still winced comically.

"We can't have that, Miss Richards." He gave her his little conspiratorial smile and held out his hand. "We have a deal."

They shook.

Lonnie and Jessie looked on with glassy stares. "Would you like to read the contract, maybe discuss it with your attorney?" Lonnie asked her.

Oh sure. Let me just call my attorney. "That's okay." She glanced at Gavin. "I don't think fine print means very much in this business."

Gavin grinned. The other two exchanged a bewildered look.

Lonnie paged her assistant, who quickly brought in a revised contract, placing it in front of Magdalene along with a pen.

Magdalene glanced one last time at Gavin Cavanaugh and, taking a deep breath, she signed.

CHAPTER TWELVE

Deathwalkers

Magdalene's head spun as Gavin walked her to the waiting car. The driver was holding the door open for her, probably sweating like a roast ham in his uniform.

"Tomorrow, I'll show you your new condo on campus." Gavin gestured toward the clusters of buildings behind them. "I hope you don't mind one last evening in town."

Magdalene raised her eyebrows. Without him she'd be homeless, and he knew it. "I'm not going to complain about another night in a luxury condo."

Gavin's grin turned wry. "You don't want to try to negotiate something better?"

She shrugged. "I've pushed my luck far enough for one day."

His grin twitched wider. "And tomorrow is a new one." Magdalene climbed into the car, and he bent down to speak to her though the open door. "Get some rest, darling. Tomorrow the work begins."

The driver shut the door. Gavin stood on the curb and watched them pull out before heading back inside.

As soon as he was out of sight, Magdalene let out a breath and pressed her palms into her eyes.

She'd just signed a three-year employment contract.

You did the right thing. Three-hundred and seventy-five grand, y'all. Were you going to turn that down?

But it had all happened so fast. The project seemed amazing, but how did she know it would work out the way Gavin said it would?

Maybe he's manipulating you like Omar said. Maybe that's why you jumped in with both feet. She didn't feel manipulated, though. This was nothing like what Omar had done to her under the cottonwood, all those many eons ago in another life.

Magdalene heaved a sigh and kicked off her heels. *It's just paperwork. If it turns out this project isn't legit, I can still leave.*

A powerful wave of longing washed over her, to sit at the kitchen table with Lynn, drinking coffee and talking this over. She closed her eyes and waited for it to subside. She couldn't go back there, no matter what.

She was safer with Gavin, anyhow. There was nothing he could do to hurt her, even if he wanted to. And he didn't want to. Instead, he apparently wanted to give her a shit ton of money and a condo.

Maybe she had signed on too quickly, but there were worse predicaments to be in.

She spent the evening soaking in the hot tub and having a nice dinner with Suzette, who was ecstatic that Magdalene had taken the job. It was hard not to have that enthusiasm wear off on her.

All her worries about ending up like her mom, about getting trapped in the endless cycle of poverty, abuse and crime were all in the past now. She was only sixteen, but she was independent. Not just independent: *rich.*

She curled up that night in her cozy bed and dreamt again of sitting in peaceful silence with Bridgett in the willow grove. She didn't wake until dawn.

Magdalene was up and dressed, drinking coffee and watching the sun rise, when Suzette padded in, wearing her glasses and with bare feet. She grabbed a muffin from the bar and sprawled in the chair next to her, grinning. "You're moving into your new condo today, which means we'll be neighbors."

Magdalene sipped her coffee. "It's so weird that he provides housing. Is that a new thing that employers do?"

Suzette shrugged. "He recruits from all over the world. Housing is expensive and a pain in the ass, plus the commute can be a bitch. Living right where you work has definite advantages. He offers great salaries, too, and the housing is just icing on the cake to make sure he gets the best people." She gave Magdalene a sidelong glance. "Still not going to tell me how much he's paying you?"

Magdalene wrinkled her nose. The woman had prodded her for details all night.

Suzette pursed her lips. "That much, huh? Damn."

"Shut up."

"Whatever it is, it must be a lot, because the word is you get one of the executive condos."

"Really?" Magdalene frowned. "How do you always know everything?"

"I gossip." Suzette stood and sauntered into her room.

"Great," Magdalene muttered.

When Magdalene's car pulled up in front of the Answers towers, a man in a suit strutted out to meet her. She cursed under her breath when she recognized who it was.

She opened her door before the driver could. "What's with the sour face?" Armando asked as she climbed out. "Don't worry, I'll be good. Suzy gave me a huge lecture."

Magdalene snorted. They started toward the building. "So, I'm working with you today?"

"Yep. I guess the Boss doesn't mind a bit of competition. I get you all day."

She sighed. "That was like fifteen seconds of you being good."

He gave an exaggerated frown.

"We going to Purgatory for some 'crowd control'?" she drawled.

They went past the receptionist and entered the elevator. Armando punched the button for the third floor. "Yeah, it might be a pretty mean scene in there today, so be prepared. Don't worry, though, we won't throw you to the ghosts on the first day. You can stay on this side of the fence."

She scoffed. "I'm not scared of them."

His eyebrows crept up. "Okay, then."

They got out of the elevator and went down a hallway to a door marked *Staging 3*. Armando entered a code into a keypad, swiped a keycard, and opened it. "You'll get your keycard and learn all the codes after your orientation."

Through the door was a security checkpoint where two guards flanked what looked like a metal detector. Armando went through it and the guards checked their screens and let him pass.

"Can I take my purse through, or will that set it off?" Magdalene asked.

Armando chuckled. "This is a resonance signature reader. It identifies allowed personnel and acts as a sort of lie detector. If someone is planning something nefarious, this handy device can sense that."

Magdalene stared at the device while every lie she'd ever told flitted through her head. Would the guards' screens give them a readout of the time she took twenty dollars from her grandma to get hamburgers with her friends? Would it tell them about the fake ID, the money laundering?

The guards and Armando were watching her. Magdalene held her breath and walked through.

No sirens went off, no gates slammed down in front of her. The guards gestured her past, and Magdalene let out the breath.

She and Armando continued down the hall. He punched a code into another keypad, slid his keycard in another slot, then opened the door and stepped aside for her to go in.

It was a tiny room with two recliners set side by side, facing a small, frosted window. There was a potted dragon tree in the corner, a small cabinet against the wall, and a desk with a computer and monitor. "Is this where we leave our bodies while we're in Purgatory?" she asked.

"Yup. We call it a sleeper room."

Magdalene perched on one of the chairs while Armando took something out of the cabinet, handing it to her.

She turned it over in her hands. It was a sleek electronic device, rectangular, about the size of her palm. It had one button and a clip on the back. "Is this the beeper?"

"Sure is." He fastened an identical one to his belt and typed something on the computer keyboard. "You just settle in your chair so you don't fall over while you're gone, push the button, and you're there. Easy peasy." He turned away from the computer and settled back in his chair.

"How do you get back if the device forces you to be unconscious?"

"The Boss is a genius. You have a counterpart beeper in the Land of the Dead and you push the button on that one in order to get out."

"Huh." She ran her fingers over the seamless plastic, then set it on the ground and leaned back in her chair.

Armando raised his eyebrows. "The beeper makes it much easier. You don't even have to wait until you're asleep." He quirked his lips. "You don't have to show off. I've already seen how amazing you are."

Magdalene rolled her eyes, then closed them.

When the scene reformed, she was standing in the empty stone courtyard in front of the Tower. Dark pavement stretched to a flat, featureless horizon and eerie silence pressed in on her as if she were the only creature in existence. She trailed her gaze up the building's sleek sides to its dizzying, distorted heights, looking away before she got to the top. It muddled her brain.

Armando blinked into existence beside her like a television turning on. A beeper was clipped to his pants, along with a holster that held something resembling a flashlight. He regarded her with startled frown, one of his eyes glowing blue. "You didn't even have time to fall asleep. And you came straight here, without your destination programmed in."

"That eye is creepy," Magdalene said. "So, where are we going?"

"We're just supposed to do our rounds." He started walking, heading slightly to the right of the Tower. Magdalene followed him, chewing her lip. Ahead, the flat pavement stretched into bright nothingness, and a pang of loneliness hit her. Was Bridgett somewhere close? Could Magdalene pierce that blank veil and find the little girl in the *real* Purgatory, where the landscape hopped and crawled with weirdness?

Could she find Omar?

Her heart twisted. She wanted to bundle up her feelings and toss them into the street. *To hell with that asshole. I'm rich now. I can find someone better.*

What had happened to the sweet, funny boy who'd helped her through the dark days after Morris's death? The guy who had broken her out of juvie, saved her from the gangsters and Stan?

That guy apparently had never really existed.

She'd been naïve to believe anyone could care about her that much. All of those stunts he'd pulled had probably been less about saving her and more about showing off his powers.

She sighed.

Armando had pulled ahead of her. He stopped, waiting for her to catch up. "You okay?"

"Yeah. Fine."

His brow furrowed, but he started walking again, slowing to match her pace. "How did you learn how to get into the Land of the Dead so quick? I still have trouble getting here without the beeper, even when I'm asleep. And I don't mean to brag, but before you showed up, I was the best Deathwalker the Boss has."

Magdalene raised her eyebrows. "Deathwalker?"

"We have to call ourselves something. It seemed appropriate."

"I guess." Magdalene shrugged. "Anyway, I don't know how I do it. Practice I guess."

"I definitely see why the Boss likes you so much, besides the obvious reasons." She shot him a glare, and he held his hands up defensively. "Just making an observation. It's not like I'd blame you for sleeping with the guy, anyway. He's rich as hell."

Magdalene wasn't sure if it was because her nerves were frayed, or because Armando reminded her a little of Stan, but her fury ignited. Raw power soaked from the ground through the soles of her feet and into her body. It felt *good*. It burned away the thoughts of the Commune, the thoughts of Omar. It made her feel invincible, taller than the Tower.

They were in Purgatory—on *her* turf. She could make this asshole *pay*.

Armando turned, the cocky look on his face quickly melting into fear as she sent a tongue of flame lashing toward him. She could feel the *crack* as it hit him and wrapped around his torso, pinning his arms.

He yelped. "What the fuck!"

Magdalene yanked the glowing rope, and he fell to his knees.

"I'm sorry," he said with wide eyes. "I'm an asshole. I didn't mean it."

She jerked the fiery rope again, and he whimpered. "I'm not fucking the Boss," she said. "He's old enough to be my dad. Neither one of us would do that."

He nodded hastily. "You're right. It was a bad joke."

"It was a really bad joke. And you should never make it again."

"You're right. I promise. I'm sorry."

She dropped the glowing rope, and it melted into nothingness. The power drained from her, leaving her empty and dizzy.

Armando got shakily to his feet, eyeing her. "Magdalene?"

She cut her gaze to him.

He blew out a breath. "I really am sorry."

Magdalene shook her head. "Forget about it."

They started walking again. The corner pillar of the Tower loomed huge before them, off to their left. It hadn't seemed so big when she'd gone inside, back when she was trying to wake Omar from his coma. She winced.

Armando watched her out of the corner of his eye. "How the hell do you *do* that?" He mimed lashing out with a whip.

She shrugged. "This is Purgatory. You can do whatever you want here."

He looked at her like she'd lost her mind. "*I* can't. Nobody else can, either. Just *you*."

She wanted to say that it wasn't just her, but held her tongue. She didn't want to talk about Omar and Bridgett, especially not with this dickhole.

"I seriously am sorry, Magdalene," he muttered. "I'm a jerk sometimes. I don't think before I talk."

Magdalene sighed. "Don't worry about it. Just don't do it again."

"I won't." A smile tilted his lips. "You're one fucking kick-ass chick, you know."

She rolled her eyes.

The Tower loomed above them, giving Magdalene the strange feeling she might fall upward and be swallowed by the silvery sky. As they rounded the corner of the massive structure, a beam of light came into view, glowing brightly blue-white against the drab horizon. It came out of the ground at a low angle and met up with the Tower near its base.

"What the hell is that?" Magdalene asked.

"It's a support beam."

It appeared solid, except it had an oily shimmer like a gas jet, making it warp and twist in on itself. As she came closer, a low hum kindled in her core. It was pleasant, like a warmth in her body.

"The Boss says not to get near it," Armando said.

Magdalene frowned. She heard him, but the hum of the beam filled her mind and made it hard to pay attention. She stepped closer. The light within the beam shone like mother of pearl, the different colors swirling in sinuous, ever-changing patterns, like water around rocks. She reached out and touched a finger to its shimmering surface.

Her skull burst wide open. Voices. Feelings. They called and screamed and sang and laughed. The Light seeped into her soul, spreading the cracks wider, revealing the places she'd kept herself together with duct tape and wishes.

They were tearing her apart. They were making her whole. She never wanted to leave, and she needed to get out of here *right now.*

Arms encircled her from behind and pulled. Magdalene stumbled backward and fell onto her butt, back into herself. Her heart pounded and her breath came fast as she blinked up into Armando's terrified face.

"What the fuck," he panted. "Are you okay?"

His arms were still around her and she pulled away and got to her feet, her legs wobbly. "Yeah, I'm..." Her mind was full of static hiss. The voices were gone, and she felt suddenly lonely, a translucent wisp of a person.

"Come on, Richards." Armando put a hand on her back and gently guided her away, veering to the right of the beam. He shook his head, laughing nervously. "Jesus, girl, you have balls."

"What is that thing?" she asked again. "What does 'support beam' even mean?"

"You'll have to ask the Boss. I'm just a lowly Deathwalker." He blew out a breath. "You scared the shit out of me when you touched that thing. You went all weird."

"Weird?"

"You started to glow. I thought you were going to get absorbed into it or something."

A chill crept slowly up Magdalene's spine. "Yikes." A whispering breeze seemed to surround her, caressing her cheeks. She felt the pull of the Light behind her, calling her back, and she shuddered and quickened her pace.

Armando looked at her curiously. "What happened when you touched it?"

Magdalene shook her head, wincing. "It was like it was alive."

Armando chuckled. "This place is a trip."

The Tower was behind them now, and the flat, barren ground was giving way to gently rolling hills. A bird with a clown nose watched them from the branches of a twisted pine with mangy tufts of needles.

"We're going to the portal?" Magdalene asked.

"Yeah. We call it the Pearly Gates, though."

She laughed. "Seriously?"

"The official name is Alpha passage. But since it goes to Heaven, the Deathwalkers thought it was a fitting name."

Magdalene wrinkled her nose. "How do you know it goes to Heaven?"

"Where else would it go? The Boss says it goes to Heaven, and he's a really smart guy."

Magdalene frowned at a butterfly flapping lazily across their path. It was wearing sunglasses and clutching a tiny cigarette in one of its legs. Gavin *was* a smart guy. But did he really know more than Bridgett and Omar? *They* weren't sure where the dark portals went.

The path led them down a hill and into a forest. Creatures peeked out from behind the trunks, but very few ventured into view. Magdalene wondered if they were spooked by Armando's creepy blue eye.

The trail ascended again, and the trees thinned. They came around a bend and their path ended at a T-junction with another. Armando led her down the righthand branch and the gate came into view.

Magdalene nodded toward it. "If you're going to give it some super fancy name like *the Pearly Gates* you should at least conjure up something nicer than chain link."

Armando laughed. "I just scare ghosts. I'm not in the design department."

They approached the gate from the inside this time, unlike the last time Magdalene had been here. How many days ago had that been? Two? Three? It seemed like weeks. She suppressed a sigh. Her heart felt like soggy toast. Even soggier than usual, in fact. She glanced over her shoulder and realized why: the inky cloud of the portal loomed there, a blankness devouring the landscape. She shuddered and looked away. She couldn't be that much closer to it than she was last time, but she could feel its presence at her back like a haunted basement.

The two Dead guards still stood inside the gate, smacking their rubbery lips and sucking their large teeth. "What are the guards for?" Magdalene asked. "Do they attack people if they get out of line?"

Armando shook his head. "They communicate with the guard captain on duty in the living world if there's trouble. That way we don't have to be here all the time. We just have to check on them every so often and be here when it's getting rowdy."

"They can make phone calls from one world to the other?"

"I don't think it's a phone, but yeah, they have some way of sending a signal."

Magdalene raised her eyebrows. "Weird." Gavin *was* a genius.

There were probably more than a hundred Dead on the other side of the fence, more than last time. A man at the front of the crowd had his head tucked under his crotch, his long arms contorted around his skinny legs as he did somersaults. A woman beside him danced furiously, her gigantic, round boobs knocking into one another like beach balls filled with pudding. Magdalene wasn't sure what protesting looked like, really, but this didn't seem to be it. "They don't look dangerous to me."

Armando gazed grimly at the scene. "They're pretty calm right now, but there are a lot of them, and that makes me nervous."

"You can't beat up on them just because there's a lot of them, though."

Armando gave her a nervous glance. "We don't beat them up, Magdalene. The shocker just scares them off."

"The shocker?"

Armando patted the flashlight-like thing in his holster.

Magdalene eyed it and crossed her arms. "How do you know it doesn't hurt them?"

He shrugged. "You can't hurt someone who's already dead."

Her brow furrowed, thinking about the battle between Stan and his victims at the rebirthing portal. Omar had said Dead people could tear apart the souls of their murderers. "I don't think that's true."

On the other side of the fence, a Dead woman rode a wheeled throne in a slow circuit around a disheveled girl contorted by violent hiccups. A flesh-colored basketball with watery eyes rolled back and forth, and a white kitten with elephant ears sat licking his paws. "Just don't use your little weapon, okay? It's not right."

"I don't see any reason to use it now," Armando replied.

Magdalene scrubbed a hand over her face, then stalked toward the fence.

"Be careful!" Armando called. She shot him a glare over her shoulder. He didn't follow.

Eyes turned toward Magdalene as she approached, and some of the Dead began to flock toward her. She interlaced her fingers with the chain link and gazed out at the strange crowd. One of the creatures raised a mauve tentacle over the heads of the others, peering at her with an eyeball clutched in its tip.

"Hi," Magdalene said.

A chorus of grunts, mumbles, and honks arose in response. "WAH!" squawked a vaguely humanoid thing toward the front. There was one clear "hello" from a thin man in a suit.

Magdalene smiled. "Why did you all come here today?"

There was a raucous burst of squawks and warbles. When it died down, the man in the suit spoke. "This is where we need to be. We want to see what's going to happen."

Magdalene nodded. "Have any of you been denied entrance to the portal?"

There was a general shuffling, and a huge BLAT like the horn of a cargo ship burst from the creature with the mauve tentacle. The man in the suit shook his head, but a hand shot up in the middle of the group. It barely reached above the surrounding heads. "I have," said a voice from its vicinity.

The hand worked its way toward Magdalene and a cute, boyish woman emerged in front, her short brown hair brushed back from her freckled forehead. Gigantic sneakers protruded from under the hem of her flowered, cotton dress. "I have," she repeated, clasping her hands behind her back.

"Hi," Magdalene said. "I'm Magdalene."

The woman nodded. "I'm Kate."

"Why didn't they let you through, Kate?"

The woman grimaced and shuffled her huge feet. "They said they had to process my request. I can't leave, and it's taking forever."

Magdalene frowned. "They're not letting you leave until they process your request?"

Kate shook her head. "No, I just can't leave." Her gaze wandered over Magdalene's shoulder to the portal, longing filling her blue eyes. "It wants me."

Magdalene shivered, glancing at the dark cloud. "I'll see if I can figure out what's taking them so long."

Kate smiled. "Thank you, Magdalene."

Magdalene walked along the fence away from the guards, and caught sight of a leaning tower of hair toward the edge of the crowd. "Hey! Barry!"

He was talking to a woman in a sequined flapper dress, but looked up at the sound of her voice and grinned. He waded through the crowd to the fence. "Magdalene? How did you get over there, girl?"

"It's a long story."

Barry's eyes were drawn by something over her shoulder and his smile faded to a scowl. She followed his gaze to see Armando standing a few paces behind her, watching her worriedly.

"What, are you with *those* clowns now?" Barry asked. "Omar is worried sick about you, and you've been off with that...thing?" He flicked his hand toward Armando as if pushing away a nasty spider.

Magdalene's insides did an experimental dance. "Omar is worried?"

A slow, insinuating smile grew on Barry's face. "Did you guys have a little lovers' quarrel? Is that what this is all about? Oh, Magdalene, he's *heartbroken.*" Barry leaned down to her level and whispered, "Listen, girl, those dinks on that side, they're bad news. You're not like them, I can tell. You need to be back over here where you belong."

Magdalene's heart pounded, and she fought desperately against the lump in her throat. *Heartbroken. Right.* She wanted so badly to ask how Barry had gotten that idea, but she knew the answer would just make her cry. *If he's heartbroken, so be it. He cheated on me. I deserve better than that.* "Why do you think they're bad news on this side?" she whispered. "They're just trying to bring order and justice."

He wrinkled his nose. "This isn't *order*." He straightened and glared at Armando, raising his fist in the air. "This is oppression. OPPRESSION!"

Armando's lips curled in a mocking smile, and Magdalene glared at him, a current of anger running through her. She turned back to Barry, speaking quietly. "Have you talked to the Chieftain yet?"

Barry nodded. "I have, and he's taking notice. There're enough people pissed off about this crap that I think he'll get involved."

Magdalene leaned against the fence, watching crowd of Dead. Barry was right: she still felt like she belonged over there. But that didn't mean Gavin's plan wasn't a good one. She just had to figure out how to convince the Dead of that so there wouldn't be "sides" anymore.

Barry's gaze focused back over Magdalene's shoulder and his lips pursed in a sour expression. She glanced back to discover Armando had come closer.

"Come on, Richards," he said. "Don't stand so close. Who knows what these things will do to you."

Barry's eyes flashed fire. "I'm going to tell Omar that you have Magdalene, and he's going to kick your narrow ass, you freaky goon!"

Magdalene's throat closed up completely. She tried to breathe evenly, but her head felt like it was going to explode.

She opened her eyes back on the Waking World and curled around her knees, cursing her own cowardice.

CHAPTER THIRTEEN

The Web

Magdalene tried to breathe. Coming back had been a mistake. Even close to a portal, feelings were so much easier to handle in Purgatory.

The image of Omar kissing Ingrid pounded through her skull on repeat, her emotions crashing over her like storm waves. That ass had the audacity to go *looking for her* after that? To tell people he was *heartbroken*?

Maybe there was some sort of misunderstanding. Maybe what you saw in Purgatory was just a projection of your fears. A knot settled in her stomach. She'd been over and over this. Ingrid had admitted to that kiss. There was no misunderstanding. She needed to stop living in a fantasy.

Armando stirred in the seat beside her and his eyes came open. "Richards? What's wrong?"

She dried her eyes and sat up, turning her face away from him. "Nothing."

"Uh huh. Why did you leave, then?"

Magdalene clutched the sides of the chair, wishing she could disappear from this world as easily as she could from the other.

She should have toughed it out in Purgatory and avoided these questions.

"Omar did something to you, didn't he?"

Magdalene squeezed her eyes shut, imagining a satellite falling out of the sky onto Armando's head.

Armando sighed. "Listen. I know it's none of my business, but you're obviously a super-dope girl, and any dude who would make you cry isn't worth your time."

Magdalene let out a slow breath and opened her eyes. "You're right, he's not worth my time."

Armando stood. "Let's go get some lunch. It's almost noon, anyhow."

She nodded and got to her feet, avoiding his gaze.

On the way to the cafeteria, the elevator stopped on the second floor and a man got in. Magdalene recognized Peter, the engineer she'd met the day before.

"Peter Rodriguez," Armando said, grinning.

"Ar-man-do Or-te-ga," Peter said. Thene he glanced at Magdalene and blinked. "And, Magdalene, right?"

Magdalene smiled. "Hi, Peter."

Armando tilted his head. "You guys know each other?"

"We met yesterday during my tour," Magdalene said.

"You guys getting lunch?" Peter asked.

"Yuuup," Armando replied. "You care to join us?"

Peter glanced back and forth between them uncertainly. "I wouldn't be a third wheel, would I?"

Magdalene snorted.

Armando winced theatrically. "Yeah, no. She's not really my biggest fan right now. Maybe you can be my bodyguard." He nudged her with his elbow. "And don't ask her if she's the Boss' girlfriend, either, she goes all haywire."

Magdalene narrowed her eyes at him. "Don't push it."

"Wait, what?" Peter's expression was teasing but curious. "You and Mr. Cavanaugh...?"

Magdalene huffed. "Jesus! Just no, okay?"

The elevator doors opened, and they got out on the first floor.

The cafeteria wasn't crowded—probably because it was barely noon—but a handful of people sat at the tables. Against the far wall, a long buffet steamed under a spotless sneeze guard. The three of them grabbed trays and started filing down the row. Magdalene wasn't hungry, but grabbed a vegetable hum bao and some Mongolian tofu just so she wouldn't look weird. Hearing that Omar was looking for her had ruined her appetite.

Peter glanced at her tray. "Are you a vegetarian?"

She hesitated a minute, and then shrugged. "I guess?" She couldn't get the idea that the souls of dead animals might eat her when she died *quite* out of her head.

"That's cool."

The other two piled their trays high with food and then headed for a table. "Wait," Magdalene said, "we don't have to pay?"

"Nope," Peter said. "Included as part of our compensation package."

"Sick," Magdalene muttered.

They sat at a table by the windows. "Pulled pork," Armando announced enthusiastically, taking a huge bite of his sandwich.

"So how do you two know each other?" Peter asked.

"I just started working with him," Magdalene replied, poking at her tofu with her fork.

Peter's eyebrows lifted. "You work *security*?"

"She's waaay tougher than she looks, take it from me." Armando sent Magdalene a covert glance; Peter obviously didn't know about Purgatory.

"I'm actually an executive assistant," Magdalene said. "I'll only work with him sometimes." At least she hoped so. Gavin hadn't really covered what her exact schedule would be. But if she had to follow Armando around all day every day, she was going to have words with the Boss. "How do *you* two know each other? You have pretty different jobs."

"We were in school together," Peter replied. "We both wanted to be in the FBI. This thug wanted to bust perps, but I just wanted to be on their cyber squad." Peter gazed at Armando thoughtfully. "Are you going to drop out, too?"

"Hell, yes. Cavanaugh pays me like a champ, and I'm riding this pony as far as it will trot." They fist-bumped across the table.

"Are you a software developer?" Magdalene asked, taking a bite of her dumpling.

Peter smiled. He had a nice smile. "Yeah, I do some of that stuff." He popped a tater tot in his mouth.

Armando gave him a knowing look. "Tell her how you got the job, Rodriguez."

Peter snickered, covering his mouth so he didn't spit crumbs. "I got into a casino's online payroll system and changed all the employee names to porn star names."

"Anita Dickin," Armando said, and he and Peter busted up laughing.

Magdalene snorted. "What? Why?"

Peter shrugged. "I lost a hundred bucks there on my birthday and I needed to regain my pride. A couple days later these dudes in suits show up on my doorstep. I thought I was toast, seriously. But instead of murdering me they offered me a job at this place."

Magdalene rolled her eyes. "That sounds like something Gavin would do."

The other two stared at her. "*Gavin?*" Armando said.

"You mean Mr. Cavanaugh, right?" Peter asked. "His name is Gavin? His mother must have wanted a puppy."

"I'm just trying to figure out why she calls him by his first name," Armando said. "I mean, she swears she's not sleeping with the guy."

Magdalene arched her eyebrows and was gratified to see a spark of fear in his eyes. "That's just how he introduced himself to me, so that's what I call him. I don't see why everyone has to treat him like some sort of king."

"Because he *is*," Peter said. "Dude is one of the richest people alive, not to mention one of the smartest." He studied her. "Seriously, no offense, but you seem really cozy around him. I'm kind of jealous, to be honest. I mean, I'm straight, but if he asked me to play bottom on his team I'd at least think about it." He and Armando broke into giggles.

Magdalene sighed. "I'm just his assistant, all right? I have a different relationship with him than you guys, but it's not like *that*. There is a middle ground between terrified hero worship and, you know, banging."

"That's what they keep telling me." Armando took another bite of his sandwich.

Peter pushed a tater tot around his plate with his pointer finger. "So, like, he wouldn't fire me if I asked you for your number?"

Armando winced. "Ooooh."

Heat crept into Magdalene's cheeks. "I don't have a phone."

Armando smirked and leaned back in his chair. "Tough luck, bruh."

Peter looked a bit stricken, and Magdalene felt bad. He seemed like a nice guy, and he filled out his t-shirt pretty well. "I'm not lying," she said. "You can give me your number if you want. I'll probably get another phone soon." She got a deep sense of satisfaction when the smug look drained from Armando's face.

Peter brightened and fished a crumpled receipt from his jeans and a pencil from his shirt pocket. As he scribbled down his number, Magdalene felt a pang of guilt. Was she leading him on just to get back at Armando?

He was hot, though. And she was single.

Her heart twisted.

Peter handed her the receipt, and she put it in her purse. She smiled at him. Maybe she'd call him. Maybe she really would.

Armando ran his fingers through his hair, looking sulky.

The two men started talking about stuff they had done in school. Armando told a bunch of embarrassing stories about Peter, obviously trying to make him look bad, and Magdalene started to hate Gavin for sticking her with him all day. He was halfway through a story about Peter passing out drunk on a pool table at a frat house when powerful dizziness swooped in and claimed Magdalene out of nowhere. Voices echoed through her skull, disjointed feelings coursed through her, and images flickered before her eyes—faces of unknown people, places she'd never seen.

Magdalene dug her fingernails into her knees, breathing steadily. *Not this again. Not this.* Gradually the voices quieted and faded into nothingness, the emotions drained out of her, and the swirl of strange images disappeared.

Magdalene blinked. The other two at the table continued to talk as if nothing had happened. She forced some food into her mouth, wondering if she had low blood sugar.

Armando checked the time on his phone. "We'd better get back. Security doesn't secure itself."

They stood, taking their trays to the caddy. Peter gave Magdalene a shy smile. "Maybe we can do lunch again sometime?"

"Yeah, that would be cool."

As they walked off, Armando, gave Peter a parting sneer over his shoulder. "No way is she going to call you, chump."

Magdalene rolled her eyes so hard they hurt. Maybe she could ditch him in Purgatory and spend the afternoon with Bridgett. Though she supposed that wouldn't be a responsible way to spend her first day on the job.

As they turned a corner into the elevator lobby, however, they found their path blocked by none other than Gavin Cavanaugh. "Miss Richards, there you are."

Magdalene smiled, overcome by a rush of...she decided she would call it relief at being saved from Armando, but the truth was, she was just happy to see him.

Gavin's little smile took on a tinge of ice as it swung to Armando. "Good afternoon, Mr. Ortega. I trust all is well at Alpha Passage?"

Armando smiled nervously. "Yes, sir. Crowd is very manageable today."

Magdalene frowned, wondering what Armando had done to piss Gavin off.

"Wonderful." Gavin raised an eyebrow sharply. "It won't be too difficult for you to cover the afternoon rounds alone, then, as I need to borrow Miss Richards here."

"Sure thing, Mr. Cavanaugh. No problem." Armando ducked his head and scampered off into an elevator.

The ice melted from Gavin's smile. "Let's go to my office. I have some matters to discuss with you."

Magdalene studied his profile out of the corner of her eye as they waited for the elevator. A thought crept into her mind about why he was mad at Armando, and she frowned, forcing it back.

Once they were on the elevator and the door had closed behind them, Gavin turned to her. "I'm sorry for leaving you alone with Mr. Ortega all morning, but I had work I needed to do."

Magdalene chewed on her lip as they exited the elevator and headed down the hall to his office, that thought sidling back into her mind despite her efforts. "Why are you mad at Armando?"

Gavin held the door of his office open for her, then gestured for her to sit at a chair in front of his desk. He settled in the leather chair behind it, putting his elbows on its burnished wooden surface and regarding her with his chin propped on his hands. "Why don't you tell me, Miss Richards?"

Magdalene clutched the arms of her chair, dread pooling in her stomach. There was a glint in Gavin's eyes that made her feel x-rayed. "Is Suzette some sort of spy? Are you grilling her about everything that happens?"

Gavin's eyebrows shot up and he chuckled. "I haven't spoken to her about you, except to make sure you're comfortable."

Magdalene squinted at him across his desk, her heart racing. The other possibilities were even more disturbing, and she half hoped he was lying.

Gavin grinned wryly and leaned back in his chair. "I don't have you bugged or electronically monitored in any way. Come, darling, you know the answer."

Cold sweat beaded on the back of Magdalene's neck. She shook her head, trying to shake the realization loose and let it float into nothingness, but it wouldn't let go.

Gavin's smile faded. "Please don't be scared. You're perfectly safe here, much safer than anywhere else you could be.'"

Magdalene clutched her head in her hands, her thoughts swimming tight circles in her skull. How could she not have seen it from the very beginning? *Had* she seen it from the beginning? Had she just been in denial?

"How do you do it?" she blurted, looking up at him. "How do you read minds?"

He gazed at her with his little smile. Magdalene had another moment of dizziness. The words seemed to flow across the desk and caress her temples. *You know the answer to that.*

Magdalene hissed between her teeth and squeezed her eyes tight shut.

You and I will make an unstoppable team.

"What are you doing to me?" Every muscle in her body was as taut as a piano wire.

"I'm not doing anything to you," Gavin said quietly. "You're just spreading your wings."

Her eyes flew open. "What's happening to me?"

Gavin gazed at her, concern etched into his features. "Like I told you, you have abilities similar to mine. I can teach you to use them."

Magdalene huffed. "I don't have any power. This is all you."

Gavin Cavanaugh sighed. His gaze wandered out the window and he rubbed the spot between his eyes with his fingers. "I remember how disconcerting it was figuring out my own powers. I can only imagine what it's like when the manifest later in life. The voices, feeling like you're out of your body and experiencing other people's feelings as strongly as your own. You probably feel like you're going insane. But you can learn how to control it and live with it."

Magdalene's heartbeat pulsed through her body. And, along with hers, another heartbeat—his. Slower, calmer. "None of that started happening until I was here," Magdalene said, her voice shaking. "You're doing something to me." Even as she said it, she realized it wasn't really true. She'd had other moments of dizziness, other times she'd felt things she shouldn't be feeling, before she came here. She hadn't thought much of it at the time, with all the things going on in her life, but...

She huffed. It still could have been Gavin doing it to her somehow. The Tower had already been raised, he was already pursuing her. There was no telling how long he'd been fucking with her head.

A sad smile curved the corners of Gavin's lips. "It can be hard to trust when no one in our life has ever been trustworthy. Our being together may be acting as a catalyst for your abilities showing themselves, but I promise you, Magdalene, I'm not doing anything to you. I've seen the potential in you since the moment I first saw you, and I've only been waiting for it to manifest."

Magdalene closed her eyes. She was trembling. But she could still feel his heartbeat—steady, dependable. A sense of calm touched her skin, then gently made its way into her nerves. She wanted to reject it, but she took a deep, shuddering breath and let that delicious feeling flow through her, relaxing each muscle, her panic evaporating with its delicate touch. She wanted so badly to trust someone. She wanted, for once in her life, for everything to be okay.

"I'll never lie to you," he said softly. "I make no excuses for what I am, but I won't insult or hurt you with lies."

Behind Magdalene's eyelids, images bloomed. Faces, landscapes, scenes. Voices murmured and whispered and feelings swam beneath the surface, roiling the waters of her mind.

She opened her eyes again. Gavin had a glint of worry in his gaze as he watched her.

She expelled a breath, laughing humorlessly. "But how do I know that? How do I know this isn't a trick, that you're controlling my mind and making this happen?"

Gavin squinted at her, and Magdalene could feel the shape of his thoughts just on the edge of her awareness. "I can't control you like I can the others," he said. "Not in the same way, to the same extent. You're different."

Magdalene swallowed. Her heartbeat had slowed, her mind had quit racing, and Gavin Cavanaugh's feelings flowed through her alongside her own. The realization grew in her: he was telling the truth. She blinked. "Who taught you how to do this stuff?"

He spun the ring on his pinky. "I didn't have the benefit of a teacher. If I had I might be in a better position now."

Magdalene scoffed. "It seems like you're in a pretty good position."

He chuckled dryly. "Money isn't everything, darling."

Another wave of the strange dizziness washed over her. Magdalene waited for it to subside. "How long did it take you to learn to control your powers?"

Gavin smiled. "I'm still learning. If you're asking how long it would take *you* to learn, I'd wager not very long. After all, you *do* have the benefit of a teacher."

Magdalene gazed at him, drumming her fingers on the arms of her chair. "Is this why you really want me here? Because you think I can control people like you can?"

"You have many skills and talents, Miss Richards, both in the Land of the Dead and here on Earth."

She chewed on the inside of her cheek. "Are they related? These...mind powers, and the fact I can stay lucid in Purgatory?"

"I don't believe so. After all, I don't have the power in the Land of the Dead that you do." His brow furrowed. "I seem to have been born with my gifts, but I didn't learn about the Land of the Dead until much later in life, from Andy."

Magdalene's eyebrows shot up. "Wait, what?"

A grin flitted over his face. "It was many years ago, when Andy was just a teenager nearing the end of his undergraduate schooling. He approached me looking for capital for his research. He had heard I was interested in the afterlife, as I was then searching for answers about the deaths of my wife and child and in the nascent phase of developing the technology that now runs this company. Andy was able to teach me enough lucid dreaming to convince me of the reality of the Land of the Dead, but I ultimately decided not to invest in his project because I mistrusted his motives. I dodged a bullet. My money would have been squandered like all the rest."

Magdalene turned this over in her mind. Andy had suspected he'd known the person behind the Tower, and he'd been right. "Why don't you trust Andy?"

Gavin grimaced. "At first, it was just a hunch. However, that hunch has subsequently been proven correct. The person who proved it to me was none other than our very own scoundrel, Armando Ortega."

Magdalene blinked. "Douchenozzle? What does he have to do with it?"

Gavin laughed. "He washed up in Andy's cult during a low point in his life. He ended up giving them all his savings, thinking he'd found the answer to all his problems and that Andy would show him a better way of life. Armando worked himself to death at that place, for no pay, and ultimately had his savings stolen for his trouble. However, the boy did end up learning a small amount of technique at lucid dreaming, which landed him a job here, so I suppose all's well that ends well." Gavin sighed, leaning back in his chair and drumming his fingers on the armrests. "Though, after seeing how he treats you, I'm re-considering his contract."

Magdalene frowned, trying to imagine Armando washing dishes at the Commune. "He's not *that* bad."

"Darling, he is *exactly* that bad."

Magdalene wrinkled her nose. "He could be much worse."

It wasn't pity that filled Gavin's eyes. It was...something else. She'd seen that look in Morris's eyes after Stan attacked her, and in Omar's eyes when he'd strode out of the dawn-washed desert to save her.

It was the look of a man determined to punish the people who hurt her.

Magdalene's brow furrowed. *Why am I so important to him?*

She knew he'd heard that thought, because a sad smile touched his lips. "You're worth protecting, Magdalene."

Magdalene couldn't stop the bitterness that bloomed like algae inside her. She'd heard promises of protection before.

"You're safe here now," Gavin said. "You may not believe me yet, and why should you? But if you give me a chance, you'll see it's true."

Magdalene sniffed. "It would be polite to wait for me to actually say things out loud."

Gavin chuckled and crossed his legs. "Other than Armando being a douchenozzle, how was your first day at Alpha Passage?"

She lifted her eyebrows. "So, you didn't watch me the whole time?"

He shrugged. "You'll find that keeping someone under constant surveillance is exhausting. But when I sense you're distressed, I can't help but check up on you."

Magdalene's foot jittered. She wasn't sure how she felt about that, but she could at least see his point. "I wanted to talk to you about something."

"Ask away."

"I spoke to a woman at the gate named Kate. She says she'd tried to get through but was told they needed to process her request. What does that mean?"

Gavin tented his fingers in front of his mouth. He had callouses and scrapes on them, and on his palms, and Magdalene wondered how a billionaire got scuffed-up hands. "In implementing a system of this level of complexity, there are bound to be hiccups. We sometimes have difficulties analyzing the merit of the Departed when they've been in the Land of the Dead for a while. That place causes peak-shifting in their signals with long exposure, and so I'm having to perfect my instrumentation." He folded his hands on his desk. "It's more difficult to get a reading of a Dead person's signal than a living person's. Since we don't have them on file if they died long ago, the program will put their request to pass through the portal on hold while it does further analysis. I'm working to adjust my waveform signature reader for the Departed so that analysis can be more easily performed."

Magdalene frowned. "If you can't get an accurate reading yet, just let them through."

"If we did that, we'd run the risk of letting murderers and rapists into Heaven, or back onto earth through the rebirthing portals."

Magdalene looked away, chewing on her lip.

Gavin smiled. "I'm confident my improved signature reader will be operational soon. If it isn't, then you and I will work together to come up with a solution that's fair for all." He leaned back in his chair again. "On a lighter topic, your condo is ready and the paperwork to transfer the title into your name has been prepared. We just need your signature, and it's all yours. You can move in immediately if you'd like."

"Wait, I *own* the condo?" Her pulse fluttered and she felt like she was floating. "I thought you were just renting it to me or something."

He grinned. "You should have followed Lonnie's advice and had your attorney look over the fine print."

Magdalene blinked rapidly. "Can I see it?"

"Of course. I'll call someone to take you there in a moment. But first, I wanted to discuss one more thing with you." His sharp gaze searched her face. "I feel it necessary to make a suggestion. You're a young woman in possession of unique talents which you don't fully understand, and which you don't know how to wield. You're in danger of misusing this power if you don't learn to control it, of maybe affecting others without meaning to. Would you consider entering into training with me?"

Magdalene could almost hear the air fart out of her balloon of excitement about the condo. Was he right? Either she was going crazy, or *something* was going on with her. If there was any chance she was manipulating others without knowing it, didn't she have an obligation to learn to control it?

She flinched as a memory flashed through her brain: a hot day under the cottonwood tree, Omar's arm around her waist, his expression twisted with bitterness. *How do I know what's real and what I've created through my abnormal force of will?*

"I...okay."

Gavin smiled. "I'll clear my schedule tomorrow and we'll work together."

Magdalene nodded, filled with strange cocktail of dread and anticipation. At least she wouldn't have to endure another day working with Armando.

CHAPTER FOURTEEN

Always Home, Never Home

Magdalene felt somewhat dazed as a woman named Marta from HR led her across campus to her condo. Marta chattered about the hot weather and her son, who had apparently just turned a year old and was starting to walk.

Magdalene nodded along, but her head was full. *He can read thoughts. He thinks I can too.*

Omar had the ability to mess with her mind, but she'd never thought about it much or worried about him prying into her head. She'd never really thought about the fact that, when he'd saved her from Stan, it had been because he'd felt her distress and come to rescue her.

Magdalene wondered if she could keep from going insane when she had no idea what was truly real. It was her early days at the Commune all over again when Omar was trying to convince her Purgatory was an actual place.

She winced. She was thinking about Omar too much.

She and Marta traversed a winding gravel path through a park. Wispy trees were planted at uneven intervals, raw earth piled around their trunks as if they'd just been put in. The housing units looked new, as well: beige stucco condominiums with huge picture windows, jutting balconies stacked one on top of the other.

Marta smiled as they entered one of the buildings and took the elevator to the third floor. "You have an executive suite."

"Oh. Wow." Suzette had been right then.

They exited the elevator in a carpeted hallway that smelled of fresh paint. Marta unlocked a door, then handed Magdalene the key. "Welcome home."

"Crap," Magdalene breathed.

The entryway opened into a furnished sitting area. It had huge windows overlooking the desert behind the compound, dry washes cutting beige veins through it and the spiky heads of Joshua trees marching into the distance. A French door opened onto a long balcony.

"This is your kitchen," Marta said brightly. It was separated from the sitting room by a vast marble-topped island.

"I have a dishwasher." Magdalene skipped over to run her fingers across the gleaming stainless-steel surface.

"That definitely makes life easier," Marta said. "My unit is nowhere near as nice as this one—only two bedrooms, and the living room is about half the size—but I was so happy when it had a dishwasher. I don't know how I'd get everything done without it, because of the baby." She laughed.

Guilt pooled in Magdalene's chest. This woman probably worked so much harder than she did, but *she* didn't have an executive condo and no one was buying *her* Gucci purses.

"Let's go see your master suite," Marta said. "I hear you have a whirlpool tub."

She did: a sunken one in front of frosted windows, with live orchids blooming on the sill. There was a separate shower. She also had a walk-in closet, where she found her clothes neatly hung, her shoes lined up on a shelf, her Gucci purse packed in a cubby.

After Marta completed the tour, she left, with plans to meet Magdalene later in the week at the pool in the middle of the complex. "You can meet the baby."

Magdalene stood staring at the door after Marta closed it behind her. Did she have friends with babies now? She felt like an imposter, but in a good way. She'd never truly thought she'd have the chance to live like this, with a dishwasher and a whirlpool tub, normal friends with normal lives. She'd grown up in a world where people were always in and out of jail, where dishes piled up in the sink and the electricity and water constantly got shut off.

Magdalene gazed around at the silent condo and a wave of unreality washed over her. It didn't feel right.

"Stop it," she muttered to herself. "You deserve this. Just because your mom never had this doesn't mean you can't."

But it wasn't just that.

Her brain was throbbing, and she couldn't shake the feeling that she was *missing* something, that an obvious fact was jumping up and down in front of her and screaming, but she couldn't hear it.

Magdalene huffed. It had been a long day. *Immensely* long. The realization about Gavin and what he said about her own powers was a lot to take in.

She sank down on her new sofa, looking out the windows.

And then there was the fact that Omar apparently was looking for her.

An unbearable urge to see him gripped her, and she had pry its fingers loose from her psyche. *He kissed Ingrid. Who cares if he's looking for me? Let him look.* She jumped to her feet again, huffing, and stomped into the bathroom for a shower.

Her new shower had four nozzles in the walls and a waterfall head in the ceiling. Fancy toiletries were lined up on the shelves. All this went a long way toward improving her mood, but her thoughts still wouldn't settle. After she'd put on some of her old jeans and brushed her wet hair, she was at a loss for what to do with herself.

A knock sounded at the door.

She opened it to find Suzette, Armando, and Peter, all of them grinning like dorks. Suzette had a bottle of wine, Peter was toting two large pizza boxes and Armando had a potted begonia. He handed it to her. "Happy housewarming."

Magdalene stepped aside to let them in. "Thanks." Magdalene blinked, her chest aching with a strange happiness. They'd really thought about her and wanted to come hang out?

Her gaze caught on Armando as the group filed past her. He'd been at the Commune. It was hard to believe.

Peter gawked around the kitchen as he put the pizza boxes on the counter. "Nice place."

"Executive condo," Suzette sang, grinning at Magdalene.

Magdalene picked at a fray in her jeans. "Aren't your places pretty nice too?"

"Yeah, but we all just have little apartments," Armando said. "Housing is included in our contract, but not *this* kind of housing."

"I don't even have housing in my contract," Peter said, "but I get a deal on rent, so I decided to take it."

Magdalene put the begonia on an end table in the sitting room, turning it this way and that until it looked perfect. "My first plant. I love it."

Suzette rummaged through the kitchen drawers. "Do you have a corkscrew? I forgot to bring one. Oh, here it is."

Magdalene scampered into the kitchen. "There's stuff in there?" She opened another drawer and found an elegant flatware set. Next, she opened the pantry, finding it stocked with flour, sugar, and spices. The fridge had milk and eggs, condiments, lettuce and broccoli. "Holy shit," she said when she opened the freezer. "There's *three kinds* of ice cream in here. Gavin thinks of everything."

Suzette gave her a wry glance as she popped the cork out of the bottle. "Yep, *Gavin* sure does."

Peter found plates and handed one to Magdalene with a cute smile. Heat crept into her cheeks, and she smiled back, wondering how old he was. Obviously too old for her. Hadn't he said something about getting drunk in a casino? That's all she needed was to be jailbait for some nice guy.

How could she trust anyone again, anyway? She'd thought Omar was kind, considerate, and honest...she wasn't a good judge of character. Maybe she should just stay away from relationships.

Suzette poured three glasses of wine and passed them out to the guys while the rest of them scooped up pizza onto their plates.

"One of them is vegetarian," Peter said.

Armando lifted an eyebrow at Magdalene. "You're vegetarian?"

Magdalene shrugged. "Yeah."

He grinned. "I guess you don't wear the leather getup when you get out the whips, then."

Peter paused with a slice of pizza halfway to his mouth.

Suzette scowled. "What the hell are you talking about, Arnie?"

"Aw, Magdalene just gave me a little lashing today, because I was being an ass to her. I totally deserved it."

Peter laughed. "I guess weird stuff goes on in the security squad."

Magdalene avoided Suzette and Peter's curious looks as they all moved to the sitting room and settled on the couch. Magdalene curled up in the corner of it with her pizza on her lap. It was sand-colored, soft and comfortable. She couldn't believe it was hers.

Armando munched a slice of Hawaiian. "I was giving her hell about her relationship with *Gavin*, and she finally had enough of my crap and let me have it."

Magdalene wrinkled her nose. "It's possible for someone to appreciate me for more than sex."

Armando winced. "That's not what I was trying to say."

"To be perfectly honest," Suzette cut in, "The *real* reason the Boss treats Magdalene like this is that she's super good at her job."

Armando grunted in agreement. "You've got that right."

Peter gestured at Magdalene's glass of water. "You don't want any wine?"

Magdalene smiled nervously. "Um..."

Suzette gave her a wicked grin. "Magdalene can't drink anymore. Not after *the incident*."

Magdalene widened her eyes at her.

Armando's gaze brightened with curiosity. "What incident?"

"You don't even want to know," Suzette said, swirling the wine in her own glass. "But maybe she'll tell you when you know her better."

Magdalene glared and made a mental note to slip some live slugs into Suzette's shoes at the first opportunity.

After her guests left, Magdalene padded into her bedroom. She found her old pajamas folded up in a drawer in her walk-in closet and put them on. She slipped between the crisp sheets of her new bed and sank into the perfectly soft mattress. Outside the broad window, the last glow of sunset still shone on the distant ridges.

She sighed. *At least I'm making new friends.*

The silence of her condo surrounded her, along with the smell of new carpets and paint. No sound of Lynn and James arguing in the sitting room. No lingering whiff of curry from the kitchen. She even missed the sound of Helena clapping her hands and calling yet another pointless meeting.

And Omar...

She shoved her face into her pillow.

Her thoughts honked in her ears, and darkness had long since claimed the desert outside by the time she got to sleep.

Magdalene wandered through dark hallways crowded with looming, staring figures, endlessly seeking something which was always just around the corner, and awoke when dawn was just beginning to dim the stars. It took her several moments to remember where she was, for her new life to settle into place around her.

She found some expensive coffee in her pantry and brewed a pot in her pristine coffee maker, then curled into a chair in the sitting room and watched the dawn grow. Thunderclouds boiled on the horizon, lightning playing along their edges, and her thoughts played tug of war in her skull. Gavin knew Andy. *Armando* knew Andy. Gavin could read minds, and so, supposedly, could she.

She felt like she was looking at a hologram, seeing one image, but if she turned her head just a little it would change into something sinister and unfamiliar.

She shook her head and got up to take a shower, telling herself she was just being paranoid. *You're not used to having money and being around normal people. You'll adapt.*

The receptionist smiled as Magdalene walked into the building. "Good morning, Miss Richards."

"Good morning." Magdalene had no idea what the young woman's name was. How long would it take her to get everyone straight?

She stepped into the elevator with three other people. They smiled at her, their gazes curious. "Good morning, Miss Richards."

Magdalene smiled back. "Good morning."

She'd never seen these people in her life, but everyone knew who she was.

They got off on the fifth floor, chatting about game night in the campus community center, while Magdalene continued to the top floor alone.

Gavin's door was slightly ajar and she knocked softly before opening it. He was sitting behind his desk, his computer screen reflected in his eyes. "Ah, Miss Richards." His gaze was intent on his screen. "Please, come in."

She closed the door behind her and sat in the chair in front of his desk.

His fingers clicked away at the keyboard. "I just need to finish this up. My code monkeys are very adept at *almost* recreating the works of Shakespeare, with only a few little errors, as if they accidentally inserted the f-bomb into Romeo's address to Juliet on the balcony."

Magdalene snorted.

Gavin didn't speak again for several more minutes and she sat quietly, watching him work. A sense of peace emanated from him. It soaked into her bones, unknotting her shoulders. Was he solving all the world's problems with his lines of code?

He tapped a few more keys and looked up at her, smiling. "Did you have a nice evening in your new home?"

She smiled. "Yes. My condo is amazing. You even got me three kinds of ice cream."

He chuckled. "I told Marcus to make sure you got some ice cream, though I certainly can't take credit for three kinds. He always goes above and beyond."

Magdalene ducked her head. "Anyway, thank you."

"It's my pleasure, darling. Now, are you ready to get started?"

She nodded. "What do you want me to do?"

He stood and came around the desk, holding out a hand to her. She took it, and he pulled her to her feet and spun her in a dance twirl. Magdalene giggled as he caught her around the waist and led her in a waltz around the room. A memory floated through her mind, of a father-daughter dance in the fifth grade. She hadn't been able to go because Morris had been gone, probably off on a drug run. He'd been the closest thing she'd ever had to a father. And, when she really thought about it, maybe he hadn't been as good a father figure as he could have been.

Gavin released her and stepped back, and the sentimental feeling drained from her as if someone had pulled a plug in her soul.

Magdalene's head swam. "How did you do that? How did you make me do that?"

He gave her his little smile, but there was something bitter in it that reminded her of Omar. "Most people wouldn't allow that I *made* you do anything."

She let out a breath. "You made me *want* to."

He studied her, then shrugged. "It's just a matter of knowing what people want and turning that to your own uses. You're helping them get what they want, and they're helping you in return."

Magdalene squinted at him. She felt hollow inside, and part of her wanted him to cast his spell again to fill that emptiness. *Where's the line between what I want and what he wants?*

Did he want a daughter? Did she want a father? She hadn't thought much about it before, because she'd been too busy trying to survive, but Gavin seemed to have unearthed that want and polished it until it shone bright within her.

But why shouldn't he bring that out in her? Why shouldn't two lonely, lost people care for one another? How was that manipulation?

Magdalene blew out a puff of air. When Omar had bent her to his will, it had been considerably less subtle. "I thought you said you couldn't control me?"

Gavin smiled dryly. "Not like I can the others. You have to already want something pretty desperately for me to get my hooks in you."

Magdalene grunted. She hadn't really needed something else to keep her awake at night.

"Power is a tricky thing, Miss Richards," Gavin said softly. "My power affects me more than it affects others. You have to surrender to it before you can wield it."

She hugged her elbows. The hollowness in her middle gnawed at her. She knew, somehow, what he meant. She had to open herself up in order to wield this power. She had to allow herself to *feel*.

"It hurts," she said, her voice raw.

He nodded. "Yes, darling. Horribly."

Magdalene took a deep breath and closed her eyes.

Her whole body was tensed, holding the dam walls against a deluge of emotion. Stan, Morris, Omar...she didn't want to feel her own feelings, much less anyone else's. She'd disintegrate like a sandcastle under a tidal wave.

"You're safe here," Gavin said.

Magdalene scoffed weakly. It came out as more of a squeak.

"I promise you," Gavin said. "You're safe."

The dizziness came in a rush, voices muttering in her head, emotions brushing hot against her heart. She took a gasping breath.

Relax. It took her a moment to realize he hadn't said it out loud. She took another slow breath, then let it out. *Relax.*

Feelings diffused into her body like ink drops spreading through water, creeping and tumbling through her veins, expanding until they took her over. Sweet longing for a girl with dark hair and beautiful brown eyes, grief for a husband gone too soon, a sizzling flash of anger, and a whole deluge of workday boredom and tedium that consumed those in the offices around her. So many feelings. They rolled over her like thick mud, and Magdalene struggled for breath.

Gavin was at her side, steadying her with a light touch to her arm. "It's okay. Breathe."

She shook her head frantically. "It's too much."

The images crowded into her mind until she couldn't see Gavin's office. She felt arms around her, but didn't know if they were around her or someone else. She was drowning in strangers' thoughts, dissolving into them. Fear spiked through her. What if she got lost and couldn't find her way back?

Gavin's soothing voice cut through the noise. "You're still here, Magdalene. Find yourself. Find your center."

"I can't!"

He chuckled. "You're still talking to me, aren't you? So, you're still yourself and in control of your own body."

She took a deep breath, concentrating on the expansion of her lungs.

"That's it," Gavin said. "Another breath, darling. You can do this."

She obeyed, feeling her chest expand against the fabric of her blouse. She could feel the sweat on her brow, Gavin's hand on her back. The chaos of noise and images became less oppressive, more like movies on a screen. Gavin's face came into focus, his bright blue eyes, his little smile. He looked...proud. Proud of her. It reminded her a little of how Morris would look at her sometimes.

A vivid image of her friend's bearded face flashed through her mind, his eyes confused and blank as they stared out at the party in the Tower.

Suddenly the voices were gone, and her head was full of the pounding of her own heart. "Morris. Where is he?"

Gavin cocked an eyebrow. "He's still with us in the Tower. Don't worry about him. He's adjusted and is quite happy."

Magdalene frowned. "You still have him in the Tower? Why?"

"He didn't want to leave you."

Grief trickled in, and guilt throbbed along with her heartbeat. With all that had been happening, she'd forgotten about her friend.

"Don't be so hard on yourself," Gavin said. "Please, sit down. Rest. You've just been through an ordeal. I know how difficult it can be before you get used to it."

Magdalene collapsed into her chair, hiding her face in her hands. Her cheeks were wet with tears, though she didn't remember shedding them. Gavin's chair gave a soft creak as he sat. "We'll go visit Morris when you're ready, but he's perfectly content where he is. I've built him a nice condo with an excellent view."

Magdalene looked up, a lopsided smile growing on her face. "You built him a condo? In Purgatory?"

Gavin shrugged. "I thought he'd appreciate it. And, one thing you can say about the afterlife, the rents are cheap and there's no HOA."

Magdalene laughed. It felt good to laugh. Her limbs ached as if she'd climbed a mountain, and her heart felt like it had been stomped on repeatedly.

Gavin smiled. "You did a very good job today, Magdalene. You'll best me at my own game in no time."

Magdalene snorted. "You played me like a piano, and then I went crazy."

He gave her his dimpled smile. "You're sixteen. Everything takes practice. And you already know how to overrule me if you wish. Your emotions just have to be stronger than the ones I'm trying to cultivate in you. You simply need to *not* want the same thing as I do." The corners of his lips curled upward. "Your stubbornness is your strongest attribute."

She raised her eyebrows. "Thanks?"

He leaned forward, studying her with his chin on his hands. "Tell me, darling, how do you feel now?"

She squinted at him. He knew exactly how she felt: small, sad, and lost. Exhausted. Empty. It felt much better to let him take charge of her emotions, to feel his heart beating alongside hers, when she felt like that. *That's your problem. You're moping around like a loser and that makes it easy for him to control you.*

But how else could she feel? She was being tossed from one situation to another, things just getting weirder and weirder at each turn. She had no idea who to trust or what to believe, and she was so *lonely*. She was just a young girl, hopelessly lost in a situation she couldn't even begin to comprehend.

Gavin's bright eyes watched her intently. He'd asked her how she felt. *You don't need me to tell you how I feel, you KNOW how I feel. You just want me to say it out loud.*

Her loneliness kindled ever stronger. She could ease it by confiding in him, by opening up, sharing her pain.

She huffed. "No."

He grinned wryly, then his smile faded. "It isn't my intent to manipulate you, Magdalene. You're just as sensitive to my emotions as I am to yours. It's called *empathy*, and we both have too much of it."

She crossed her legs, studying him over the expanse of his desk. "Right."

He laughed.

She chewed on the inside of her cheek. "How does all this work? Why can we see into other people's heads, but no one else can?"

"Every person has a vibrational signature, Miss Richards. To know what they're thinking and feeling you just have to let it resonate with your own. Everyone does it to a certain extent, unknowingly, but you and I are special cases. For some reason you and I...and your friend Omar...operate over a broader spectrum, incorporating a higher level of energy."

Magdalene winced. "If Omar can do this stuff, too, why don't you have *him* here?"

Gavin's eyes glinted like the heart of a glacier. "Because he's dangerous."

Her eyebrows crept up. "You're scared of him."

A humorless smile flitted across his lips. "So would you be, if you knew what I know."

Magdalene dug her fingernails into her chair arms, hardening herself against the oncoming pain. "So, tell me what you know."

Gavin sighed and leaned back in his chair. "Mr. Omar Arif, as you know, has a great deal of power to change and manipulate the flow of energy in this world. He is a strange phenomenon. It seems that the physical laws of the living world are bent and twisted in his presence. Here, in this world, things are more ordered, less chaotic, than in the Land of the Dead, but Mr. Arif seems to be a conduit that transmits the chaos of the other world here. I fear that, though he may not yet know it, he could ultimately destabilize this plane. I worry that, where I would build and bring order, he would destroy and bring confusion."

Magdalene's stomach soured. "That's a pretty heavy accusation. He may be a jerk, but I don't think Omar wants to destroy the world."

"Perhaps not," Gavin said quietly. "But sometimes, with what we see as the best of intentions, we end up causing pain. At any rate, he and I are opposed on a fundamental level: Mr. Arif does not wish for the universe to be a place of order. He believes that life is not fair, and he would keep it that way even when presented with an alternative. It is in his nature, built into the fabric of his being. So, yes, I do fear him."

Magdalene tapped her painted fingernails together. Gavin was right. Omar was all about doing the best he could within the system that existed. And wasn't Omar himself afraid of his own power?

Gavin winced. "I didn't bring you here to upset you, believe it or not. Let's continue the lesson. You can see into others' minds. Now let me show you how to intervene in their will and thought process."

Magdalene's heartbeat accelerated. "You want to show me how to manipulate people?"

"Manipulate is a strong word. But you'll control people whether you want to or not, so you should learn to recognize when you are. After all, there are times when it's ethical and times when it's not."

The image of Stan's face rose in her mind. Magdalene shoved it away, her stomach roiling. If these abilities had shown themselves earlier, could she have stopped everything that happened?

"There's no use wondering what could have been," Gavin said gently. "There are bad things that we can't prevent, no matter how hard we try."

A darkness pressed against Magdalene's chest, alien yet familiar—the weight of Gavin's feelings, and so she knew he wasn't just talking about Stan.

"However," Gavin continued, "if events hadn't taken the turn they did, you wouldn't be here now. Sometimes fate is stronger than we are."

She rolled this over in her mind. "How do we know what's fate and what isn't?"

Gavin's gaze turned inward, and Magdalene could feel his pain in the air between them like raw, exposed skin. He twirled the ring on his pinky. "That's something only time can teach you. It's a lesson I've had to be taught over and over again." He smiled, and the darkness around him was gone, whatever memories had troubled him tucked away neatly out of reach. "Now, Miss Richards." He gazed at her across the desk, a flash of challenge in his eyes. "I want you to find the connection between us."

Magdalene closed her eyes. It was there, a unity of their feelings, as if it had always existed. The weight of her sadness and uncertainty lifted as their minds came together. Then, there was another connection, another presence: voices, images, feelings. Magdalene could tell it was a woman, sitting at a desk, cheerful and bored. She was curious about something, a little idea dancing on the edge of her thoughts.

Magdalene sensed Gavin's energy flowing into that curiosity, nudging it to the forefront of the woman's mind until, with a twinge of embarrassment, she realized what the woman was wondering about: herself and Gavin.

Maybe I should go check if they need any coffee, the woman thought. *Maybe then I can see what they're up to.*

Magdalene's eyes flew open and she glared at Gavin. He raised his eyebrows, the corners of his lips twitching up.

There was a knock at the door. "Come in," Gavin called.

Marta stuck her head in. "I was just wondering if you two wanted anything to drink."

"Some coffee would be lovely, Marta," Gavin said. "Anything for you, Miss Richards?"

Magdalene huffed softly. "Coffee for me, too."

Marta retreated and the door clicked closed.

"You have a intercom, Gavin," Magdalene said. "Do you really need to rummage around in people's brains to get a beverage?"

"That wouldn't be very instructional, would it?" His little smile faded. "You just have to know people. Knowing them allows you to forge an empathic pathway into their mind. It's that simple."

"You look around in their heads until you find a way to make them *want* to do whatever it is."

"In a manner of speaking, yes."

"Isn't that a little problematic?"

He shrugged. "Only if the power is abused. You have to be careful that you're not acting out of anger or hurt or jealousy. Everybody has to learn to control their emotions and behavior, but it's more critical for those like you and me."

There was a knock on the door and Marta came back in with a coffee tray, which she put on the desk. Having already been in her mind, Magdalene could feel the woman's presence more acutely, could sense the murmuring of her thoughts. Magdalene watched her as she bustled back out again. "She's jealous," Magdalene muttered after the door clicked closed. "You know what they say about us, don't you?"

Gavin chuckled darkly. "Yes, darling. I know."

"Doesn't it worry you? I'm sixteen. It could cause you a lot of problems."

He lifted an eyebrow. "You've chosen to keep your age secret, however, and I'll respect that, for now. But no, it doesn't worry me. You may have noticed I'm a very powerful man, Magdalene, and their gossip can't hurt me. The only person in the world who can hurt me is *you*."

Magdalene blinked. "What do you mean?"

He gave her his mysterious little smile. "You might be too young, and too new at this, to fully appreciate how wonderful and terrifying it is for someone to have a direct link to your mind."

Magdalene stirred cream and sugar into her coffee. "I don't want to hurt you."

And she realized it was true.

Maybe it was terrifying, and maybe she still didn't trust him entirely. It was hard to trust people. But the connection she felt with him wasn't something she wanted to give up. Whether that was something he'd forged through his own will, or something that had arisen from her own nature and her loneliness, she wasn't sure.

In the end, it was all the same to her.

CHAPTER FIFTEEN
Understanding

It was only four in the afternoon, but Magdalene slumped into her condo and kicked off her cute shoes, tossed her fancy clothes into a corner of her closet, and put on her pajamas. The lesson with Gavin had left her exhausted.

She flopped onto her bed and stared up at her ceiling. *It can't be right, manipulating people that way.*

But what if you only do it for their own good, and for the good of others? She sighed, pulling the blankets over her head. She didn't know the difference between good and evil anymore. She was so tired, and her heartache had flooded back even worse than before the moment she was out of Gavin's presence. She couldn't stop thinking about Omar, even though it made her want to chew glass.

Was Omar really a destabilizing, chaotic force like Gavin thought? It was true Omar had never believed in messing with the natural order. *Justice is a dangerous concept, in this world and the next.* But wasn't justice better than injustice? If it was possible for life to be fair, shouldn't you at least try to make it so?

Anger, grief, and confusion hammered her brain, but she couldn't find the strength to hate Omar. She just wanted to see him so she could have this argument with him in person. *Why is he looking for me after what he did?*

She drifted off to sleep.

Bridgett waited for her under the willows, the breeze ruffling her golden hair. Magdalene sat down beside her, feeling as thin and flimsy as cellophane. Even in Purgatory she felt tapped out.

The little girl looked up, frown lines bracketing the blank patch of skin where her mouth should be.

"Something's wrong," Magdalene said.

Bridgett shook her head, looking off into the distance with a furrow between her brows.

Magdalene hugged her knees. "Bridget, I want to see Omar." Just admitting it out loud made some of the weight lift from her chest.

Bridgett whipped her head around to stare at Magdalene wide-eyed. She pounded the ground with her fists and shook her head.

Magdalene frowned at her, unease creeping up her spine. "But why?"

Bridgett just shook her head again, her gaze pleading.

Magdalene's throat closed up and she buried her face in her knees. Had Barry been lying about Omar looking for her? In reality, did he never want to see her again now that he'd found someone better?

Magdalene felt a hand on her arm and looked up to find Bridgett offering her a tissue, her eyes full of compassion. Magdalene gave a watery snort as she wiped away her tears. She was in Purgatory, and the tears weren't even real.

Except they were.

Her longing for Omar seared through her chest. She hated herself for it, but she wanted to see him.

Magdalene took a deep breath, prying herself loose from that longing, letting it drain out into the breeze through the willows. Bridgett sat silently beside her, comforting her with her presence.

Eventually Magdalene fell out of Purgatory and into a normal dream, out of reach of her worries.

Armando showed up on her doorstep at eight thirty the next morning. Gavin had warned her they'd be working together again but had promised the young man would be on his best behavior. When Magdalene saw the nervousness in Armando's smile, she wondered what Gavin had said to him.

She fought a headache as she slipped her shoes on and went out the door. Her desire to see Omar filled her, and she couldn't stop wondering why Bridgett didn't want her to.

"Where were you last night?" Armando asked. "You stay out late with the Boss?"

She locked her door behind her. "I just went to bed really early. Like, *really* early." She could hardly believe she'd slept as long as she did. She must have been exhausted. "Did you guys stop by?"

Armando nodded. "Since we couldn't roust you, we hung out at Peter's place, playing video games. So lame." He examined her and frowned. "You okay?"

She nodded. "Yeah, I'm fine."

His gaze lingered on her a moment longer, and he shrugged. "Look, I *am* really sorry about how I treated you—"

"Don't mention it," Magdalene cut in. "Just don't do it again."

He nodded, seeming as happy to drop the subject as she was.

They crossed the campus, went up the elevator in the office tower, and sought the shelter of the sleeper room. Armando strapped on his beeper while Magdalene simply closed her eyes and appeared in the vast empty courtyard in front of the Tower. Armando blipped into existence a few moments later and they began their trek to the gate.

As they passed the support beam, the hum sang through Magdalene's bones, calling to her. A warmth stretched out from it, clasping Magdalene's heart in teasing fingers, and voices whispered secrets on the edge of her hearing.

"Magdalene," Armando said sharply.

She blinked. She was standing in front of the beam, reaching out to touch it again. "Shit." She pulled her hand back and clutched it to her chest.

Armando looked her over worriedly. "Come on, let's keep going."

They put the beam on their left and kept walking. As its vibrations diminished behind them, sadness settled over Magdalene again.

She missed her friends. She missed Omar. It didn't make sense, but it was as if her body felt the pull of his, calling her across the dimensions and the space that separated them.

Magdalene swallowed the lump in her throat.

There was a fluttering of wings and a sparrow flitted out of the silver-grey sky and landed on her shoulder, its tiny claws poking into her skin.

Magdalene stopped, her heart hammering. The bird hopped down her arm to peer at her with a shiny black eye. Its jewel-bright plumage of red, yellow, green and purple glinted in the light, ethereal and beautiful in contrast with the barren plain. It ruffled its feathers with a papery sound and chirped softly before breaking into a liquid song.

The notes forged music out of the raw silence and struck the chords of her heartache. Her vision blurred with tears. After a moment, the bird fell silent, then fluttered away and disappeared into the silver-grey again.

"What the hell was that?" Armando breathed, watching it go.

Magdalene shook her head, hugging herself and fighting the urge to wake up in the sleeper room. Had that been a projection of Omar's mind, or her own? She was guessing her own. The plain stretched out straight and wide around them. There was no one else around.

She just couldn't get Omar off her mind.

Armando shifted on his feet, then laid a hand gently on her shoulder. "It's okay."

She dried her eyes on her sleeve. "Sorry."

He looked at his feet. For a moment, the asshole she knew fell away, and he seemed almost human. "I don't know much of your story, but I'm guessing you've been through hell. I get the impression that a bunch of bigwigs are fighting over you like you're a commodity."

Magdalene blinked.

"Come on. Let's keep going," he said.

They started walking again. Magdalene tugged at a tendril of her hair. "You were out at the Commune with Andy Clayborn, right?"

He grimaced. "Yeah, I was out there for a little while, a few years ago, back when I was a stupid little turd. It didn't end well."

She nodded. "Was Omar there yet, when you were there?"

"You mean the violent kickboxing jerk Omar who makes you cry? No, he wasn't there when I was."

"Have you seen him at the gate at all since I got here?"

He studied her, and her guts cringed away from the pity in his creepy, mismatched eyes. "Nope. I haven't seen any living people on the other side of the fence at all."

Magdalene wanted to ask him more questions, but the gate came into view and distracted her. Even from a distance it was obvious there were more people than the last time she'd been here. Her heart pounded in her ears as she scanned the area around the crowd, looking for a mess of brown curls, a teasing smirk, but he wasn't there. *If he's looking for me, he's not looking very hard.*

The guards watched her as she approached the fence, their elastic lips forming into bizarre shapes. The Dead on the other side regarded her curiously. A man with his eyelids sewn shut lifted the hem of his wifebeater to reveal an eyeball in his navel, which peered at Magdalene intelligently. Another man kept sucking his blue lips so far in that his face collapsed into itself, leaving him pinheaded with jutting ears and bulging eyes.

She couldn't see Barry anywhere, but spotted a familiar, boyish face pushing toward her through the crowd. Kate broke through and hobbled up to meet Magdalene at the fence, grinning. "You came back."

"Of course. I spoke to Mr. Cavanaugh about you—he's the man who built the Tower."

Kate frowned and there was an outbreak of agitated muttering in the crowd.

Magdalene tensed, eyeing them. "He's built a program to regulate who gets through the portal based on how good of a person you are. It's not working correctly yet, but he's promised to fix it soon."

"What do you mean by that?" Kate asked. "The portal is calling me. It needs me. It obviously thinks I'm a good enough person to enter. How can this Mr. Cavanaugh stop me from going?"

Magdalene chewed the inside of her cheek. Would the portal still call to someone who didn't deserve to be called after Gavin's program was fully functional? Would they be stuck here, unable to leave, but unable to pass through? "What does it feel like, to be called by the portal?"

Kate's eyes shone. "It feels good. Like everything is going to be all right, and like everything will make sense soon." She stared longingly at the darkness behind Magdalene. "I need to go," she said, her voice almost a moan.

Magdalene nodded, her jaw tight. "I'll do everything I can."

But she didn't even know what that meant. What would she do if Gavin's system ended up denying Kate entrance to the portal? She sighed. "I'm sorry for what you're going through."

A wisp of smile flitted across Kate's face. "Thank you for helping us."

The ache in Magdalene's heart eased a little. It felt good to be able to do something for someone like Kate. But how would she feel if she ultimately couldn't get the woman through?

Maybe you could give Gavin a taste of his own medicine and make him want to open the portal to her.

But she didn't have that sort of power yet. And even if she did convince him to let Kate through, how many others would be stuck here?

Magdalene endured more stares from the other employees as she made her way to Gavin's office. The gossip seemed to be getting worse, not better, and she had an urge to stop in the middle of the hallway and scream *I'm not fucking him.*

Though she supposed that probably wouldn't help matters much.

Gavin's door was closed, but he answered her knock. "Good morning, Miss Richards."

Magdalene's shoulders relaxed and she smiled.

He stepped out into the hallway with her. "I want to show you my lab." They started down the hallway. Everyone looked like they were hard at work and ignoring them, but she could sense the eyes on her back after they passed. She and Gavin exchanged an amused look. "Ignore them, ," he said. "Great and powerful people are always objects of gossip. You'll get used to it."

Magdalene frowned, but didn't say anything.

Gavin took her to the same wing where the sleeper rooms were located. The guards at the security checkpoint waved them through with smiles. Gavin went to the very end of the hall and keyed a six-digit code into a keypad and swiped his keycard.

The door clicked open, and he held it so she could enter.

They stepped into a long, windowless room cluttered with instruments and machines. Gavin waved toward a corner where, between a lab bench and a heap of wires, a huge, molded plastic box the size of a refrigerator stood. It had buttons and a dark screen on one side.

"You're already familiar with the waveform signature reader, which we just passed through," Gavin said. "The WSR detects each person's unique resonance signal. However, the type at the security checkpoint only works on living people. This, on the other hand," he patted the plastic box, "is a WSR for the Departed. When fully functional, its counterpart in the other world will be able to accurately analyze the signals of all those wishing to pass through the portals, even those who have been dead for some time."

Magdalene ran her fingers along the smooth side of the machine. For a hunk of plastic, it was beautiful. "How long will it take you to finish it?"

"If I'm lucky, a week or so."

Magdalene nodded. A week wasn't too long. She'd talk to Kate. Hopefully she wouldn't be too frustrated about the delay. "How did you capture *my* signal?" Magdalene asked. "When I passed through the WSR the first time to go to work, they already had it."

"I was able to program you into our system manually."

Magdalene raised her eyebrows. "What does that mean?"

He shrugged. "I can see the signals that people give off. I have to study a person quite comprehensively in order to grasp the subtle nuances—it's generally much easier to just let the machine do it—but in your case I didn't have much difficulty. I know you and your signature quite well."

"You can see…"

He leaned back on the bench, crossing his arms. "Yes. It's a very efficient way to know people."

Magdalene plucked at a button on her sleeve. It had been unnerving to know he could read her thoughts, but this was a whole new level. He could see her *soul?* "What does that look like?"

"It's a pattern that makes up the fabric of a person. Since I've never seen people any other way, it's hard for me to know how it's different from what other people see, and hard to describe. I was seven years old before I discovered that how I perceive the world is unique."

Magdalene squinted at him. "I don't see people that way. At least I don't think so. So, I don't have the same powers you do."

"Perhaps not, but it doesn't seem to hinder you." He smiled, then straightened. "I have another of my projects to show you."

They took the elevator to the lobby and he led her out into the blazing sun, through the park, and to the residential buildings. They entered one of the complexes and took the elevator to the top floor.

There was only one door off the hallway, and Gavin opened it, letting her into a condo even nicer than hers, with wood floors, dark blue walls, and antique furniture.

"Is this yours?" she asked.

"Yes, this is my residence while I'm here. And I've been here most of the time lately, due to the amount of work involved in launching this project." He led her up a set of stairs. "I've been developing an easier and more elegant way of entering our headquarters in the other world." They took a door off the landing into a room filled by a large worktable littered with wires and gages and gadgets. "The transition is rather rough on some people, as you might imagine. Please, sit." He gestured to a pair of recliners against the wall, similar to the the ones in the sleeper rooms.

Magdalene sank into the soft cushions and propped her feet up. Gavin fiddled with a small tablet computer, then brought it over with him and sat in the other chair. He watched the screen, a slight furrow between his brows. "Would you like to go see your friend Morris?"

She nodded.

Gavin pressed a button on the device.

Magdalene gasped as the room around her disappeared into darkness. She felt a tug, as if her body were caught in an undertow, then the world came back into existence around her.

She sat clutching the arms of a chair identical to the one in Gavin's house. The room, however, was much different, with walls of white plaster and a Persian rug on a floor of black marble. Gavin sat beside her, watching her with his sharp gaze.

Magdalene took a steadying breath. "Are we in the Tower?"

Gavin nodded. "You feeling all right?"

"I'm fine. I just wasn't expecting that."

He grinned, shaking his head. "I'm working at making the entrance smoother. Everyone, myself included, loses consciousness the first few times. But not you, of course." He stood. "Let's go find your friend."

They went down a hallway into another elegant room, where they found Morris sitting on a loveseat, gazing out a window at the jumbled landscape of Purgatory far below. He glanced up as they came in. "Hi, Little One," he mumbled. Then his gaze wandered back out the window.

Magdalene sat down beside him on the loveseat and Gavin settled into a club chair. "How are you?" Magdalene asked.

"I'm good, I guess. Better now that you're here." He smiled. The ghost of his old twinkle was in his eyes, but he seemed distracted.

Down below on the wide plain, the strange city of the Dead writhed and morphed. "The view is different up here than it was in your field," she said.

"It's different here, but I felt it was time to move on." His brow furrowed, but he smiled at her again as Magdalene took his hand. His palms were as rough and solid as they'd been when he was alive, though without warmth.

"I miss you, Morris," she said, and her friend squeezed her hand and caught her eye. He looked worried for a moment, as if he was trying to think of a way to tell her something, but then he just smiled again.

"It's going to be okay, Little One. It's going to be better than ever, I promise."

A lump rose in Magdalene's throat. "What do you mean?"

Morris tugged at his beard and gazed back out the window, as if he hadn't heard her.

A trickle of unease crept through her. Then the feeling exploded within her and Magdalene was seized by the sudden desire to leave. She blinked, trying to get her breathing under control, but it was no use. She squeezed Morris' hand. "I'll come back later. I love you."

Morris nodded and glanced at her. There was a flash of something deep in his gaze. Something that looked like a warning. Then she opened her eyes back in Gavin's house.

Dizziness washed over her, her heart pounding, every beat like a command. *Run. Run. Run.* Magdalene dug her fingernails into the chair arms, gasping for air. What the fuck was happening to her? She sat pinned under the weight of her terror, unable to move.

Slowly, her heart settled into its normal rhythm and the feeling lifted. *Maybe it's just the transition, or something to do with being in the Tower.* She shook her head to clear it.

Gavin opened his eyes and sat up. "Are you all right, darling?"

"What was wrong with Morris?" Her voice was still shaky.

He studied her for a long moment. Magdalene could feel his pity and guessed the reason for it the moment before the words left his mouth. "He's thinking about going through the portal into the next life."

"No!" Her chest tightened. "No." Her eyes smarted and she pressed the heels of her hands into them.

"Don't cry, Magdalene," Gavin said softly. "I know it's horrible to lose the ones we love but think of the wonders that await him on the other side."

She shook her head frantically and glared at him through her tears. "How do you know what's through the portal? There could be nothingness, or something horrible."

Gavin nodded, frowning. "All I have is my faith, which is enough for me. I know that's useless to you, though, and I wish I had something of substance to show you."

"Have you ever gotten close to a portal? Because I have, and it sucks. It doesn't feel like heaven."

He nodded. "My work has brought me very close to the passages near the Tower. I agree, it's not that pleasant. It seems, however, that it's only terrifying to those not prepared to enter. And I'm not prepared. If I were to die today, Magdalene, I don't believe my own program would allow me entry." He twisted the ring on his pinky. "I haven't completed my work or atoned for my past sins. I'm not worthy of entry into Heaven. That's why the experience of going near a passage is uncomfortable for me. For you, it's merely your age and your fear of death that make you feel that way. You have so much more to do before your time, so the portal warns you away."

Magdalene hugged herself, every muscle in her body tensed against the grief that lashed at her. "How do you even know that Morris wants to go through the portal? Maybe it's something else."

Gavin shook his head. "People look different when they're preparing to enter the next life."

Magdalene frowned. "Their pattern changes, their signal, or whatever you call it?"

He nodded.

Magdalene squeezed her eyes closed. She heard Gavin get up and felt him approach her. She opened her eyes to see him kneeling by her chair, his gaze sad.

"Why does everyone leave?" Her voice broke and her chest felt like it would burst.

Gavin reached out and took her hand. His palm was rough and calloused against hers and his presence soaked into her, his thoughts and feelings like a raft bearing her up. Another spasmodic breath filled her tight lungs.

"I'm so sorry," he said.

And suddenly, Magdalene couldn't hold the dam any longer. The pain roared through in a deluge, crumbling it to gravel. Gavin pulled her into his arms, and Magdalene crumpled to the floor and curled up in his embrace, sobbing. The feelings buffeted her from all sides. Her grief from losing Morris, and now losing him again. Her anger at Omar, at Stan, at her mom. But Gavin's presence was like a grounding wire. He took those feelings into himself and let them flow out into the earth. His mind was there with hers, and she could see his life laid bare before her, what he'd been through, the grief he'd endured. He'd spent his life intimately aware of what everyone around him was thinking and feeling, and yet he'd been alone. How can you be close to anyone when you know them better than they know themselves, and when you're forever affecting their emotions just by your presence?

Had his wife truly loved him of her own free will, or only because Gavin had wanted her to? She'd died without him ever knowing the answer to that question. Magdalene saw it and felt his grief and guilt as if it were her own.

Instead of making her own burden heavier, though, it seemed to lighten it.

She wasn't alone.

Eventually, the floodwaters of pain subsided, but Magdalene stayed where she was, her cheek pressed against Gavin's chest, listening to the steady beat of his heart and feeling the rise and fall of his breathing. Morris had never held her like this, nor had her grandmother. Magdalene had always been strong so that they didn't have to comfort her. They'd had enough to deal with without her causing more drama. But there were no secrets between her and Gavin, no lies, no subterfuge, and no need to be strong. Their minds were one.

And that, she saw, was why Gavin really wanted her there, why he'd gone to so much trouble to find her. She was the only one who was his equal, who could know him as well as he knew her.

Magdalene sat up, wiping her eyes, and they looked at one another, a universe of understanding passing between them in a moment.

"How did you find me?" Magdalene asked. "How did you even know I existed?"

Gavin smiled. "I sensed you. I knew you were out there somewhere, and I couldn't rest until I found you."

Magdalene knew it wasn't the whole story. She felt a secret lurking in the depths of his mind, just out of reach. But she didn't push him. He'd tell her eventually.

"Will the computer program let Morris through?" she asked. "Does he qualify?"

Gavin's smile faded. "If you wish it."

Those words settled around Magdalene's shoulders like a slack noose, waiting to be tightened. She knew exactly what they meant, and how deep that meaning went.

CHAPTER SIXTEEN
Love is Blinding

Magdalene lay curled on her couch, staring at her blank TV screen. She hadn't bothered to turn it on and the remote lay forgotten in her hand.

Did Morris really feel the pull of the portal the way Kate did? Magdalene remembered the longing in the woman's face as she'd gazed into the dark cloud. Morris couldn't feel it that strongly—if he did, he would have left the Tower, right?

Maybe the pull would get stronger. And what would Magdalene do if it did?

She sighed, pressing her face into the cushions. She knew Morris had done some sketchy things. He'd been a drug runner most of his life. But he'd been so kind to her, always doing his best to make her feel loved and cared for. And in the end, he'd sacrificed himself to save her and give her a good life. How many people would do something like that?

Morris had been born into poverty, with parents a lot like Magdalene's. He'd never had much of a chance to be anything other than what he was. Despite that, he'd been a good person, with so much more heart and courage than most. Some people's easy, banal lives were laid out before them like a red carpet. All they had to do was put one foot in front of the other. They didn't need to have courage in order to be good people. They didn't have to work at it. A good life just *happened* to them. Morris had done what he needed to do in order to survive. How could that make him a bad person?

If he wanted to go through the portal, it would be injustice to hold him back.

Magdalene wanted to know whether Gavin's program would deny him. But she knew what his answer had meant, when she'd asked whether Morris would qualify for passage. The decision wasn't up to the program, it was up to *her*.

Magdalene flopped over onto her back and stared up at her vaulted ceiling. It wasn't fair to leave that decision up to her. How could she possibly decide to let her friend walk into that dead darkness, into the unknown?

But how could she possibly hold him back if he was being called?

Sighing, she heaved herself up. She needed something to do to keep her mind off things.

Her feet took her into the kitchen. Throwing open cupboards and rummaging through the contents, she found an assortment of brand-new springform cake pans. Lynn made the best yellow cake in the world and had taught her the recipe.

It was almost three in the afternoon and Lynn would be starting dinner soon. Would Ingrid be helping her?

Magdalene ignored the squeezing of her heart and started searching for baking powder.

The cake layers were cooling on the counter and Magdalene was whipping up cream cheese frosting when there was a knock at the door.

She opened it to find Armando, Suzette and Peter smiling at her. She stood aside and let them in.

"It smells amazing in here," Armando said. "Are you baking something?"

Suzette had come with two bottles of wine this time, and Peter had a large paper bag full of Chinese takeout. As he passed Magdalene, he paused to wipe something off her nose with a fingertip. "I *hope* you're baking something. Otherwise, that was cocaine."

Magdalene's cheeks burned. "Probably flour. I'm baking a cake, and I didn't put any cocaine in there."

"But cocaine cake's my favorite," Suzette complained.

"You know how to bake *cake*?" Armando stood in the kitchen, staring at the three round pans. "Magdalene, you are the most awesome person I know."

"It's just cake," Magdalene said.

"Yeah, but who makes homemade cake?" Peter said. He smiled at her, and Magdalene couldn't stop herself smiling back. He really did have a cute smile.

Suzette caught Magdalene's eye and gave her a stern look. When the other two had their backs turned, laying out the takeout cartons on the kitchen island, Suzette whispered, *Knock it off, jailbait.*

Magdalene's smile faded. Suzette was right. It wasn't fair to lead Peter on, and not just because of her age. Her heart felt like it had been left in the middle of the freeway during rush hour, flattened into grisly jerky. Another relationship was not what she needed right now.

Suzette poured three glasses of wine, and they all loaded up on food and sat in the living room.

"Did you hear about the plague in Salt Lake?" Armando asked as he slurped up noodles. Suzette and Peter nodded grimly, but Magdalene shook her head, frowning, her mouth full of egg fu young.

"Five people have died so far, about fifty people in the hospital," Suzette said, frowning at her glass of wine. "It's kind of freaky, actually. It started so suddenly and is spreading so fast."

A chill ran down Magdalene's spine. "How far is Salt Lake from here?"

"About five hours," Suzette said.

"They have them quarantined, it'll be fine," Armando said. "We're in no danger here."

"I hope not," Suzette murmured.

There was a heavy silence until Peter cleared his throat. "Speaking of fun subjects, they have me working on the team designing a new dating website. It's weird."

Magdalene exchanged a confused glance with Armando and Suzette. "A dating website?" How exactly did *that* align with Gavin's goals?

Peter chuckled. "Yeah. I don't know, man. The code is really interesting, don't get me wrong. It's just that they're gathering a *scary* amount of information from people. And the questions they want to ask the users..." He shook his head. "I wouldn't join the thing."

Unease threaded through Magdalene's nerves. Data collection. *That's* how it aligned with Gavin's goals.

"You'll need join it when Magdalene never calls you," Armando said, taking a bite of Mongolian beef.

Peter glanced at Magdalene. It was hard to tell with his skin tone, but it looked like he was blushing. "Don't hate, Armando," he said.

Magdalene's food was only half-eaten, but she jumped to her feet, ignoring Suzette's pointed look. "I'm going to go frost the cake."

"Now look what you did, Armando," Suzette complained. "You chased her off. Don't take any crap from him, Magdalene. Just get your whip out again."

Magdalene shot her a glare over her shoulder. Suzette smiled sweetly, sipping her wine.

It was almost ten o'clock by the time the three of them said goodnight and left, each of them taking a second piece of cake for the road (a third, in Peter's case). Magdalene cleaned up the kitchen, rinsing the expensive-looking china and placing it in the gleaming dishwasher, then wiping crumbs off her flawless countertops.

She was such an *adult*. It was weird.

As she nestled into bed, the silence of the apartment pressed in. Magdalene stared up at the dark ceiling, emptiness blooming inside her. How long would it take her to get over Omar? How long would it take before she forgot about Lynn?

If I could just see Omar one more time...

Magdalene huffed to herself. What would the point be? Bridgett was right not to let her see him. All it would do is make her feel worse.

Bridgett was waiting for her, sitting cross-legged in the fragrant grass next to the willows. Magdalene wondered if she was standing guard, keeping her from Omar the way she had when he was in a coma and fighting Stan in Purgatory.

Magdalene stretched out next to her in the grass and they sat in silence together, contemplating the distant mountains. Magdalene wondered if she could walk there, if this world that Bridgett had created was that complete and detailed.

Her heart ached. What if she just walked into those hills and never came back? She could leave her body to rot in Gavin's fancy condo and stay in Purgatory, wandering through fields of alpine flowers for all eternity. She was so tired. Tired of being thrown around from one stressful situation to another, tired of making friends and losing them, tired of the hurt the universe kept dishing out.

Footsteps sounded in the grass behind them. Bridgett turned, and her eyes sparked fire.

Magdalene's breath stopped. Omar was on the edge of the field, striding quickly toward them. The wind blew in his dark curls and his deep eyes were fixed on her with an intensity that made her pulse race.

Magdalene jumped to her feet, feelings pushing at one another in their race to her heart. She'd missed him so much. She wanted to punch him. She wanted to run into his arms. She wanted to run away.

As if he'd heard this last thought, Omar stopped, holding a hand up in entreaty. "Magdalene, please don't leave. Please listen." Blue glints danced in his hair, a halo of his power all around him, even more of a godlike creature than the last time she'd seen him in Purgatory. The sight of him left her breathless and awestruck.

Bridgett leapt up, her gaze hard. She made a swiping motion and a shimmering curtain fell between them an Omar.

Omar pressed a hand against it. He glared at Bridgett and his mouth opened in a yell, but no sound reached them. He thrust out a hand and a blast of blue fire flowed from his fingertips and exploded silently against the barrier. Curls of flame billowed out and dissipated, leaving the barrier unharmed.

Magdalene stepped toward him, her heart in her throat. All her doubts about him evaporated, replaced by a longing so powerful it felt like it would split her in two. "Bridgett, please. Please."

Omar turned his gaze back to Magdalene and held it, his eyes glinting like black ice. *We've been tricked*, he mouthed. *Magdalene, I love you.*

Bridgett whirled on Magdalene, making another violent swiping motion, and Magdalene woke up with a gasp in bed.

Her heart pounded in her ears. For the first time in days, she allowed the scene of Omar kissing Ingrid to unfurl in her head, and she cursed, pounding the mattress with her fists.

How had she missed it? She'd been too upset perhaps, or too convinced deep in her heart that someone like Omar could never love her. Maybe that's why she'd never realized that, in that vision, Omar had looked like Omar in the Waking World. Plain, human Omar, with his brown curls and teasing smile. Not the figure of dark, godlike power, wreathed in the electricity of his magic, that he was in Purgatory.

We've been tricked.

A knot of fear formed in her stomach.

CHAPTER SEVENTEEN
If Your World Falls Apart

There was a knock on Magdalene's door at eight thirty the next morning and she opened it to find Armando smiling lopsidedly. "Good morning, chief. You ready to do the rounds?"

Magdalene nodded. Her head and heart pounded as she stepped out and locked the door behind her.

As they crossed the park toward the office tower, Magdalene squinted against the sun. After seeing Omar in Purgatory, she'd lain awake the rest of the night, wondering what the hell she was going to do.

We've been tricked. She'd been over and over it in her head, and she didn't know how it had been done, or why, but she knew Omar was right.

Had it been Gavin? She flung that idea away. Gavin didn't have any power in Purgatory. All he had was his gadgets and his genius. How could he possibly have created an illusion that elaborate and convincing? Besides, she'd been in his head. She would've sensed some trace of a lie that big lurking in the shadows of his thoughts.

Had it been Ingrid? She'd said she was a lucid dreamer. Did she have power like that? Maybe she'd just wanted to get Magdalene out of the way so she could have Omar to herself.

"Are you okay?" Armando asked.

Magdalene emerged from her thoughts and tried to smile. "I'm fine. Just didn't sleep well."

"Ah." Armando grimaced. "I hate it when that happens."

Magdalene chewed on the inside of her cheek. She wanted to ask Armando for his phone to call the Commune, but she stopped herself. She didn't know what was going on yet. If she tipped off whoever was behind this that she knew about the lie, would they do something else to keep her from Omar? If it was Gavin...

He wouldn't trick me. He wouldn't do that.

Distant thunder rumbled. Dark clouds were amassing eastward by the gap leading to Lake Mead. "Wonder if we'll finally get rain," Armando muttered.

They entered the office tower and waved to the smiling receptionist before getting in the elevator. As they headed up, Armando frowned. "Reports are that stuff is getting pretty crazy again at the Pearly Gates. We'll have backup today."

A new wave of dread washed over her, temporarily crowding out her other worries.

They were silent as they passed through security. When they entered the sleeper room, Armando took his beeper out of the cabinet, along with a pair of steel batons with buttons along the sides. He handed one to Magdalene. "Press this button before you enter the Land of the Dead," he said, indicating the largest one. "I'll show you how to operate it once we're there."

She perched on one of the chairs, frowning at the thing. "What is it?" It was seamless and smooth, and it felt good in her hand. Gavin must have made it; it had the characteristic elegance of the things he designed.

"That's the shocker," Armando said.

Magdalene dropped the device as if it were about to vomit on her slacks. It tumbled onto the carpet and rolled toward Armando. "No way. No. I'm not doing any *crowd control*."

Armando studied her, a furrow between his brows. "It doesn't hurt them, it just scares them off and keeps them from mobbing us."

Magdalene swiped a tendril of hair from her face so she could glare at him more efficiently. "How do you know it doesn't hurt them? And why are you scared of the Dead, anyway? They can't do anything to you. They're only spirits and your body isn't even in their world."

Armando winced. "I don't want to think about what they could do to your soul, even if your body is left intact here in the real world."

Magdalene pushed that thought away and shook her head. "Gavin asked me to be an ambassador, not a member of his goon squad."

Armando gave her a long look, then picked up the dropped shocker and hooked it onto his own belt. "You know how to take care of yourself, I guess. And if worse comes to worse, I won't let them hurt you." He settled down on his chair and clipped his beeper to his pants. "Who knows. Maybe if I save your soul from being torn apart by those goblins, you'll let me take you to dinner tonight."

Magdalene stretched out on her own seat. "You're such a dingus."

She closed her eyes.

The landscape of Purgatory melted into focus behind her eyelids: the wide, empty plain with the Tower in the middle like a dark pillar holding up the silvery sky. The silence and stillness fell over her suddenly. She'd almost gotten used to the desolation around the Tower, but today it made her uneasy.

Armando blipped into existence beside her and they started toward the gate.

"Please don't go running off to talk to the Departed today like you usually do, at least," Armando said. "I don't want to risk you getting hurt."

Magdalene scowled. "They won't hurt me."

"You don't know that." Armando scrubbed his face with his hand. "Besides how bad I'd feel if something happened to you, just think of what the Boss would do to me. He'd probably chain me up in his dungeon and have his minions roast my nuts with torches."

Magdalene shrugged.

They walked a few steps in silence and Armando sent her uncertain glances. "The Boss is, like, in love with you, Magdalene."

Her pulse stumbled, and she crossed her arms. "Would you please shut up? You don't know shit."

"I've seen the way he looks at you, heard how he talks to you. It's all over the company. People barely talk about anything else."

"Don't you guys have anything better to do than talk about us? You know, like work or something?"

Armando laughed. "Do we have anything better to do than talk about a reclusive billionaire genius in love with a drop-dead gorgeous girl almost half his age? Of course not. Tea doesn't get hotter than that."

Magdalene whirled on him, her face burning. "How many times do I have to tell you to *stop*?" Her heart pounded, her lungs constricted. "I'm not even half his age, all right? I'm fucking sixteen, and Gavin knows that. He's like...he's like my dad." She swallowed.

A flurry of emotions chased one another across Armando's face, and he turned visibly green. "You're sixteen?"

She huffed. "You should actually know that. Didn't you try to frigging abduct me after I escaped from juvie?"

His Adam's apple bobbed as he swallowed. "I didn't know it was juvie! It's not like I've ever been there. I thought it was regular jail." He winced.

Magdalene started walking again. Armando followed suit, matching her pace with long strides.

"I thought you were at least twenty-one," he said weakly.

Magdalene stared straight ahead, her jaw tight.

"That's why Suzette won't give you drinks?"

Magdalene just sniffed.

Armando studied her out of the corner of his eyes. "I'm sorry, but that actually just makes it creepier."

Magdalene turned on him again and jabbed her index finger into his chest. A spark flew from the impact point, and Armando stumbled back, his eyes wide. "Gavin isn't a creep," Magdalene hissed. "He's never been like that with me. Believe me, I know what it's like when older men..." She winced, then continued walking, Armando trailing after. "He's not like that."

The support beam loomed beside them, and its light and warmth flowed over Magdalene like a caress, a whispered promise of joy and peace. She was so tired. The knots in her shoulders ached and her unease had curdled in her stomach. She didn't know who to trust. She didn't know what was real.

Magdalene realized her footsteps had slowed. The light swirled around her nerves and tugged at her, its hum singing in her bones. *You don't have to carry those burdens any longer*, it said. *Your worries are an illusion. I'm the only thing that's real.*

Magdalene gathered her hands into fists and forced herself to keep walking. As the beam's music faded and its grasping tendrils released her, she felt emptier and more confused than ever.

"I'm sorry," Armando muttered. "I'm not trying to make you mad, Magdalene. Just make sure you're safe, okay? Suzie, Peter and I—we're here for you if you need us."

Magdalene nodded. "Thanks, Armando. That means a lot."

They crested a small rise, and the gate came into view.

Magdalene's breath stopped. The crowd was huge, and the racket of it washed over her. It was like the sound of a vast flock of animals, honking and roaring and trumpeting.

She and Armando exchanged a glance. "I've never seen it like this," Armando said, "and I've seen it bad."

They quickened their pace, the din growing louder as they approached. The guards stood motionless in their places, like always, as if they weren't aware of the commotion. There were two other living people inside the gate, a man and a woman, both of them with shockers on their belts. Their expressions were grim, their right eyes glowing blue.

"Armando, thank fuck you're here," the woman said as he and Magdalene jogged up. She was tiny and young-looking, with thin lips and a boyish haircut. The man stood next to her, tall with shoulder-length brown hair and a cropped beard.

"Magdalene, this is Joy and Irving," Armando said.

Irving smiled. Joy nodded, giving Magdalene only the briefest of glances.

Armando frowned at the crowd. "I heard we were having trouble, but we didn't know it was this bad or we would have come earlier."

A roar went up and the Dead surged forward, pushing and clawing at the chain link. The fence held steady, and the crowd broke against it like an ocean wave. Magdalene could barely distinguish one creature from another, it was just a solid, tumbling, boiling mass of strange beings, stretching so far back that she couldn't see where it ended.

Where had they all come from and why were they here? Surely all these people couldn't feel the call of the portal?

"We've had to use the shockers a couple of times," Irving said, and Magdalene tore her eyes from the fence to glare at him. "But they just keep coming. There's a huge guy that I've never seen before. It seems like he's their leader or something. He keeps bringing them back when we scatter them."

Magdalene's scalp tingled, and she stood on her tiptoes, scanning the crowd. *The Chieftain.* It must be. That's why there were so many people.

The Dead were standing up for themselves.

"Maybe if we all activated our weapons at once, it would have more effect," Joy said, skimming the crowd with an emotionless gaze.

"No." Magdalene fixed Joy with a hard look. "Let me talk to them."

She marched toward the fence. "Magdalene, no!" Armando yelled, but she ignored him.

The roar of the crowd filled her skull. As she got closer, she spotted Barry smooshed between the fence and a man in a teal bodysuit who had a rooster comb flopping around his head. A herd of tiny rhinoceroses wriggled around their feet. Another man near Barry had his lower half suspended in a clear bubble, his naked legs dangling inside. Magdalene wondered how he got around.

Another roar rose from the crowd. Magdalene looked out at the sea of faces, all of them screaming or hooting, distorted with emotion. They surged forward again, and the fence shook with their weight. But, when the wave retreated, it still held.

For all her bravado, a chill of fear slipped down Magdalene's spine. It was more overwhelming than she'd expected. But she wasn't about to lose face in front of Armando. Taking a deep breath, she headed toward Barry.

Barry spotted her and grinned. His lips moved, but she couldn't hear him above the noise. As Magdalene got closer, a hundred appendages slithered through the chain link, reaching for her. Magdalene's heart rose into her throat, remembering Armando's words: *I don't want to think about what they could do to your soul.* She was on the enemy side of the fence. Would they see her as a threat?

But then Barry thrust his hand through the fence, grinning, and Magdalene took heart. She straightened her shoulders and closed the gap, clutching Barry's hand in greeting. Other arms and tentacles and trunks found her, caressing her limbs, sniffing around her ears, petting her head. Magdalene made herself stand fast, fighting the urge to pull away. It was unnerving, but it didn't hurt. No one seemed aggressive.

"You came to help us!" Barry said. A short man, his belly hanging ponderously over a white loincloth, honked like a foghorn. Barry gave him a snide look, and he quieted, smacking his lips together with a wet splat. Barry turned to the rooster-comb man next to him. "Hey, Magdalene's here!" The rooster man blinked at Magdalene and made a perfect "o" with his lips. His mouth stretched toward her like a fleshy tube, his black eyes glittering.

"I saw Omar last night, and I told him that the slimepiles behind the fence have you," Barry said, grinning. "He'll show them a good time now!"

Magdalene's heart skipped, then stumbled. Had Omar not known where she was before? An odd feeling crept into her stomach. What would he think of her, that she'd run off with the man behind the Tower? Her guts tangled up into a mess of knots. *We've been tricked*. But by who, and why? And what was she going to do about it? Was she going to leave Gavin? Gavin and Omar each thought the other was dangerous, but that's because they didn't know one another. Was there any way to get them to work together?

Magdalene pushed those thoughts away. She didn't have time to think about it right now.

Barry leaned even closer until his lips smashed up against the chain link. "The Chieftain's here. He came! We're going to get this fence down!"

"Yeah, I heard," Magdalene said. "Barry, have the people on this side been hurting you? Do their weapons hurt when they use them?"

His smile faded and he mumbled something she couldn't hear. She leaned closer, pressing her ear to the fence. "What?"

"It's horrible," he said, his mouth tickling her ear. "It's like your brain is wiped clean and all you can think of is getting out of there. I always recover, but some of the more floppy-minded people, it sends them gibbering off, and I don't know if they get better."

Nausea gripped her stomach.

A voice rose above the crowd. "Magdalene, get away from there!"

She turned to find Armando beckoning to her. Joy stood beside him, watching Magdalene with her dead-eyed stare. Irving shifted on his feet and watched the fence warily.

Magdalene shook her head sharply and turned back to Barry. A familiar face caught her eye behind him as Jeffrey shouldered his way through the crowd toward her. His robe had come untied, and Magdalene could see the undershirt, boxers, and knobby old man knees beneath. He nudged aside the rooster man and took his place, a slow grin spreading over his face as he gazed at her. "Here's the star of this shit show."

Barry looked askance at him, wrinkling his nose.

"Listen," Magdalene said. "You've got to stop this before they hurt you." She gently brushed away a tentacle that was trying to get down her shirt.

Barry raised his eyebrows. "We're not stopping nothing, girl. Not until they take this fence down."

"We've squawked our grumbling remonstrances, but their ear-tubes are writhing with maggots and stale toast and half-chewed and dusty nuggets of beef, their minds are composting under the weight of their personal trash," Jeffrey added.

Barry cocked an eyebrow. "Exactly."

A grin rose to Magdalene's face despite her sadness and confusion. She glanced back to make sure Armando and the others were still out of earshot before leaning as close as possible to Barry and Jeffrey and suffering a renewed assault of caresses. "We'll fix the problems with the gate somehow. If we can't, then I'll be back on your side soon to help you fight. But for now, you've got to call off the riot. They've got weapons. *Please.* I don't want anyone else hurt."

Jeffrey's face twisted in an odd scowl, his chin disappearing.

Barry frowned. "You really want to stop this party, Magdalene?"

She nodded desperately. "There has to be a better way than this."

Barry looked around at the crowd. "I can't tell these people what to do. You can try talking to the Chieftain, though."

"Where is he?" Magdalene asked.

Barry held up a finger to tell her to wait before melting into the fleshy mass of the Dead as if he'd been swallowed whole. Armando yelled Magdalene's name again, and she whirled. "Wait a minute! I'm talking to them!"

Something grasped Magdalene's arm and she squeaked in surprise as she was jerked toward the fence. A blue hand clutched her bicep, pink fingernails digging into her flesh, and a strange sensation crawled through her arm. Armando stepped toward her, but Magdalene shook her head. "Stay back."

The hand clutching her belonged to a blue, gumdrop-shaped blob with a mass of blinking eyes piled atop its head. Magdalene gently pried the fingers loose, sighing with relief when the creature let her go and drew its arm back inside the fence. She took a few steps back and glanced over her shoulder. Joy was scowling and tapping her shocker against her open palm. She said something to Armando, but Magdalene couldn't hear her over the racket. Armando responded, his brow furrowed in anger, and Joy rolled her eyes at him. *They're not going to wait long,* Magdalene thought with a prickle of fear.

She turned back to the fence in time to see the front lines of the crowd part and disgorge a startlingly large man. A tangled mass of brown hair spilled over his bare, muscled torso and his pillar-like legs were encased in leather breeches. The roar of the crowd diminished, then fell into a hush.

Magdalene knew this was the Chieftain. His whole being radiated power like a glowing stove. He stood gazing impassively at Magdalene through the fence. Barry emerged from the crowd to stand at his side, grinning. The peak of his bobbing hair barely reached the huge man's shoulder.

The Chieftain's lips curved in a half smile. There was something odd about his eyes— they were in constant flux. Magdalene couldn't say what color they were, only that they were all colors at once. They reminded her of someone she knew but couldn't quite remember.

Armando's yell split the sudden quiet. "Joy, stop!"

Magdalene turned. Joy was glaring at the Chieftain, her shocker in her hand. Armando tried to grab her arm, but Joy sidestepped him and raised her weapon.

Armando turned panicked eyes to Magdalene. "Move! Get out of the way, now!"

Joy pushed a button on the side of her device and a loop of light appeared at the head of it. Magdalene thought bemusedly that it looked like a luminous ping-pong paddle. Armando made another grab for Joy's arm, yelling again for her stop, but Joy dodged him once more. The crowd began to murmur.

Magdalene's pulse raced, but she crossed her arms and stood firm, shielding the Chieftain from Joy's weapon. The crowd noise grew louder, and hands and tentacles began to caress her again.

Joy, her mouth twisted in a bitter sneer, brought the shocker down in a sharp arc.

There was a flash of red light. It spread out and swelled into a translucent shock wave that rolled toward Magdalene, bending the light around it. Armando bellowed a warning.

Hot fury spiked through Magdalene, and power surged up from the ground into her body, blazing through her. The shock wave from Joy's device approached as if in slow motion, and Magdalene welcomed it, she wanted it, she let it wash into her. It couldn't hurt her, and it couldn't pass through to her friends. She was shielding them. She was their protector.

Magdalene's lips curved in a triumphant smile. Joy was about to burn in her own fire. She raised her arm, letting the force gather in her fist, then she thrust it toward Joy with a yell. Power exploded from her in a burst of white light. Joy's scowl melted into terror as it hit her, lifting her off her feet and throwing her back. She hit the ground with a sickening thump and lay spread-eagled and motionless, her weapon falling from her limp fingers, its glowing head singeing the earth around it.

Magdalene gasped. The power flowed back out of her, leaving her empty and weak.

The Dead erupted in a roar of triumph. "Avenging angel!" Jeffery yelled. "Beautiful and terrible!"

Stan's face filled Magdalene's mind. She saw Omar's lightning bolt hit him, saw Stan's eyes go blank, saw him fall to the ground.

Irving ran to Joy's side while Armando stood, gaping at Magdalene.

Magdalene swallowed, feeling nauseous. She glanced behind her. The crowd was roiling with a million bobbing heads and grappling arms, legs, wings, tentacles and feelers. Barry was screaming and jumping up and down, Jeffrey was laughing out loud, his face thrust skyward.

The Chieftain's strange gaze was fixed on Magdalene, and he gave her an approving nod.

Magdalene didn't feel triumphant. She felt small and weak and terrified. She forced her feet to move, to run to Joy's side.

Irving glanced up as she approached, and Magdalene could see the glint of fear in his eyes. Joy's eyes were closed, her body limp. Magdalene shuddered as the vision of Stan's dead face flashed through her mind again. "Is she okay?"

Irving's adam's apple bobbed, but he didn't answer. Magdalene fell to her knees and took Joy's hand. Could someone die in

Purgatory? She shook her head frantically to dislodge that idea. "Get her back home. She might need a doctor."

Irving nodded and fumbled at the beeper attached to Joy's jeans, pushing the button. Joy disappeared, and he followed a split second later.

Magdaline got shakily to her feet. Armando touched her lightly on the arm as if he wanted to make sure she were real. "Are you okay?"

Magdalene nodded, not able to meet his gaze.

"I told Joy not to do that shit, she wouldn't listen. She wanted to hit that big guy, he's their leader, the one who has been causing all the problems."

"And she got exactly what she gave." Magdalene's voice was hollow. "Will you believe me *now* that the shockers aren't harmless?"

Armando winced, then squinted at her. "You look...weird. You're glowing."

Magdalene glanced at her hands. A pearly halo surrounded them. Probably something to do with all the power she'd funneled. "Go back, Armando. I'll follow you in a second. Go see if Joy is okay."

He regarded her doubtfully, then glanced back at the Dead, who were pushing at the fence, their din more deafening than ever.

"I can handle them," Magdalene said. "Go!"

Armando gave her a long look, then nodded. He pressed the button on his beeper and vanished.

Magdalene glanced at the guards, who stood impassively as always. She remembered what Armando had said, that they were there mostly to transmit information to the Waking World. She wondered exactly how much information they could transmit.

Magdalene gathered her hands into fists. Gavin had hired her as an ambassador. She was just doing her job. But she couldn't silence the voice whispering in her head: *You don't know whose side you're on.*

She huffed. *There shouldn't be sides at all.*

Magdalene went back to the fence to where the Chieftain stood, towering over the rest of the crowd. He gazed down at her, and the crowd's racket slowly fell into a charged hush. All eyes were on Magdalene. Her pulse raced, adrenaline surging through her.

The Chieftain lifted his chin, a faint smile curling his lips. "Bright Girl." His rich voice boomed through the silence.

The back of Magdalene's neck prickled. Bridgett was the only one who'd ever called her that. Maybe he'd spoken with her before she lost her mouth.

"Thank you for coming to us," the Chieftain said. "It is a thing foreseen."

The crowd gave a small rumble of agreement.

Magdalene gazed up into his strange eyes, her brow furrowing. She wanted to ask what that meant. She had a sense that this man would have an answer to so many of her questions, but an even stronger sense that it wouldn't be easy to drag those answers from him.

The Chieftain glanced up and down the fence that separated them. "You will choose on your own time, as a woman always does."

Barry laughed, then quickly stifled it with his hand.

"I'll come back soon," Magdalene said, "and we'll talk about what needs to happen with the gate. Until then, can you please call off this riot? Otherwise, people might be hurt."

The Chieftain glanced over his huge shoulder, surveying the crowd. "You fought to protect my people. We'll wait. We'll talk with you." He studied her for a moment, then smiled. "I want Bright Girl on my side of the fence."

His words rolled over Magdalene like a deep river of crystal-clear water, and she dissolved into them, into the weight of centuries, the force of generation after generation of people living and dying, loving and fighting. Then the words passed through her and away, leaving her empty and confused as the Chieftain continued to gaze down at her with a smile.

Magdalene thrust her hand through the chain link and the Chieftain grasped it in his huge, heatless paw. "You will come back. We will talk." His eyes glinted, and she found it hard to look away.

This wasn't a man she could win over easily, and certainly not with bullshit. *In order to make him believe, you have to figure out what you believe first.*

She released his hand and stepped back from the fence. "I'll be back soon."

Magdalene opened her eyes in the Waking World. Armando's chair was empty. The silence in the sleeper room seemed weak and watery after the frenetic energy of the crowd.

She sat up and pressed her palms into her eyes, taking steady breaths. She'd find out if Joy was okay. Then...then she had to go face Gavin.

We've been tricked.

She shook her head. "He wouldn't trick me."

Magdalene realized she was literally trying to convince herself. She straightened her shoulders and stood.

Before she could go out, however, the door lock clicked and Armando burst in. When he saw her, he let out a relieved breath. "You're back, you're okay."

"Have you seen Joy? Is she hurt?"

Armando shook his head. "She's a bit dazed, and she's pissed off as hell, but she's perfectly okay." The corners of his mouth twitched into a grin. "That was hardcore, Magdalene. I thought for a second *you* were the one that would get hurt, but..."

Magdalene snorted. "I'd like to see her try."

Armando snickered.

"I have to see Gavin," Magdalene said. "I have to tell him what happened."

Armando's smile faded. He nodded. "I'll go with you as your witness. Joy shouldn't have discharged her weapon like that with you in front of her. You were just defending yourself."

Magdalene considered him a moment. Most of what she had to say to Gavin had to be said alone, but she could use the moral support in the meantime. She nodded. "Thanks, Armando."

He stood aside to let her out, and they went down the hallway.

After they'd passed through security, he turned to her, his brow furrowed. "I thought for sure the Departed were going to do something horrible to you. But you just walked right up to them. And you *defended* them."

She raised her eyebrows at him. "The Dead aren't our enemies."

He shot her an uncertain look.

When they reached Gavin's office, Magdalene stood before the door for a moment, gathering her resolve, then knocked.

Gavin Cavanaugh opened the door. As soon as his gaze met hers, Magdalene realized he knew.

He knew *everything*.

CHAPTER EIGHTEEN

And There's Gonna Be Trouble

Gavin Cavanaugh gave them his little smile, his gaze lingering on Magdalene. "Miss Richards, Mr. Ortega. What a pleasant surprise. Please come in."

They stepped inside his office and Gavin shut the door behind them. He didn't offer them a seat or sit down himself. He simply raised his eyebrows and waited. Magdalene's heart pounded.

Armando took a breath. "Mr. Cavanaugh, I wanted to explain something that just happened at the gate."

Gavin listened as Armando recounted the tale, his expression impassive. But Magdalene could sense his feelings smoldering below the surface. She clutched her hands together in front of her, her mind racing.

"I just wanted to make sure you understood it wasn't Magdalene's fault," Armando concluded. "Joy discharged her weapon against my orders when Magdalene was in the line of fire. Magdalene was only protecting herself."

Gavin smiled. "I have no doubts as to Miss Richards' innocence or the integrity of her actions. She will suffer no reprimand from me. Quite the contrary."

Armando's shoulders relaxed.

"Now that that's settled," Gavin continued, "could you please allow me Miss Richards' company for a moment? I need to speak with her about a private matter." He glanced at Magdalene and a chill ran through her.

Armando nodded. "Sure thing. I'll head back to the gate. It's unattended at the moment."

"I think you'll find matters there much improved, thanks to Miss Richards," Gavin said.

Armando grinned. "You knew what you were doing when you hired her."

"I certainly did," Gavin said. "I usually do."

Armando stepped out and the door clicked shut behind him.

Gavin and Magdalene faced each other in silence. The office grew dimmer; outside the windows, thunderclouds had rolled over the sun. Magdalene's heartbeat pounded in her ears. She kept her expression neutral, she held his gaze, but she knew it made no difference. She might as well have been a glass display case for her emotions.

Gavin gestured at the sofa. "Please sit."

Magdalene sat, pressing her hands between her knees.

Gavin sat in a club chair facing her, crossing his legs and regarding her with his little smile. But Magdalene could sense the ice in his gaze. His anger and fear pulsed in her own veins.

"The lovely Miss Richards," he said. "You bring more people under your spell every day. Not even the Chieftain is immune."

Magdalene narrowed her eyes but held her tongue. There was a lot more going on here than she was aware of, and she was fumbling in the dark.

"That was an admirable thing you did at the gate, shielding the Departed from that young woman's attack. I wish I could have been there to see it in person."

"You shouldn't hurt the Dead," she said. "You shouldn't let your guards do that. It's wrong, Gavin."

Gavin studied her. "I understand how you feel, Magdalene. But you have to understand that not all of us are as skilled as you are in talking to the Dead. Sometimes my guards have to use force to protect themselves."

Magdalene pressed her heels into the floor to keep her legs from jittering. She still couldn't see what lay in wait around the next corner of this conversation. Gavin's thoughts were shrouded figures in the fog, and Magdalene suddenly felt very young and stupid. How could she have ever believed she knew the entirety of Gavin Cavanaugh's mind?

But there were some things she did know. For one, Gavin wouldn't hurt her. Not ever. She drew herself up, holding his gaze defiantly. "If you're really trying to help people and make the world a better place, then you shouldn't hurt people. I thought you were trying to stop people from being hurt."

Gavin twisted his ring. "Not everyone will benefit from the world being a better place. Those who stand to lose their privileges and power are bound to fight my new order. I'm not setting out to hurt people. I'm just doing what needs done, and others are fighting *me*."

"But they aren't bad people, Gavin. They're just confused. If you'll give me time to explain it to them…"

"I didn't have the benefit of your negotiating skills until today. I've been doing the best I can without you, but now you're here, I'm certain things will be different. That's why you were meant to come to me."

The fog lifted, and Magdalene saw it in his mind: his steadfast belief in his system. The determination forged by years of pain, emptiness and loss. She felt it as if it were her own.

And she saw *exactly* how far he'd been willing to go to get her there.

We've been tricked.

Magdalene's chest tightened. She'd been so naïve. "You don't need me that badly." Her voice was thick. "You have so much power. You don't need me at all."

His expression darkened. "Magdalene, I will *always* need you."

Thunder rolled through the building, rattling the windows. Magdalene squeezed her eyes shut, battling the lump in her throat. So much pain, so much loss, so many mistakes that could never be washed out. She hugged herself, a tear rolling down her cheek. She wanted to run away. She wanted to run into his arms, to make it better for him, for both of them.

But how could she make it better, when all she had to offer him was her own pain, her own bitterness and anger? She understood too well his need to control, to prevent more hurt, to keep the remaining tatters of his heart intact. She knew the burning desire to crush those who had destroyed his life.

They were of one soul. And it was terrifying.

"Your kindness will help me succeed where I alone would fail," Gavin said. "Only you can bring balance to this project and show me the right path forward. I'm nothing without you, Magdalene."

Magdalene shook her head. "You tricked me into coming here."

"I had to get you away from those frauds. I'd do anything to make you safe."

Magdalene groped around in her feelings, trying to grasp her own anger in the haze of his pain. She glared at him. "They aren't bad people at the Commune."

Darkness flickered in the depths of his blue eyes. "You're wrong about them."

Her heart thundered in her ears as another roll of thunder boomed outside. The world spun around her, a tornado of emotions, words, images. Magdalene concentrated on the rise and fall of her breathing, on finding herself in the maelstrom. "You hurt me, Gavin," she said quietly. "You tricked me." She took another breath, letting her own heartbeat fill her. She could feel his mind, and her own. She could feel the connection between them like a luminous rope, and she grabbed hold of it.

Her own heart flowed into his. *You hurt me. You tricked me.* Her pain and anger and loneliness crashed through them both and she felt its impact in his heart. Then those feelings drained away in dark rivulets and she was filled with lightness, relief. *But there will be no more hurt, no more betrayal, no more lies now that we're together.*

"Don't," Magdalene gasped. The warmth inside her shattered and she was left with emptiness and raw pain.

Gavin gazed at her sadly. "I'm sorry, Magdalene. I can't help what I am. All I know is trickery and manipulation. That's why I need you. You make me a better person."

Magdalene shook her head, barely trusting herself to speak.

"I've been trying to change the world," he said. "But when you came here, I realized what really needed changing was *me*." He winced. "You're right. I'm selfish. I'm egotistical. I was willing to trick and manipulate you just to have you here. I was naïve enough to think that it wouldn't matter. That once you were here, you'd be happy. That you'd be able to forgive me." He gazed at her. There was no more connection between them, no tug of war. Just his plain words laid out for her inspection. "I make no apologies for what I have done. I wouldn't blame you for leaving. But God brought us together. You can save me, Magdalene, and then, together, we can save the world."

Magdalene's heart now beat alone in her breast, and the only feelings she felt were her own. And she felt empty. Lonely.

Gavin had hurt her, but he truly thought he'd been doing the right thing. He might be wrong about Omar and Andy, but were his fears about them really so illogical?

Magdalene knew what she really wanted: to have it both ways. To have Omar back without giving Gavin up.

A flash lit the room, and thunder cracked.

"Give me another chance," Gavin said. "No more secrets or tricks. I shouldn't have gone about this the way that I did, but I was a stranger to you and had no idea how to get you trust me without resorting to some kind of deception. Even if I could have come to the cult without Andy and his attack dog running me off, you would never have listened to me. I would have just been some lunatic telling strange tales."

Magdalene gazed at him across the distance that separated them, her heart twisting. She still wasn't sure why she was so important to this man, why he was willing to risk so much in order to have her here. There was still something going on that she couldn't see, something he was keeping hidden. But their connection was real, and the strength of it resounded in the roots of her being. She was more certain of it than she was of the floor beneath her feet. This man would never abandon her. He'd follow her into death and beyond if he had to. He'd protect her, no matter the cost.

Magdalene had spent her whole life being tossed away, forgotten, used, and mistreated. She'd had her heart stomped on as thoughtlessly as if it were sidewalk trash. But here was this man who had everything: power, money, armies of minions jumping to his every command at any hour of the day. And yet, what he wanted most of all, the only thing in the universe he would exchange all that money and power for, was *her*.

Even if she didn't yet know the reason for it, was that something she was willing to give up?

Gavin smiled, and Magdalene smiled back, the emptiness within her evaporating.

Then, the door clicked open, and her heart stalled.

In the doorway stood Omar, his eyes flashing black fire. His gaze met Magdalene's and a torrent of feeling rushed into her, filling her like a breath of air after being trapped underwater.

Omar turned his eyes on Gavin and his lips curled in a cruel smile. "Good afternoon, Mr. Cavanaugh. It's so nice to finally meet you in person." Lightning flashed again, and thunder cracked like a shot, making Magdalene jump. The rolling shockwave made the pictures rattle on the walls.

Gavin studied Omar with his cold gaze. "Mr. Arif. I won't ask how you got past security, as I know your talents for deception and subterfuge."

Omar's smile widened. "I can only assume that's a compliment when it comes from you."

Magdalene stood frozen, her heart pounding.

"I assume you have come to rescue Magdalene," Gavin said. "I assure you, she's in no need of rescuing."

Omar's smile faded. "I'm not here to rescue her. I'm here to ask her to come back with me." He turned his gaze back to Magdalene. The hardness drained from it, and Magdalene could see in his eyes all the same anguish and angst she'd been wrestling with herself since she'd walked out of the Commune. "I don't know exactly what he did to get you here," Omar said, "but I'm guessing it was a trick, because I know what he did to me to stop me from looking for you. I won't force you or trick you, but I want you to come back with me." A sad smile flitted over his face. "So badly."

Magdalene pressed her head between her hands. She wanted to try to reason with them. She wanted to tell them they each had the other wrong and that they should work it out. Thunder cracked again, and she twitched.

"Omar is a dangerous man, Magdalene," Gavin said. "He'll only end up hurting you. You'd never have chosen to be with him in the first place if you'd been in possession of all the facts."

Omar flexed his fingers and electricity crackled between them. "You're one to talk about *facts.*"

Gavin's eyes were chips of ice. "You would destroy the world just to protect your own ego."

Yeah, no. She probably wasn't going to get them to work it out today. Maybe with time.

Omar glared at Gavin. The halo of his power surrounded him like a dark cloud, making the hair on Magdalene's arms stand on end. Her heart stuttered. She didn't want a fight.

"He doesn't love you, Magdalene," Gavin continued, his gaze still fixed on Omar. "He only wants you because your powers augment his own."

"Interesting accusation," Omar said. "I'm guessing you're saying that because it's true for *you*. But it my case, she was slowing their expansion."

Gavin's gaze flicked to Magdalene, a warning in it. A moment later, the door flew open and three men in security uniforms burst in. One of them grabbed Magdalene and hauled her toward the exit as another, a blond guy, lunged at Omar. Omar stepped back, flicking his fingers toward him, and the guard yelped and fell to the ground.

Magdalene struggled against the arms holding her. The third security guy, a redhead, made a move for Omar while the blond guy scrambled to his feet and grappled for the taser on his belt. Magdalene yelled a warning, and the blond went skidding across the room, crashing into Gavin's desk. The redhead stopped as if his feet had turned to stone and stood watching Omar with wide eyes, his chest heaving.

Magdalene thrashed against the guy holding her. "Let me go! Stop this bullshit!"

Gavin stood with his arms crossed, glaring at Omar. He shot Magdalene a glance. "I don't want you caught in this nonsense. I don't want you hurt."

Without taking his eyes from Gavin, Omar flicked a hand in Magdalene's direction and the man holding her yelled a curse, his grip slackening. The blond was trying to extricate himself from the rubble of the desk, but Omar glanced at him and he slumped to the carpet, where he lay struggling against invisible bonds.

Magdalene finally wrenched herself free from her captor. There was a thump as he crumpled motionless onto the floor from whatever spell Omar had thrown.

Magdalene surveyed the wreckage of the office, the two guards on the ground, and the one standing immobile in the middle of the floor staring at Omar with animal terror. Gavin watched it all with cold fury and the light of retribution in his eyes.

She wasn't going to broker any peace deals here today. But if the choice was hers, she knew what it would be. "Gavin."

Gavin turned his gaze on her. "Don't, darling." His voice was thick. "Don't leave." His anguish flooded her. His desperation, his fear, his love, so strong they left her blinking and breathless. And there was something else in his mind. Something about her, the secret she'd sensed before, lurking in the shadows of his thoughts. Magdalene reached for it and found herself abruptly shut out.

She and Gavin gazed at one another, and Magdalene's empty heart wrenched. "I'm sorry."

Lighting flashed and thunder shook the building's foundations. Rain began to patter the windows, quickly increasing to the roar of a deluge.

Omar raised his eyebrows at her, and Magdalene nodded. He took her hand, and they ran.

Heads turned as they sprinted down the stairs and out into the lobby, but no one made a move to stop them. They dodged out the front door and into the pouring rain, and there was still no pursuit.

It made Magdalene more nervous than if he'd sent an army after them. She knew she hadn't seen the last of Gavin Cavanaugh. She knew he wouldn't give up. So, what was his game now?

Through the thick veil of rain, Magdalene saw the Prius waiting in the lot. They ran toward it, their feet splashing in the puddles.

The hair on Magdalene's arms stood up and a feeling of foreboding came over her. Omar pulled her into his arms the moment before the world split open with a blinding flash, a deafening crack. Magdalene screamed, and Omar held her, the rain pouring over their heads and between their bodies. She gasped, then let out a breath. Wherever it had struck, it hadn't struck them.

"You okay?" Omar asked.

Magdalene looked up at him. His curls were flattened to his head and rivulets of water streamed down his face. He gazed down at her and smiled, pushing a sodden lock of hair off her forehead.

He brought his lips to hers, kissing her as the rain poured over their heads, flowed between their bodies. Magdalene pressed closer to him, the pain and angst that had filled her since her false vision dissolving into the heat of his body and the taste of his tongue, the feeling of his hands on her.

Her heart was a complex place, but she'd made the right decision.

Lightning flashed, thunder boomed.

They jumped into the car and Omar started the motor. They sped out of the parking lot and onto the highway, the rain drumming the roof and windows, the wipers working overtime.

Magdalene glanced back one last time. The Answers Industries compound sat, the buildings no more than looming shadows in the ferocious monsoon. No figures rushed out the doors, no cars pulled out of the lot after them. If she hadn't known Gavin better, she would've thought he had given up.

Omar wiped the rain from his face and shot her a grim look. "He won't have anyone follow us. He'll have a better plan than that."

Magdalene hugged herself and gazed past the windshield wipers at the lightning flashing over the desert. Omar was right. Gavin wouldn't try sending thugs after her again. He didn't need to do that anymore.

Because he knew her, and she knew him.

She sighed, squeezing her eyes shut. Omar put an arm around her, and she nestled against him, feeling the warmth of his wet skin. "I saw you kissing Ingrid in Purgatory."

He tensed and cursed. "I'd wondered what trick he'd used on you. It never happened."

"I finally figured that out, after I saw you in Bridgett's field. I don't know how Gavin created that illusion, but he did."

Omar was quiet for a while, gently threading his fingers through Magdalene's wet hair. "At first I thought you'd just left." His voice was dull. "Then we figured out Ingrid and Matthew worked for him."

Magdalene sat up. "Wait, what?"

Omar's mouth tightened. "After they took off, we did some digging around. They're both employees of Answers Industries, and Andy happened to recognize the CEO."

"No way would I just leave you," Magdalene said.

He smiled sadly. "And no way would I cheat on you. And yet we both fell for it, didn't we?"

Magdalene winced. "I guess when you can read people's minds it's easy to play on their fears."

Omar ran his hand over his wet hair. He had circles under his eyes and lines of strain around his mouth. "I was in Purgatory a long time the night you left. I went to another portal to see if he'd been working around that one. He hadn't blocked it yet, but there was a girl there. A living girl, with a glowing blue eye. I spent a long time talking to her, but it was like trying to pry information from a block of wood. I'm sure Mr. Cavanaugh sent her there to keep me occupied long enough to get you away.

"When I came back, you were gone. But there was a note on my dresser." He opened the center console and pulled out a wrinkled and smudged piece of notebook paper, which he handed to her.

Magdalene unfolded it. It was written in a flowing hand very unlike her own uneven scrawl.

Dear Omar,

I've had a chance to think about our relationship over the past couple of days. When Matthew arrived, it was like a light turned on, and I was finally able to see what was going on around me. I thought I had feelings for you, but I think what was really happening is that you were manipulating me, making me feel the way YOU wanted me to feel. I might have felt something for you, but I don't know which feelings were real and which ones weren't.

"What the fuck is this bullshit?" Magdalene exclaimed.

Omar sighed.

Magdalene resumed reading.

When I met Matthew, I knew how I really felt. I don't know how else to explain it. He's not controlling like you are, Omar. When I'm around you, my every move and thought seems to be dictated by what YOU want. It's really frightening, and I have to get away from you in case you try to twist my mind again and make me believe I want to stay with you. So, I'm leaving, I'm going away with Matthew, who lets me be who I am. I hope that this is a wakeup call to you, and that you learn to be a better person so that you don't hurt other girls like you've hurt me.

Very Sincerely,

Magdalene

Magdalene flung the note away from her, and it fell to the floorboards. "That's utter crap. Did Ingrid write it? Do you know?"

"Probably," Omar said. "By the time I read that, not only were you gone, but Matthew and Ingrid were, too. I shouldn't have believed it. I should have known you better than that."

"It is exactly the shit you're primed to believe, and Gavin knew that," Magdalene muttered. "He knows our insecurities better than we do."

Omar gave her a searching look before turning his gaze back on the road. "I did have a weird feeling, though. Ingrid wasn't acting quite right. And Bridgett is…"

"Yeah, what the fuck is up with Bridgett?"

Omar chuckled dryly and shrugged. "Good question, but it was another clue something weird was going on, because she obviously was trying to keep us apart, playing some dramatic role, whatever she thinks fate wants her to do." He scrubbed his brow. "Then Barry found me and told me where you were. When I thought about it, I finally came to my senses. Or, at least, I knew I had to find out for sure."

Magdalene took Omar's hand, interlacing her fingers with his. The feeling of his skin on hers, damp and warm, brought all the emotions she'd been trying to block out flooding back in.

"I'm so glad you're back," Omar said.

Magdalene smiled. "Me, too."

And she was. But the image of Gavin back in his office, alone, wouldn't leave her mind.

Magdalene was so tired. She laid her head on Omar's shoulder. He released her hand and put his arm around her again.

She felt like she was surrounded by a fog. It weighed down her thoughts, tangling through them and tearing them apart. It made the world seem so far away.

It had been a hard week. She just needed sleep.

Epilogue
PULLED IN

Omar let Magdalene sleep. She'd been through a lot and was probably exhausted. He was just glad to have her back. They'd have time to talk everything over later.

A sharp curve loomed up out of the pouring rain, and Omar realized too late he was going too fast. He whipped his arm from around Magdalene's shoulders and put both hands on the wheel, then tapped the brakes. The tires skidded on the wet pavement, but he managed to stay on the road as he careened around to the left.

At the edge of the curve, Magdalene's body slid in her seat and flopped listlessly against the passenger window, then fell forward against her seatbelt. Omar's chest tightened. "Magdalene?"

She didn't answer.

He skidded to a stop on the shoulder and put the car in park, then gently shook her. Her small body was a dead weight. "Magdalene?"

But she wasn't going to wake.

She was gone.

END OF BOOK TWO

Author's Notes

T hank you so much for everyone who helped me with this book. Mom, Dad, Faith, Ayla, Paul, Will, Mark, Richard—you're troopers. Thank you for listening to all my bullshit and hanging in there.

Thank you to my critique groups, of course.

Thank you, Malenko—I'm going to call you your government name. I hope it's not what your mom calls you—for answering my messages at 3:30 a.m. my time and talking about the world and nothing and everything. Your work keeps me going, and I stare at it when I feel the heart going out of me. And I mean *your* work, not the work you're doing for me. Someday, it will be part of the arcane knowledge that you did the covers of these weird little books before you got Big. You're a genius.

Gavin...stop looking at me like that. You helped. Always.

Other Books By Author

As I said, if you're waiting for *Death's Door* (Tales from Purgatory Book 3) to be out, just go to TalesFromPurgatory.com and contact me. I'll send you an ARC!

<u>Other books by Liz Roderick:</u>

TALES FROM PURGATORY SERIES:

The Commune

<u>Other books by Elizabeth Roderick:</u>

Love or Money

Hoodlum Army

Gracie & Zeus Live the Dream

THE OTHER PLACE SERIES:

The Hustle

The Other Place

Love and War

Synchronicity

SHORT STORIES

Mirrormaze Anthology

Somniscope Anthology

Go to TalesFromPurgatory.com for links, news, and new releases!